To Bob & Alice,
Love you guys)
Enjoy this.
Lydia xo
Hoya, Hoya!

WHO'S AFTER SAMANTHA?

Lydia T. Ponczak

Lydia T. Ponczak

WHO'S AFTER SAMANTHA?

Lydia T. Ponczak

Weaving Dreams Publishing
Watseka, Illinois

Weaving Dreams Publishing

Copyright © 2012 by Lydia T. Ponczak

ISBN # 978-1-937148-06-5

Library of Congress Control Number
2011941260

ALL RIGHTS RESERVED

www.weavingdreamspublishing.com

Cover Art by
Carl Tocwish

Printed in the United States of America
10 9 8 7 6 5 4 3 2

Dedication

To my awesome son, Glen, my pride and joy

and

to Joni, a dream of a daughter-in-law

and

to my unmatchable son, Jeff,

who was taken from us too soon.

Acknowledgements

As an author of a first book, I could fill pages with names of people to acknowledge but foremost my deepest thanks to my writing group, The Southland Scribes. Special kudos to my mentor, Helen Osterman, who tirelessly answered my questions and never considered them dumb, as she guided me through every phase of publication. Heartfelt thanks to Scott Doornbosch, who encouraged me to write another 4500 words and then suggested a possible way to do it; to Julie Hyzy who pointed out the rough spots and urged me on from Day One; to Sherry Scarpaci whose valuable suggestions improved many a chapter. My deepest appreciation, also, to Linda Cochran, Ralph Horner, Ryan O'Reilly, Sandi Tatara and George Kulles for their constructive critiques and advice.

A personal shout-out to my son, Glen, for creating awesome publicity materials and grateful thanks to him and my daughter-in-law, Joni, who encouraged and supported me, and lessened my frustration with computer problems. Love ya, guys.

Warmest thanks to my dearest friend in the whole wide world, Irene Gutsell, who spurred me on throughout my arduous journey and knew when I needed a night out. You're the best, Irene!

My gratitude to (Ret.) Sergeant Michael Black of the Matteson Police Department and (Ret.) Chief Nick Sparicino and Sergeant Alexander Curlee of the Oak Forest Police Department for patiently explaining police procedures and protocol. Any errors in that field are strictly my own.

Thanks to my publisher, L. Sue Durkin of Weaving Dreams Publishing, who was never too busy to explain, explain, explain. I am fortunate to have pitched my book to her at the *Love Is Murder* writers' convention.

And, last but certainly not least, a warm thank-you to Lee who suffered hunger pains for months when breakfast, lunch, or dinner was delayed or forgotten because a scene or a chapter needed to be revised. Without his patience and understanding, this book would never have been finished.

Chapter 1

I dialed 9-1-1 and chilled. No way was I going back upstairs. The poor woman who fainted had to take her own chances in the room with the probably-dead body.

How could a commonplace writing seminar turn into a slaughter zone?

The food I enjoyed during the two-hour lunch break between sessions threatened to reappear. I took a deep breath and swallowed hard. I looked up and down the street for squad cars. What was taking Chicago's finest so long to get here?

With my stomach churning, I approached a bunch of my fellow seminar attendees when they returned from their lunches. "Do any of you know what to do for a woman who has fainted?" I asked. "She's upstairs and needs help. I also think there's a dead woman up there." My breathing increased with each word, but I was determined not to hyperventilate.

The small crowd froze at my words and then became abuzz with excitement. Two women and a man volunteered to go upstairs to see if they could help.

I advised the others to wait with me for the police.

Most ignored me. They were too curious and excited not to see the situation for themselves.

Jeez, you'd think authors would know better than to contaminate a crime scene!

It didn't take them long to run back down to the street, wide-eyed and scared. Questions were thrown at me from all sides. I just shook my head and clammed up. I was waiting for the cops to show up; it seemed like hours since I called them.

When the squad cars finally appeared, I told the officers the little I knew. They immediately radioed for help with crowd control, and separated the conference attendees from the other assembled onlookers. The police began taking names and addresses, and told the group to remain until the detectives showed up. They separated me from the others and left an officer with me.

When the plainclothes arrived, another policeman pointed me out to the detectives "Stay put," one of them barked in my direction.

I stayed put.

Although I stood in the ferocious sun, the scenes from the upstairs horror flashed through my mind and caused me to tremble inside my skin. I would've trembled more had I realized the murderer would turn my world topsy-turvy and hurl me into life threatening situations.

Waiting for further instructions from the police, I calmed myself by replaying the day in my mind.

The morning started off sanely enough.

My Mother's Day gift from my sons was an all day seminar, *Self-publishing: Refreshed & Updated*, which was to be held in July on Chicago's northwest side.

Through the years I authored short stories, some of which brought me monetary awards from writing contests. I included the winners and also-rans in birthday cards to my friends and relatives who seemed to enjoy them.

Now, taking advantage of an early retirement package from the Chicago Board of Education, I made up my mind to finish, then pitch, my first mystery novel to publishers at an upcoming writers' convention. Having just birthdayed on the wrong side of fifty, I was determined to pursue a writing career before I added on another year. So, I was excited about attending the seminar.

Living in Oak Forest, a lovely southwest suburb of the city, for almost twenty-five years, I had little idea of what Chicago neighborhoods were like. Over recent years, young professionals moved into many old communities that were reconstructed and remodeled. Was the northwest side seminar site in gang and drug territory or in yuppieville? I didn't know which category covered the Diversey and Lincoln Avenues vicinity.

Besides I'm a South-Soxer, where the Chicago White Sox is the reigning baseball team. I was headed into *enemy* territory. The Cubs ruled on the Northside.

"Will I have to take a bat with me for protection?" I asked Jeff, my younger son.

"Oh, for heaven's sake, Mom. The worst that can happen is some yuppie will throw his Starbuck's latté cup at you. The area is upscale. You don't have to worry about your safety."

Silly us, with no inkling of the chaos awaiting me.

I shuddered and stopped daydreaming. Why are the cops staying up there so long? I wondered. The July sun was beating down on my wilted body with enough force to melt my skin.

"Excuse me," I asked my own special boy-in-blue. "I'm dying in this heat. Can we move into the shade or into my car so I can turn on the air?"

The kid-cop gawked at me as if I were inviting him to engage in an illicit act. Since the youngster looked fourteen and a half years old, he could forget any solicitation on my part. My teacher friends and I never understood women who became involved with their teenage students. We agreed we didn't even want to touch some of those boys' papers, let alone their *kruszkies*.

"Best we stay here," he said, in the curt way I soon discovered was standard police talk.

I honored him with an exaggerated sigh and an exasperated look. With nothing better to do, I continued my reminiscences.

Darling Harry had a fit that I was going such a great distance to a seminar. "Those sons of ours have no common sense, Samantha. Just like the rest of your family. Why couldn't the boys find classes for you on the Southside?" he grumbled.

Anything farther than seven miles is cross-country to my Harry.

"You can't find your way around the block," Darling continued.

"How the hell are you going to find this place? Where are you going to park?"

I received further comments regarding my stupidity for going, and our sons' weird ideas coming from my side of the family. Yada, yada, yada. He also presented me with encouraging words such as "you're never going to publish a book anyway," as well as other disapproving commentary, ad nauseum.

I became use to Darling's complaints through the years about anything *different* that I might set out to do. I was determined to make the most of this seminar, regardless of his negative attitude.

Jeff made out a detailed map for me with none of that *turn north, turn west* junk. He provided me with *turn right, turn left* instructions with names of the streets and intersections. The directions were printed out in very large letters, because he knows I hate to wear my glasses.

"I'll keep my cell phone on all day," Jeff said. "Don't call home because dad will just start ragging you. Call me if you get lost, and I'll get you resituated."

I, therefore, felt pretty confident I'd be okay. And I was, arriving at my destination with not one false turn. Jeff got my whispered thanks for the super directions.

I also had no trouble finding a nearby parking place in the congested, but attractive, Northside neighborhood.

My Oak Forest community consisted of homes spread out from each other. I was never farther than a couple of blocks from spacious forest preserves. I knew long ago I could never move back to a jam-packed, over-flowing, big, bad city neighborhood, no matter how charming it was.

Walking the short distance to Unique World, the building where the seminar was held, I noticed the structure did not appear updated or rejuvenated like its neighbors. In fact, it was the only dilapidated, old-looking building on the block. The cornerstone listed 1867 as the construction date. Not a single improvement seemed to have been made since then.

Just my luck, I thought. The outdoor temperature was ninety-eight degrees with humidity to match. I bet myself there would be no unique air-conditioning in Unique World. Born and bred in Chicago's Bridgeport community, which was built up in the late 1800s, and teaching all my life in Chicago public schools constructed during the same era, I knew how these old buildings retained heat and clamminess.

If I realized then that concern over conditions of Unique World would shrivel in comparison to my next couple weeks, I would have never entered the building. I would've taken my blond-headed, short-skirted, five-foot six-inches and gone back to Oak Forest. But, oblivious to the tangled web awaiting me, I opened the ancient, heavy door and crossed the threshold to meet my fate.

The even hotter air and humidity hit me like a blast furnace. If that wasn't bad enough, the old, three-storied building didn't have an elevator. I began the climb up steep, rickety, wooden staircases that had no railings. My Arrid Extra Dry almost gave out as soon as I rounded the first stairwell. There were still two more flights to go.

Promising the gods I'd work on being a better wife if there was a water fountain near the seminar area, I entered. No fountain. Whew! No need to improve my status quo as Harry's patient, loving mate.

The seminar room felt like a windowless sauna. Had I stepped into hell? More heat slammed into my face as my deodorant completely gave out. About twenty other people of varying ages, ethnic groups, nationalities, and, I think, genders and sexual preferences, were present already.

No one gave me a friendly glance. In fact, one woman gave me the evil-eye. No, it was more than that. If looks could kill, I'd have been slashed, quartered and hanged from a hook! What the hell was her problem? I wondered.

As I sought an empty seat, a few older women eyed me from head to foot and whispered to each other. I gave them a bright smile, but they weren't having any of it. I often got those looks from women my age. I dismissed them as being jealous old broads, because I still had my figure under control, a flair for fashion, and a youthful hairstyle. Appraising them, I thought these gray-headed, tightly-curled, matronly-looking babes could do without the Cokes and donuts laying in front of them. I wondered how a couple of the heavy gals made their way up the steps without calling the paramedics. Meow!

I chose a seat at a long table as far away as possible from the

Killer-look Woman. She was a big mama of truck driver proportions. I didn't want to tangle with her.

Chapter 2

Ah, the detectives returneth. I let out a sigh of relief. Maybe now I could get out of this friggin' heat.

I approached the plainclothes men.

My fourteen-and-a-half year old guardian put out his hand to block my way. "They're not ready for you yet. Please stand back," he said.

Jeez. Must be true what I read in mystery books. The detectives are prima donnas and shielded from the peons approaching them. I bet it'd be easier to get an audience with the pope.

I decided to continue my reverie. No doubt it'd get me ready for the recounting of my day, later, to the detectives.

If possible, the seminar room grew more uncomfortably hot by the minute. Someone brought in a large fan, which made the room buzz with a loud, annoying sound. I figured the instructor would shut it off when the lecture started, or no one would hear a thing.

I glanced over my shoulder at Killer-look Woman and, sure enough, her searing glare was enough to penetrate my heart. Hatred oozed from the woman's eyes. I tried not to let her unwarranted animosity upset me.

In front of the room stood a person of questionable gender whom I figured was the speaker. Attire consisted of baggy khaki pants, shapeless blouse or shirt, and ugly shoes. A short, severe hairdo topped the face, which sported not a trace of makeup. No jewelry adorned ears or fingers, although one wrist displayed a masculine-type wristwatch. Piercings or tattoos were not visible, but nowadays who knows what hidden nooks and crannies sport those treasures. I put on my glasses to get a clearer look at the person, but still couldn't figure out the gender.

Clothes and grooming are very important to me. Besides being a retired teacher and a frustrated, but aspiring, writer, I am program director and host for a monthly community television program. The appearance of some of the women I interview always amazes me. I would think they'd want to appear their best for TV. But many women chose outfits with unbecoming colors; some didn't even wear lipstick, let alone a little makeup. Others looked like they could trace their hair style back to the Reagan administration. Meow, again, I guess.

Ohhh-kay. I sighed, and started looking over my booklet and materials.

I stopped my recollections, took a tissue out of my purse, and blotted my face. If I didn't get into some shade or air-conditioning soon, the police were going to have another dead body on their hands.

I tapped my guardian on the shoulder. He turned around quickly, and made me almost lose my balance. The baby cop looked like he was ready to pull out his gun or his handcuffs. He couldn't have been on the job too long.

"I'm sorry I startled you, Officer. If the detectives are much longer, I need to sit down or something. I must be old enough to be your mother; would you want your mama to be tortured like this?"

The policeman looked at me, and saw my extreme discomfort. "I'll see what I can do, Ms. Lisowski." Moving away, he spoke into some kind of gadget.

For God's sake, was it going to take an act of Congress to get me into a cool place? I began fanning myself with some seminar material that wasn't bloodied-up and continued my flashback.

"May I have your attention?" the instructor said. "Everyone is here, so we can get started."

The lecturer turned out to be female. She spoke, as I suspected, *sans* fan, for a couple of hours.

Long before the first break, I knew self-publishing was not for me. The procedure seemed to be similar to setting up a business from scratch. Everything an agent would do for an author, from negotiating with a company to printing the book, to distribution and publicity, would have to be done by the writer, only more so. Exhaustion set-in just thinking about all the steps in-between. My impression was all I needed to do was get a disk from Microsoft, type out my stories, bind them, and away I'd go. How naive was that! I certainly didn't want to start my own business. I just wanted a few friends to enjoy my short stories or that mystery book down the line.

Because my sons paid for the full day of lectures, I decided to stick it out in my uncomfortable surroundings, hoping to pick up a few hints here and there.

Innocent of what awaited me, I discovered a two-hour break coming up. Maybe I'd ask killer-look to lunch.

Well, maybe not.

Since no introductions or attempts at friendliness between attendees took place, I ventured out alone to find a restaurant.

My first encounter with the natives was a woman a bit younger than I; lately, unfortunately, almost everyone appeared that way. She wore a crazed smile on her rubiest of red lips, her eyes concealed by enormous, dark, Elvis-like sunglasses. Pitch black hair brushed her shoulders like a dirty waterfall. Her skirt was even shorter than mine! On one leg was a white, opaque, long stocking, continuing under her skirt, but her other leg was bare. She wobbled on at least four-inch heels.

"'Afternoon," she sang. "Lovely day."

I smiled and nodded my head as I kept on walking, using all my strength not to look back at her in case she was turning around to get another glance at me.

Next I passed a couple of immaculately dressed young men who walked with arms around each other, holding each other's butts as tightly as though those parts of the anatomy would fall off if they let go. They furtively glanced at me as I passed, and I could swear I saw condescension in their eyes. They probably fingered me as being one of those tough, low-class, south suburban White Sox broads. Too bad I didn't have a 7-Eleven coffee cup to hurl their way just to prove them right.

Waiting for the red light to change so I could cross the street, I spotted a couple of grubby guys with creepy tattoos and multiple face piercings wearing Chicago Cubs t-shirts. I was surprised, because Cubbie fans like to lord it over Sox fans, claiming themselves to be the elite, clean-cut crowd. It was probably best I didn't have on my top that stated: *I'd rather have my sister on drugs than have her date a Cub fan.* What an interesting situation I'd have created at the crosswalk.

Without further encounters with uptown's more quaint population, I found a great restaurant where I reveled in the air-conditioning and drank the largest, coolest, chocolate milkshake on the menu. As I slurped up the last fantastic sip and paid my bill, I needed all of my will power to pull myself back to the sweaty dungeon.

I had passed a magnificent Catholic church on my way to lunch, and I decided to make a short stop to check it out. The minute I entered, I found the cool interior breathtaking in its statuary, pillars, beautifully-painted ceiling and stained windows. The church reminded me of St. Mary of Perpetual Help Church in Chicago's Bridgeport community, where I received my sacraments and took my wedding vows.

But one aspect was added.

Killer-look Woman!

She was on her knees in a pew. Head bowed, she appeared to be either shaking with laughter or crying violently. As if she sensed a presence, she raised her head, turned and glared into my eyes!

I gasped and skedaddled.

"We can move into the shade by my squad car."

I nearly jumped out of my panty hose. I was so intensely involved in my mental meanderings that the patrolman's voice startled me. His professional manner actually cracked for a moment. He smiled in a sheepish way.

"Sorry if I surprised *you* this time, Ms. Lisowski. I said we could move to a cooler place if you'd like."

Wasn't that what I'd suggested, let's see. I consulted my

wristwatch. Exactly twenty-eight and a half minutes ago?

I was happy to see that the young cop's face was as flushed as mine, and that beads of sweat were oozing down from under his hat. We moved, although I thought the sun had glued my feet to the sidewalk. A large canopy, from the building where his squad car was parked, created a slight but refreshing relief from the sun's direct rays. A wide, wooden window ledge allowed me to park my body for a while.

"Psst, psst. Miss, miss." A strange-sounding voice came through my consciousness.

The cop and I turned around to identify its source. The body attached to the words was the odd- looking woman I had encountered on my way to lunch. She stood, smiling, behind the yellow police tape. Her dirty black hair had frizzed up from the humidity, but other than that she looked like the heat had no effect on her.

"Would you like some water, miss?" she asked. Without waiting for an answer she tossed a plastic bottle to me. Her aim was bad and the bottle nearly clipped an ear off of the cop.

"Hey," he yelled at her. "Move away. This is a crime scene." He looked around for a fellow policeman to help.

"I know a secret; I know a secret," chanted the woman, tottering on her high heels. "But I have to get my hair done first." She pirouetted and nearly fell off her shoes. "I can't tell you my secret until tomorrow." Her grotesque smile was freaking me out, as if I needed any further freaking-out-ness. She attempted to go under the yellow tape to get to me.

My cop made a bee-line for her. He grabbed her arm and summoned help. A female police officer came to the rescue, gently leading the poor woman back under the tape and away from us. Another cop dealt with the excited crowd of on-lookers who had flooded the area, no doubt eager to witness bloodshed.

The woman looked over her shoulder as she was led away. "Remember. I've got a secret. I won't tell. I won't tell till tomorrow."

"Well," I said to my keeper. "What was that all about? Are you going to hold her for questioning? Do you think she might know something about the murder?"

"Depends." His face and manner remained stoic.

As he was back to his non-responsive mode, I tried to handle the incident by storing it in a compartment of my brain. I opened a different compartment in my head and pictured what had happened when I returned from lunch. Although I was thirsty as hell, there was no way I'd drink the water from the bottle that Ms. Looney-tunes threw my way.

Chapter 3

When I re-entered the airless seminar room after lunch, I sighted only one occupant. She appeared to be asleep, head and arms spread out all over her materials, and mine. As I approached Sleeping Beauty, I noticed, spilled on some of my booklets, something that looked like a thick reddish-brown V-8 drink, which I hate. I became further irritated when I saw some more of the stuff dripping onto my chair and the floor.

Damn! I began to salvage what I could.

I jumped as a piercing scream interrupted my progress. The jungle cry came from a woman who entered the room. Her eyes bulged and her mouth gaped. She looked back and forth from me to the woman stretched across the long table. The air in the room absorbed her fear as she kept on screaming.

I looked again at the slumped-over figure and reality hit me. Upon closer scrutiny I determined that the woman's bearing somehow looked wrong and that the thick, sticky stuff around her was not the dreaded V-8. It was blood.

Blood!

I caught my breath, and with red-soaked manual in hand, moved toward the frightened woman, who seemed frozen in the doorway. As I approached her, she screeched, "Murderer, murderer!" and fainted.

I'm no Florence Nightingale in the best of circumstances, and these were the best of nothin'. I didn't know what to do. Head up, legs lowered — legs up, head lowered. I couldn't remember that damned first aid fainting tip. I didn't want to worsen matters for the woman. Instead, I gingerly stepped over my accuser and ran down the rickety steps to get help as fast as my high heels would allow, praying I wouldn't break my neck in the process.

Each floor, and then the lobby, were empty. Go figure. Slaughtering going on and no one around to help me.

I ran outside. The only person who approached me was that crazed-looking woman I had passed earlier. What the hell does she do? I wondered. Just keep walking around the block, singing to herself?

Figuring she'd be no help, I remembered my cell phone. I know, I know. I should've thought of it upstairs in the dead zone, but I only used that phone for family emergencies and completely forget about it otherwise.

I misdialed 9-1-1 a couple of times because my fingers were trembling and had a mind of their own. As I punched and re-punched the numbers I felt myself getting weak in the knees. I leaned against the building as I finally got through to the police operator.

My kid cop interrupted my flashback. "The detective is ready for you," he said. He escorted me out of the shade into the bowels of hell once more.

I wondered if plainclothes men were oblivious to heat rays. The detective I approached looked cool and collected in his sharp sports jacket, perfectly creased trousers and immaculate shirt and tie. In fact, he looked mighty fine. I wasn't under so much stress that I couldn't appreciate a tall, good-looking man. I could almost smell the power that surrounded him. His sexy persona wasn't bad either. He reminded me a bit of Pierce Brosnan of Double 07 fame.

"Ms. Lisowski, is it?" he asked. "I'm Detective David Kelly from Area A, Chicago Police District 18. I understand you found the body?" He eyed me from head to toe. Maybe he was looking for blood splatter on my clothes or cuts on my skin. His manner unnerved me. "I'd like you to make yourself available for a while at headquarters."

I blinked. He requested my presence "downtown?" Boy, that didn't sound good! Should I ask for a lawyer? No, that was stupid; I didn't do anything that required a lawyer. But don't all suspects in the books I read always feel they don't need legal advice and then talk themselves into jail?

My voice quavered as I asked, "May I call home first, Detective? If I'm delayed, my husband may worry."

Hah, fat chance of Harry worrying. Darling always complained that once I left the house, he never knew when to expect my return. But I was a bit shaky, and I knew that after lecturing me, Harry would come up with sensible words to calm my nerves.

"You can make the call now. I'll be right back. Don't move," the detective cautioned.

That didn't sound good either.

My young, non-responsive policeman again appeared at my side.

I took out my trusty cell and called home, leaving a short, panicky message on our land phone's voicemail, which Harry would never retrieve anyway because he doesn't know how. Harry and the phone — no strike that — all modern equipment, don't exactly get along. He'd just have to figure out by himself that something was wrong when I wasn't home by dark, if he wondered at all.

As I have no sense of direction, I asked Detective Kelly, upon his return, to be sure that I was following him in my car on the way to headquarters. He instructed me to leave my vehicle parked where it was, and that I would be driven to the district in one of the squad cars. My protests were met with an icy stare. That was one stare too many in one day for me, so *the person of interest* meekly accepted the ride back to HQ with one of Chicago's finest.

Wow, I was beginning to use words like a real criminal already!

"Tell me how you happened upon the body," Detective Kelly said, as I settled into the uncomfortable chair in an interrogation room.

Jeez, I thought, where's the spotlight?

"I understand you were the first person to enter the crime scene and later made the 9-1-1 call. What did you touch before leaving the room?"

I told him that I only tried to gather some of my materials to keep them from getting messed up further by what I thought was a spilled bottle of that gooey V-8 stuff.

The detective looked at me skeptically, an "Oh, yeah?" look on his face.

I met his stare and continued. I stated that I didn't touch the woman sprawled over the table or the woman who fainted, and was she okay?

"That woman is Jean Thorpe, who accuses you of murder. She says she saw you trying to remove the knife from the victim's body."

"Knife? What knife?" I screeched. I didn't see any friggin' knife stickin' out of any friggin' body! Damn. I'd better wear my glasses more often.

Detective Kelly gave me another cynical look, like "I've heard that song before." In a bored voice, he asked, "Would you like some water, Ms. Lisowski? Or coffee, soda?"

I told him I was okay and wasn't going to panic, that it was just because he shocked me with the knife stuff. I added that I didn't even know the name of the victim.

"Carole Langley. From Orland Park. That, I believe, is a neighboring community of yours. Did you ever see her before, or come into contact with her?"

"No! As I said, neither her name nor her face is familiar to me. Why did this Thorpe person accuse me of murdering her?" I began to get agitated again.

He ignored my question. "Did you speak with the victim at any time during the seminar?" he asked.

Was Detective Kelly not listening to me? I'd already answered that question. Maybe he was hoping I'd slip up on some detail or confess to the murder.

I wanted to go home and unload this awful day on Harry and my sons and my best friend. I didn't want to keep being repeatedly asked the same stupid questions.

"Please start over again at the beginning. Don't think any detail too trivial. We want to get the whole picture here. Start with how you happened to be in this class."

I breathed out a full-scale sigh. As I reviewed the morning's events for Detective Kelly, I again held back about Killer-look Woman. I wanted to consider her intense stares later, once I got home and my emotions settled down. Her murderous scowls might have been headed toward the soon-to-be victim instead of toward me, but at this point, I couldn't be sure. No way was I going to get Killer-look into trouble without first thinking things through.

Although I did my best, Detective Kelly seemed unhappy with my re-enactment. Maybe he had a gut feeling that I was holding back relevant information about the crime.

Finally, he had someone type up my statement, had me sign it, stated that he'd probably have to contact me again and told me I could go. I found him condescending and coldly unfriendly. Just like those detectives on TV shows who never show emotion or smile or make a warm comment to anybody.

I couldn't resist a jibe. "Are you going to say, 'Don't leave town?'"

Detective Kelly was not amused. So I decided not to ask him for directions to the woman's restroom. He sent for an officer who eventually returned me to my parked car.

To this day I don't know how I drove the long distance home in the darkening hours while in my agitated state. It must have been dumb luck.

Fate protects menopausal women to make up for night sweats.

Chapter 4

"Harry," I yelled entering the house. "I'm part of a murder!"

"Why must you always talk to me when I'm somewhere where I can't hear what you're saying?" Darling complained as he walked down the stairs, settled into his favorite chair, and turned on the TV. "How come you're home so late? I thought that bullshit seminar only lasted till four o'clock."

Ah, my Harry. He is always so concerned about my welfare. No wonder I've kept him around some twenty-five years. And, see, I was right. He didn't retrieve my phone message from the answering machine.

"You won't believe this, Harry."

Darling immediately rolled his eyes and impatiently tapped his foot. That was always a sign he was set to be bored out of his mind with some situation I was about to relate, and that his precious stock market quotes would be interrupted.

"I was just saying that I walked in on a murdered woman."

The foot stopped tapping, the remote clicked on mute, and Darling actually looked at me. "What?"

After enlightening him, he didn't reach out to hug or comfort me. His first comment did not display any concern for how I must be feeling. "How do these bizarre things keep happening to you?" he grumbled. "This sounds like something out of one of your short stories. Are you bullshitting me?"

"If a man calls on the land phone asking for me, don't hang up," I said as I walked away. "It'll be Detective Kelly from the Chicago Police Department. My lover has instructions only to call me on my cell phone."

Harry followed me. "Don't get cute, Samantha. I want to know more about what happened."

It takes a murder for Darling to finally be interested in my existence.

The third degree Harry gave me was much worse than Detective Kelly's, making me feel that the murder was somehow my fault. And I swear he left the den's bright lamp shining in my eyes on purpose. Where do women on TV programs get those husbands who radiate comfort and affection toward them for merely developing a hangnail between manicures?

After the ordeal with Harry I had to tell someone who would react as excitedly as I did or I'd burst.

Reenee! Yes, my best friend, my soul mate, Reenee.

I raced to the phone. As soon as I got her on the line, I spewed out a synopsis of my adventure in three minutes flat, without taking a breath.

"Wow. You're not calling from the hoosegow, are you, girlfriend?" Reenee, asked. "I love ya, but I've got the godchild for the night and I can't come bail you out."

"Not yet," I told her.

As I figured she would, Reenee reacted with gasps and screams as I slowed down and repeated my experience, this time giving her a blow-by-blow recap of the day. We had a merry old time for the next hour.

Harry was nearby and in his regular agitated state when I got off the phone. "You sounded like a giddy teenager," he complained. "You both giggle like schoolgirls when you talk to each other."

To keep peace at the O. K. Corral, I bit my lip and refrained from telling him that he could've moved away from the phone. He didn't have to listen to my animated conversation. Men!

"Well, what did the Great Advisor counsel you to do?" he asked.

"Get a divorce," I quipped and went upstairs.

Even though it was now quite late, I wanted to call my sons with the news. I knew they were home, even though it was Saturday night and they were both young and restless. They were busy renovating

Glen's apartment, where Jeff stayed through his summer breaks from college, and then they had planned to spend the evening relaxing with Miller Lite and cable sports. But I knew they'd want to know how I made out with their gift.

The boys listened without interruption on one of their speaker cell phones. This being my fourth rendition of the day's events, I think I may have exaggerated things a bit. Each of my sons shared in my excitement.

"What an experience," Glen said. "Were you badly scared? Have you calmed down? Are you sure you're okay?"

I assured him I was all right and that the detective's interrogation shook me up almost as much as the murder scene.

"Write down your feelings as soon as you can," Jeff added. "Your experience could make a great plot for a mystery novel. What does Dad think about all this?"

They laughed as I asked if they really needed me to answer that question. Glen and Jeff knew their father.

After I finished talking to them, I booted up my computer and sat thinking in front of it. I calmed myself and, objectively, went over the day, step by step. During my interrogation at the precinct, I received a copy of the seating chart of the attendees. I was told the information might help me remember some important detail as I looked over the seating arrangement. Now I again tried to visualize faces.

Mentally I rolled up my sleeves and let my imagination take off. I set up two columns. In the first I listed the attendees. In the second column I typed in information about their appearance, demeanor and anything I felt could be pertinent. Then I studied the seating chart in relation to me, the victim and Killer-look Woman.

Yes, I speculated; I could've been mistaken. Damn, I should have been wearing my glasses more that day. The scowler's fierce looks could've been directed not at me, but at the woman sitting next to me, soon to become Ms. Murder Victim. I also became a little uneasy about failing to mention that possibility to Detective Kelly.

But, on the other hand, who was I to point a finger? Maybe everyone who came into the meeting room was greeted by those unsettling looks. Maybe it was this woman's natural disposition.

I looked at the seating chart for her name. Frances Morrow. Well, maybe Frances always walked around with squinted eyes, passing out evil looks.

That's the trouble with being a Libra — she considers every side of a situation and is unable to make a decision. Nuts. This Libra was going to break the Zodiac rule. Decision: Keep speculations to myself; let Kelly do his own investigating.

"Christ!" complained an apparition standing in boxer shorts at the doorway. "It's two in the morning. Once you get on that damned computer, you never quit."

"Just go to the washroom, Harry, and don't worry about me. I'm solving a murder case."

"My ass," he grumbled. "Go to bed."

About an hour later, I did.

From the information given to me at the police station, I knew that Frances Morrow, the Killer-look Woman, lived in Tinley Park, a community adjacent to my Oak Forest neighborhood. I passed this tidbit on to Harry as we were finishing breakfast the next day, then said, "I found a Morrow, J's, address in the phone book. Probably Frances' husband. Let's go drive past their house."

"I'm not going on a wild goose chase," Darling said. "You don't even know if you have the right address or the right Morrow. That's a common name." His face tightened and he clenched his teeth. "Just drop it, Samantha. I intend to watch the stock market this afternoon."

Humph, what else is new? And where the hell does he find market quotes on a Sunday? I quickly cleared off the table, washed my hands and took my car keys off the kitchen hook. "Bye!" I yelled, before Harry could start his tirade about why I shouldn't go.

Orchard Lane was a typical Tinley Park area: flowers galore, nourished, sprawling lawns, shade trees and lovely homes. I drove by J. Morrow's house a few times. No signs of the life were apparent.

I debated walking up to the house and ringing the doorbell, but what would I say? What's with those killer-looks at the seminar? Or, thought I'd stop by to ask about the big ol' butcher knife you stuck into Carole Langley?

On my sixth drive by, Frances Killer-look Morrow herself emerged from the house. I jammed on the brakes and almost hit my chin on the steering wheel.

Now what? I thought. Offer her a lift? Ask her to lunch?

Step on the gas and get the hell out of there before she spots me?

Bingo!

Chapter 5

Arnie Kendall, a reporter from CLTV, called later that morning, shooting questions at me over the phone. Did I know the Langley victim? Why did Jean Thorpe accuse me of murder? Would I be available for an interview on or off camera?

Now I have to say that I don't shun the limelight. In fact, I thrive on it. Because of hosting my own TV program, I'm no stranger to the camera. My poor mother in heaven probably can't believe how I turned out. She told me that as a toddler I wouldn't smile for the camera. I cried or remained stubborn and keep a frown on my face instead. In fact, one time my dad almost socked a professional photographer because I didn't win the "Cutest Little Blond Toddler" contest, even though the scowl on my photo face was strictly my fault and not the poor man's. Now I welcome the camera whenever the opportunity arises. I'm really a ham at heart.

Besides, being interviewed on CLTV meant metropolitan-wide exposure. Maybe I could get in a plug for my TV show? Wouldn't that be a blast!

When I told Harry that I'd agreed to an interview, he had a fit. "Why do you always get yourself involved in things? Unlike you, I don't want this house surrounded by the press with lights and cameras." Darling's harangue continued, but as I was busy planning my wardrobe, I barely heard him.

The phone rang again. "It's probably Hollywood calling," he said, sarcasm dripping from each word.

Unfortunately it was only Detective Kelly. I was surprised that he was working on a Sunday, but I guess one day of the week is like any other for the cops. He requested my presence at headquarters for further inquiries. I asked if he could come to my house instead. Stone silence gave me a clue as to what he thought of that suggestion. He then briskly told me that a car was on its way and would be there within the hour.

Harry was pleased with the arrangement. With gas prices soaring, he was happy to have the City of Chicago pick up the tab for the fuel to the Northside. He actually offered to go with me, but I vetoed that. He'd just try to boss me around, telling me what I should or shouldn't say, act or do.

I called the CLTV reporter, Arnie Kendall, and rescheduled my interview for later that evening. He wasn't too happy about the delay, as he had deadlines, yada, yada, yada.

"Take it or leave it," I told him, although I wasn't thrilled either about possibly not appearing on a Chicago metropolitan TV channel. "I'm sorry, but I'm sure the police won't change their time schedule so that I can be on the evening news."

Reporter Arnie reluctantly agreed to postpone the interview. He said he would use footage from the crime scene for the evening news and that my interview would be saved for the follow-up story for the next day.

The squad car that came for me was in a plain brown wrapper. I was disappointed. I'd pictured blaring sirens and flashing red lights so that my catty neighbors would have something more to talk about besides my short skirts and long earrings.

I opened my door to the cutest officer, whose nametag read "Patrolman Richter." He reminded me of my younger son. I yelled "bye" to Harry and I was on my way.

Once in the car I tried to get Patrolman Richter to use the siren or lights just once, but that didn't happen. He wasn't interested in chitchat either. So I filled my brain with deep philosophical thoughts such as: would my sons get a rebate on the seminar; would Harry, "You have more clothes than a boutique, Samantha," have a coronary when he saw the new dress I'd purchased for an upcoming wedding; why did one false nail always break a whole week before the next manicure; can I convince Darling to take me out to dinner when

I get back home — and before I knew it, we had arrived at our destination.

Down through history, deep, philosophical thinking has always helped time fly.

I was directed to a waiting room. The door soon opened, and another hunk of a police officer said, "Okay, miss, Detective Kelly will see you now."

I immediately liked this policeman. In fact, his curly hair reminded me of my older son. At my tender age, any young man who called me "miss" instead of "ma'am" can do no wrong. His cute butt wasn't bad either. I always did like men in uniform.

The officer ushered me into the same interrogation room in which I was questioned the day before.

"Am I a suspect?" I asked Detective Kelly upon entering.

"Why do you think that?" He gave me a piercing look, as if I'd put the idea into his head. "We're in early stages of interrogation. At this time, everyone who was at the seminar is a person of interest." He motioned me into the identical uncomfortable chair with the cracked vinyl seat I remembered from my last visit and got right down to business. No small talk from Mr. Detective.

How could someone so handsome be so unpleasant?

"I just want to review your story. Sometimes a person remembers things a day or two after a traumatic experience." He looked at me as though he suspected I had manufactured most of my account the previous day. "Before your lunch break, did anything unusual happen?"

"Everybody kind of minded his or her own business," I told him. Suddenly, Killer-look Woman popped into my mind. I had more or less decided not to say anything about her, but Detective Kelly must've noticed a change in my facial expression.

"Yes, what?" he asked.

I didn't want to cast aspersions on anyone just because I found her creepy, but Detective Kelly insisted I tell him what had given me pause.

"There was this woman who gave me the *kruszkies*."

"What? Krusz. What?"

"Sorry. I coined that word and use it when I can't think of a better word fast enough. I mean she gave me the willies." I paused to see if that word was in his vocabulary, then continued. "As I entered the seminar room yesterday morning, her venomous glare almost stopped me in my tracks. If looks could kill, I'd be the one in your morgue right now."

The detective questioned me about the fellow attendees world without end, amen, but focused on Frances. I think her killer-looks intrigued him.

No, I didn't know Frances Morrow. No, she didn't look even slightly familiar. No, she never spoke to me. No, no, no, I had no idea what her problem was. In the end, I merely stated that maybe she recognized me from my TV show. Maybe she didn't like something I'd said or someone I'd interviewed on the program. Perhaps she'd stopped me in the past to put her name in the Fan Jar for prizes and I'd failed to do so. How stupid did that sound!

A whole new scenario opened for the detective, and I had to go into the entire story about the program I host. The ordeal was exhausting. I needed a martini, damn it, not the acidy coffee that was offered me, *sans* cookies.

"Could this woman have been glaring at someone else? Perhaps the eventual victim who was seated next to you?"

I had considered the same idea late last night but dismissed it as speculation, because I thought the woman also gave me the killer-look as I came into the room. Confusing ideas spun around in my mind like Indy-500 cars on the racetrack. Was the eventual victim perhaps entering behind me? Did we arrive at about the same time? Or did everyone who entered the room get the look? I racked my brain in vain. Hey, that rhymed. Maybe I should become a poet, not a writer. And screw these stray thoughts when I should be keeping focused.

"I didn't have my glasses on, Detective, so I can't be sure her every malevolent look actually came my way."

"Frances Morrow. A woman possibly giving you wicked looks. A resident of Tinley Park, a neighboring community of yours. Does any of this have special meaning to you?" His gaze bored into mine.

Dear lord, I thought. Here we go again with "does that seem familiar" crap. I wanna go home!

I told him no, and hesitated. I couldn't decide in that split second whether to tell him about seeing Frances Morrow in the church during lunch or not. If I said I found her there either violently sobbing or hysterically laughing, Detective Kelly would probably have the poor woman in hand irons before I could shove the words back into my mouth. But he had the story out of me within seconds. I guess that's why he gets the big bucks.

Again Kelly questioned me every which way but loose about the church situation. I think he was still convinced I was withholding crime-solving evidence. I had learned my lesson. My mouth would remain closed to extraneous information trying to ooze out until further notice.

After signing my statement, I was told that I could leave. As Detective Kelly was brisk with me and also seemed to be annoyed, I didn't bother checking out his butt. Judging from the rest of him, though, I bet myself it was a "10."

On the way back to the squad car, I berated myself for exposing poor Frances. Even the cute officer with the cute you-know-what couldn't cheer me up during the drive back to my house. And I still faced an interview that night with Arnie Kendall from CLTV.

Upon arriving home, I needed a cool martini with floating olives in a chilled glass, and a rubdown with a satin glove.

Instead I got Harry with a scowl on his face and no decanter in his hand, let alone a fashion accessory.

"What took so long, Samantha?" Darling was full blast into his aggravated mode. "This house sounded like an office with the phone ringing all day. How many interviews did you agree to do?"

"Don't start with your lectures." I gave him the uplifted hand, the Samantha look, and went upstairs to fill a warm bath full of my favorite bath salts.

Refreshed, new makeup intact and in a great outfit, I was ready for the CLTV interview.

Chapter 6

The reporter, Arnie Kendall, turned out to be a jerk, obviously in love with himself. He primped and posed and watched himself on the camera screen as the interview progressed, almost oblivious to my answers. I was unimpressed by his style and arrogance. Even after only a year or so of interviewing guests on my TV show, I felt I could've done a much better job.

Ah, I remain an undiscovered treasure.

Kendall's first question was, "How did you feel when you found the body, Ms. Lisowski?"

I hate when reporters ask such a question when a serious crime is involved. I should have sarcastically countered, "Like dancing in the streets, dodo head. How the hell do you think I felt?" But instead I smiled sweetly and said, "Please call me Samantha." He answered my smile with a stiff, false one of his own. I felt like bopping him on the head, but I controlled myself and continued. "At first I thought Ms. Langley was just taking a nap in some spilled, sticky V-8 stuff."

Did the guy follow up on this remark? No! Did he not want to know why I couldn't distinguish a sleeping body from a dead one? Instead of pursuing my statement, he came up with a question that had nothing to do with my response.

"How did you find out about this self-publishing workshop?"

Was he not interested in how I could have mistaken V-8 stuff with your daily twenty-three vegetables and thirty vitamins in it for blood? Did he not realize that inquiring minds would want to know?

Kendall reminded me of a story my college writing class professor told us liberal arts students as an illustration of how not to interview:

A reporter asked Ernest Hemingway, back from an African safari, about his scariest adventure.

"*I was coming out of my tent at dawn one day,*" the author said. "*As I emerged, I came face to face with a Bengal tiger! I was so frightened I couldn't move.*"

"*What do you think of the African situation, Mr. Hemingway?*" the clueless reporter asked.

As I didn't think Kendall would appreciate my mini-lecture, I kept my lovely painted lips shut. He continued asking inane questions that I hoped I didn't answer insipidly. Arrogant Arnie hemmed and hawed a lot through it all.

Although Kendall was at the house for more than an hour, I knew the bit would run thirty seconds, tops, on the morning news. I also knew that the plug I managed to sneak in for my own TV program would end up on the cutting-room floor.

"Well, that took you long enough," Harry said after the reporter left. "I suppose the phone will be ringing off the hook tomorrow with calls from your friends, reporters and God knows who else. You never think how I feel about the commotion you cause in my life."

As Darling just about never answered the phone, I didn't know how I was causing any discomfort at his end. He'd be at work all day anyway. I ignored his grumbling and went upstairs to call Reenee and the boys. I wanted to make sure they'd catch my debut the next morning on a major TV channel.

Glen and Jeff thought it was too cool.

Reenee, on the other hand, expressed concern for my safety. "Aren't you worried that the killer might see the interview and think you are a threat to him?"

"Don't be silly," I said. "I have absolutely no inkling about who committed the murder."

"But what if the killer doesn't know that? What if he gets it into his head that you saw something that could identify him? I'm surprised you haven't thought of this possibility, considering all the police programs you watch and the detective mysteries you read."

I blinked. Damn. She might be right. Maybe that interview wasn't such a good idea after all.

"You've got a point, Reenee," I told her. "I was so wrapped up in myself that I never considered possible, dangerous side effects. See what I get for not discussing things with you before I jump into doing them?"

"Well, just be careful, Sammy. And ix-nay on any more stories to reporters. Let all this die down."

I assured my friend that I'd follow her advice and told her I was looking forward to our get together the next day.

As I needed a break from murder and mayhem, I was glad Reenee and I had long ago planned a visit to the Chicago Bears summer training camp in Lake Forest the following day. We loaded her ten-year-old godchild and my nine-year-old godchild into her van and were on our way. I don't know who was more excited about the trip — the boys, or Reenee and me. Besides men in uniform, she and I love football players, in or out of uniforms.

We spoke little about the murder. The kids were wild about seeing the Chicago Bears up close. Reenee and I were wild about checking out the tight ends with our binoculars. One of the players must have spotted us, because he flicked his tongue over his lips and flashed a big toothy smile our way. We nearly fell off the bleachers! He probably felt he was doing his job of keeping menopausal women happy.

When the Bears started practice skirmishes, we moved from the bleachers to sit on a blanket on the grass behind a taped-off area. Believe me, ladies, there is nothing so exciting as being at ground level as tough, muscular, sweaty linemen rush toward you! The boys were in heaven, and we two silly women almost swooned with ecstasy.

After the training sessions ended, we joined the crowds seeking autographs. Like shameless fifty-something hussies, Reenee and I winked and flirted with any players who looked our way. They seemed to get a kick out of it. Probably couldn't wait to get home and tell their girlfriends about the two older broads making asses of themselves.

When we finally returned to the van, we were bowled over to find a black rose under the windshield wiper. We looked around trying to spot someone watching our reaction to finding it there. Crowds were milling about in the parking lot, but no one seemed to be interested in us.

"Looks like we impressed the hell out of one of those football players, Sammy. I bet it was the one who was slurping his tongue all over his mouth whenever we looked his way. I guess we still got It, kid."

"Don't get too hyped up, Reenee. More probably a player put the flower there as a dare from his teammates or as a joke — to get a kick out of seeing two old broads react like they'd have young football players even remotely interested in them. Besides, don't you think it's weird that someone could find a flower at a training camp, let alone a black rose?"

Regardless of the intent, we giggled like high school cheerleaders, put the rose behind the visor in the car and made up preposterous fantasies about the guy who'd left us the flower.

We stopped at a restaurant on the way home and gorged ourselves on fried food and milkshakes. Our godchildren were keyed up about having their pictures taken with their favorite players and getting their autographs.

"You're the bestest godmother in the whole wide world," little Steven told me.

I hugged him and told him he was the bestest godchild in the whole wild world.

Saturated with good old fat and sugar, we headed for home. All the way, Reenee and I took turns putting the black rose in our hair and behind our ears. Even the pricks from the thorns didn't curb our enthusiasm. We had a merry old time.

Murder was the farthest thing from my mind.

Murder became foremost on my mind the minute we arrived at my house.

Detective Kelly was perched on my porch.

Chapter 7

Reenee took my godchild home, saying she'd talk to me later.

Although I offered refreshments, Detective Kelly was not interested in tea and crumpets, or even coffee and Oreos. He preferred to remain perched on my porch. He appeared more brisk and agitated than the last time we spoke. His main annoyance seemed to be with writers who, he felt, treated crimes as fodder for their next novels. Secretly I was pleased that he put me in an author category, but surely he couldn't accuse me of holding back information and trying to solve the murder on my own?

I couldn't figure out why he was telling me all these things. I was absolutely truthful with him. Didn't I enlighten him about Killer-look Woman?

And did I smell alcohol on his breath?

"We have whittled down the persons of interest to five," he said. "Although you are not one of them, I expect you to be at headquarters on Thursday at 9 a.m."

"Me? I don't know anything more than what I've told you. What about Frances Morrow? Did you talk to her? What did she have to say about all those killer looks headed my — or somebody's — way?" My arms moved frantically and my long earrings jangled in agitation. I was incensed to be inconvenienced with more interrogation sessions when all I did was find the body. "Did you discover why that woman who fainted, that Thorpe person, why she accused me of murder? How did she know the Langley woman was dead, having only entered the room herself?"

Throughout my tirade, Detective Kelly gazed at me with a silly smile on his face. Did he find my rantings humorous?

I continued my third degree. "Did you look into the murdered woman's background to find a link with anyone at the seminar? Did you consider the possibility that someone from outside the group could have killed Langley?" Wow, I was good at this interrogation business. Maybe I should seek a detective's career instead of a writer's? "And who're the other persons of interest?"

A smug expression accompanied his reply. "We ask the questions, and we don't entertain queries about an on-going investigation."

Great, I thought. Now he's using the royal *we*.

I wondered why Kelly was delivering this message personally. He had driven a great distance to be here on my porch. My mind began to create scenarios. Maybe he had a girlfriend in the southwest suburbs. Maybe he did his drinking miles away from his district. Maybe he was having a breakdown. Maybe I should pay attention to what he was saying.

"Do you understand?"

Oh lord, understand what? I looked at him like he might have the words written on his forehead.

"You've got me so upset that you'd better repeat the last part."

"Don't act flustered. You know what I said. The car will be here Thursday at eight in the morning."

Jeez, I thought. Just what I need. Another grouchy man in my life.

Suddenly his demeanor changed.

"Would you consider having lunch with me after the meeting?"

"What?" I took a step back and almost fell off the porch! Detective Kelly grabbed my arm to steady me. His hand lingered, caressing my skin. I was speechless.

"Think about it. I like your sense of humor and your sauciness." He winked, leaving me with a look that stripped me naked.

I stood on the porch in shock until his car left the driveway. Then I yelled, "Yikes," and flew into the house to call Reenee.

"Detective Kelly hit on you?" she screeched, after I related the whole scenario. "What're you gonna do?"

"What do you mean what am I going to do? I'll either ignore his pass or report him."

"Or go to lunch with him. I'm sure you noticed how sexy he is."

"Reenee!"

"We're not getting any younger, Sam. What would it hurt? Order the most expensive entrée on the menu, sip your martini and enjoy the attention."

"Right," I replied, throwing in a lot of sarcasm as I continued, "and return to his office, swish the paperwork off his desk and lie across it in as seductive a pose a fifty-ish woman can muster."

"Yeah! Wear some Victoria's Secret undies — black, or red." Reenee began to giggle. "Spray on your Fay-Tel perfume."

"Turn on that sexy station full of police calls," I giggled back.

"Caress his gun."

"Fondle his shield."

"Nibble on his armored vest."

We worked ourselves into a sniggering fit as we kept topping one another with ribald comments.

"Thanks, Reenee. I needed that. You're better than a shot of Jack Daniels. You always know how to lighten a situation." I wiped the happy tears from my eyes. "But, seriously, what do you think I should do?"

"Maybe you should discuss this with Harry."

"Are you crazy? He'll turn it around and insist that I'm responsible for Kelly's pass. Maybe I should ask my attorney-cousin, Paul, to accompany me?"

"Wouldn't it seem suspicious to haul a lawyer along? My gut feeling is for you to attend the meeting alone and pretend the lunch invitation never happened. It was probably the booze talking anyway."

"You're most likely right. Lord knows I made stupid statements many a time in a boozy haze. By the way, thanks for taking Steven home. And that was something else with the black rose, huh? Oh, well, I think our godchildren had a good time at the Bears training camp."

"Not as great a time as we had." Reenee started to giggle again.

Chapter 8

The next afternoon, Khara, an acquaintance of mine, gave me a jingle.

"I wanted to call you ever since I saw your interview on CLTV," she said. "You looked great on the tube, by the way. Me — I'd be sputtering all over myself. But then, you're always so comfortable in front of a camera."

"Thanks. Kendall carries on a lousy interview, but that's another story. I'm glad you called me, because I intended contacting you today. Talk about two great minds, huh?"

After we caught up on each other's news, I asked if she knew a Frances Morrow who lived a block away from her. I told her the woman was at that writing seminar where the murder took place, but I didn't go into details about her venomous looks or her performance at the church.

"Oh, yes, I know *of* her," Khara said. "Frances is the neighborhood's subject of gossip and speculation. Has been for years. I understand that in the past she was a social butterfly, active in the writing and publishing community, friendly and fun to be with."

"Are you sure we're talking about the same Frances Morrow? The woman I'm talking about seemed to frown a lot." Boy, was that the understatement of the year.

"Yes. It's sad to hear how she's deteriorated in the last thirty years or so. Put on loads of weight, unfriendly — kinda out of it. Frances is practically a recluse. I didn't think she had time to treat herself to a movie, let alone attend an all-day seminar."

This phone call was paying off. It seemed that Khara knew a great deal about Frances.

"What in the world happened to her?" I asked. "Why *wouldn't* she have time for a seminar?"

"I've been told that she drastically changed her lifestyle due to a horrible, debilitating disease that her daughter contracted. Lori is totally incapacitated. Frances and John, her husband, are Lori's primary, and probably only, caregivers, absolutely devoted to her."

"How terrible. Life can sure suck. Has Frances always lived in Tinley Park?"

"No, her former place was on Lake Shore Drive and was supposed to be a doozy. I'm told she used to throw lavish cocktail parties at her home for well-known authors. She even had movie stars at her get-togethers."

"Was she a professional woman?"

"The word is that she wrote for a magazine or worked for a publisher in some high position. No one seems to know for sure."

"What a change in her life, huh? Her finances must have taken a tumble. Medical bills and therapy sessions have been known to wipe out fortunes. What's Lori's condition called?"

"I can't remember. It's got some kind of long name. My sister's pal has an aunt who's kind of a close friend to Frances. I can ask and check out the latest buzz if you'd like."

I told her I'd like and would be in touch.

Later in the evening, with Harry gone on his overnight business trip, I decided it was time to do some serious writing. Being mentally and physically involved in a real-life murder was exciting, but deadline beckoneth, the bell tolleth and all that stuff. I put the whole Detective Kelly thing on the back burner of my brain.

Almost five months ago I entered a writing contest sponsored by a magazine that published male/female relationship articles. The entry rules stated that stories could be serious, dramatic or humorous. My submission fell into the latter category. I was thrilled when my cynically-amusing vignette was awarded first place. Part of my prize allowed me to submit stories once a month for possible publication. My dark humor and caustic dialogue seemed to appeal to the editors. Each effort I sent in since winning the contest had been published.

After six months, a favorable review from the magazine's board could result in me being hired as a regular contributor. I had one month left before the powers-that-be determined my fate.

My stories were based loosely on my life with Harry. Over our married years together, he's provided me with a lot of "ammunition" upon which to expand and exaggerate. I changed names, however, to protect the guilty. Also, I used a pen name for my submissions, as I intended to kill "Eddie/Harry" in one of my future stories. Still and all, I considered myself fortunate that Darling wasn't interested in reading my articles. Otherwise, I might have WWIII on my hands if he'd read how I embellished his every idiosyncrasy.

Or maybe not. The magazine paid fairly well. Harry tends to forgive a lot when money is rolling in.

A couple of ideas for the next piece spun around in my head. Let's see what conflict I can stir up this month, I thought.

Am I not a super individual who could so easily shift gears? Harry is so lucky to have me. If only he knew it.

Creative juices flowed as I sat down at the computer. The murder/Detective Kelly upheaval seemed to stimulate my psyche. My fingers flew over the keyboard and the words had nothing to do with murder:

THREE LITTLE WORDS

There are three little words that I hate to hear.

No, the three little words are not "I loathe you" nor the dreaded commitment of "I love you," or "Please marry me."

The three little words I hate to hear are, "Here, you drive," as my husband, Eddie, tosses me the keys to the car.

Eddie really doesn't mean, "Here, you drive." What he really means is "Here, you drive, so I can criticize everything you do."

Not too much later I sat back and congratulated myself. Done, and it was barely midnight.

Save. Proofread. Edit. Forward. It felt good to send the article on its way.

And then the phone rang.

Midnight.
Phone ringing.
Home alone.
Involved in a murder.
I got the *kruszkies*.

Chapter 9

Although apprehensive about answering a midnight phone call, ninety-eight percent of me figured it was Harry or Reenee. Both knew that I stayed up till all hours of the night. I don't have caller ID on my phone because, like my kitchen appliances and most of my furniture, the Lisowski household is a close second to pioneer days, or maybe life in the Dark Ages, when it comes to new and improved living.

Two percent of my brain considered current circumstances and didn't want to answer the call, but the ninety-eight percent of me won.

"Hello?" I said in a brave, matter-of-fact voice.

The caller wasn't Harry or Reenee.

A soft, eerie voice chuckled out my name as a simultaneous flash of lightning and a nerve-racking clap of thunder almost made me jump out of my Minnie Mouse pajamas. Few things are more frightening to me than being alone in a big house on a stormy night and receiving a phone call from some weirdo.

Instead of being sensible and hanging up, I reacted like the goofy women in TV movies. "Who is this? Harry, is that you? Are you trying to be funny?"

"No-o-o," exhaled the breathy voice. "I'm watching you. It's such a pleasure watching you!"

"Drop dead!" I yelled and hung up the phone, which immediately rang again.

Was the caller Killer-look Woman? Or, Jean, the Accuser? Or — oh, my God, not Detective Kelly!

I picked up the receiver, slammed it down and then kept it off the hook. I wasn't going to cooperate in the caller's game. I could strangle women in movies who'd keep answering the creepy calls, asking "who's there" over and over while getting more scared by the moment.

But the caller unnerved me.

Try going to sleep after that!

I tried, after turning on every light in my bedroom. Under the covers I dove, like a little kid who thinks her "blanky" is going to keep her safe. I had almost re-introduced myself to Mr. Sandman when the doorbell began ringing non-stop and a banging on the door made me want to dive further under the comforter.

Being the gutsy broad that I am, I knew I'd have to go downstairs and check out the disturbance, whether the person on the other side of the door was a serial killer or a magazine salesman. Considering the hour, the first was more likely.

I quickly walked down the stairs, stopped in the kitchen for a frying pan and cautiously approached the front door. Damn you, Harry, I swore in my mind. I told you over and over again to buy a door with glass inserts. How the hell can I distinguish through a windowless door whether the bell-ringer/door knocker was male, female, friend or foe? Damn you, Harry.

"Who's there?" I asked loudly in a quivering voice. "I have my cell phone in hand and just have to press the last number to call the police."

"Samantha, it's Reenee. Are you okay? Let me in."

"Reenee? What the shit are you doing here at three in the morning? Are you crazy coming out on a night like this! Is something wrong? Did you have a fight with Wally?"

"Will you just open the friggin' door and stop asking stupid questions? It's raining like hell out here."

As soon as I opened the door, Reenee smothered me with a bear hug.

"I'm so glad you're okay, Sammy! I was just falling asleep when it dawned on me that you might be in danger over all this murder stuff."

"What in the world — oh, lord, you're all wet."

Reenee looked like a drooping ice sculpture. She seemed worried and stressed out. "I had to come here."

"Not another word," I told her. "Take off those soaked clothes while I dig up some towels and a bathrobe for you. We can put your wet stuff in the dryer."

After she snuggled into the warm robe I brought her, Reenee plopped on the sofa as I scurried to switch on all the lights in the house and re-cradle the phone. I knew Wally would be calling here once he discovered his wife was gone. I also brought some wine back for the both of us. As soon as I sat down, an avalanche of words tumbled out of her.

"I figured that if you could find Frances' address in the phone book, then she could find yours. She's gotta be aware of you after your interview played on TV. She must be under overwhelming pressure from the stress of the murder or from the police, and decided that you're her next victim. I decided to phone and warn you."

She shivered as she spoke. I told her to slow down and drink some more wine. After a few sips, she continued in a more rational manner.

"I called you, but the line was busy. I called fifteen minutes later and it was still busy. I waited another half hour, and when I still couldn't get through, I called the operator. She said the phone lines in your area were not down and perhaps your receiver was off the hook. That's when my imagination took off."

Words churned out of Reenee faster than an auctioneer's chatter. "I could just see it. The assailant broke in. She snuck up to your room. She saw you at your computer. You turned around and screamed. There was a struggle. You reached for the phone. The killer banged it out of your hand. You tripped. She attacked. You lay on the floor, your life oozing away, your throat slit by that big ol' butcher knife!"

I looked at Reenee in astonishment. Who was the mystery writer here anyway? Her imagination was more inventive than mine.

She gasped and finished breathlessly, "Your energies invaded my psyche. I could feel your vibes in my bones. You were dying and I had to save you. I threw on my coat, left a hurried note for Wally and drove over here like a bat out of hell."

"Oh, Reenee," I said with a catch in my voice. "You truly are my soul mate. Could a person have a better friend?"

I hugged her. This marvelous woman had driven twenty miles by herself during a vicious storm in the wee hours of the morning just to see if I was okay. Shades of the ghastly experience in our youth flickered through my mind. I shook myself mentally. No way was I going there tonight, but I knew Reenee felt the waves of nostalgia, just as I did. We looked intently at each other, silently recalling grisly, dark moments of thirty years ago. A few tears and holding tight to each other's hands settled us down.

"Circumstance call for more nectar of the grapes," I said with a little laugh, trying to ease the tension.

During our third glass of California's finest, I related my midnight experience. My situation didn't seem as scary now that Reenee was next to me. We discussed possible phone call suspects.

We just started to get comfortable with the idea that all's well in God's world, when a ferocious flash of lightning struck, and the lights went out. Almost on cue the phone rang. We both jumped. We grabbed hands as I cautiously answered the call.

"Sam! Please tell me that Reenee made it there." Wally's panicked voice soared over the phone. "I woke up to go to the bathroom and saw that she was gone. Good thing she left a note for me on the toilet seat or I would've called the police. What the hell is going on?"

I assured Wally that everything was okay, and turned the phone toward Reenee, sharing the receiver with her. She quickly explained the situation, summing it up by pleading, "Please don't be mad, Wally. I'm sorry I worried you, but I had a chilling feeling that Sam was in trouble. I just had to come here immediately. I wasn't thinking straight."

We both pulled our ears away from the receiver as Wally vented his anger and fear.

"Oh, honey, I really am wretched over my stupidity. But do you mind if I stay here for the night? It's brutal outside, and now the electricity's off. We're both really scared. I don't want to leave Sam alone."

After further "discussion" regarding his dissatisfaction about his wife's nocturnal activities, Wally stated that he was coming over to stay with us.

"Watch for my car, and do not answer the door for anyone else. Call the police if either of you feels uneasy. Let them dismiss you as two silly women with unfounded fears if nothing comes of it. Better that than you doing something to endanger yourselves. I should be there in forty minutes."

Wally and the electricity arrived at the same time. My night of panic faded with the darkness. I chastised myself for being a silly old broad.

My punishment was preparing a giant-size breakfast the next morning for my overnight guests.

Did I ever mention that besides cleaning house, I hate cooking?

Chapter 10

Harry walked in from his overnight business trip while Reenee, Wally and I were enjoying our breakfast buffet.

"Hmm," he said. "When I smelled food, I thought I was in the wrong house. I should have known that we had company." Harry observed the bacon and eggs, pancakes and syrup, the oatmeal and the coffee. "Sam never cooks an elaborate breakfast just for me."

"I'm trying to keep your cholesterol and weight down," I quipped. "I want you around for a few more years, because who'd be my polka partner if you're in the hereafter?"

Ah, another day in the war of words. Note to self: Remember Harry's dumb statement and Samantha's clever retort, for use in an upcoming story.

Harry attacked the food feast. I don't cook often, but when I do, I make enough to feed the entire U.S. Marine Corps. Darling was on his second helping of pancakes when it dawned on him to ask why we had company at ten o'clock in the morning.

We all spoke at the same time, giving him our own versions. The chatter sounded like cackling time at the hen house. Harry kept looking at one or the other of us, trying to figure out what the hell we were talking about.

He finally called out, "Stop. Everyone stop. One at a time."

I took first dibs because I wanted last night's episode told so as to put me in a favorable light. Then Wally and Reenee had their say.

Harry looked at me in exasperation. "You see what happens, Samantha, when you get involved in a mess? I told you not to agree to be interviewed on TV or go sneaking around that Morrow woman's house. You call your detective and tell him about the phone call. It's got to be related to the murder."

"He's not my detective, even though he made a pass at me — oops, shit!"

Darling glared at me. "He what?"

"Now just relax, Harry. I think it was just the booze that made him do it."

"The booze? You gave him a drink? Or did you meet him at a bar, Samantha?"

This whole thing was getting out of hand. Reenee glanced at me with knowing eyes and said, "Let's go, Wally. I'll pick up my clothes from the laundry room and we'll be on our way. Call you later, Sam."

"What are her clothes doing in the laundry room, Samantha? Was Detective Kelly part of this shedding-of-the-clothes experience, too?"

By now my head was spinning. I was dead tired since I only slept a few hours, and last night's wine marathon didn't help my morning blahs. I wanted to lie down for a while, but Harry insisted I tell him everything, starting from the time he left the house yesterday.

I fell asleep in my oatmeal while Harry was still in his lecture mode.

I received the silent treatment the rest of the day. To say that Harry was not pleased with me would be the understatement of the millennium. I made several attempts to appease him until I came to my senses.

Hey, I thought, why isn't he more empathetic toward me? How come he's not showering me with concern and sympathy over that scary phone call? Why can't we discuss this Detective Kelly situation so I know what to do about tomorrow's meeting at the police station, instead of him giving me a hard time?

I decided the hell with it. As usual, I'd figure out a solution for myself.

Without a goodbye to Mr. Wonderful, I grabbed my purse, got in the car and went shopping. Nothing like a nice outfit from head to toe to lift a girl's spirits.

I treated myself to a massage, too.

Harry could make his own dinner. An elaborate breakfast was

enough cooking for me in one day.

In the words of Marie Antoinette, "Let him eat cake."

Chapter 11

Six-thirty Thursday morning came too fast. I had slept soundly but with crazy dreams. Chasing murderers with knives and forks and being chased by them in return resulted in one haggard body. And I still had to decide what to wear for the meeting at the police station. I intended to tone down my usual attire so the good ol' detective wouldn't think I'd dressed provocatively just for him.

I hoped Harry wouldn't awaken while I was getting ready. I didn't want to discuss anything with him. He'd had his chance the day before.

Besides, I didn't want his words of wisdom to start my day off any worse than it was already proving to be: I had to change my pantyhose twice because of two runs; the zipper on my skirt caught on my tucked-in blouse, which ripped the fabric; I couldn't find my favorite earrings or my lucky wristwatch; a heel from my shoe fell off as I walked down the hallway stairs, and I nearly killed myself on the steps. If these were omens, maybe I should get back into bed and call in sick. But being the valiant person I am, I merely sang *We Shall Overcome*, and I did.

Minutes later my "chauffeur" rang the doorbell. I took a deep breath, said a quick prayer to Our Lady of the Bewitched, Bothered and Bewildered and answered the door.

I expected a paddy wagon to be my chariot, filled with the persons of interest, but a lonely unmarked car was parked in the driveway. I supposed the powers-that-be wanted us in separate vehicles so we couldn't talk to each other or compare notes. My designated driver, who looked only a little older than the kid-cop who'd watched over me at the crime scene, wasn't vocal either. So I sat back in the car and recalled Reenee's advice. We'd decided that I should act nonchalant and avoid Detective Kelly's baby blues.

"Be like Jack Web in the old *Dragnet* series," she had quipped, "and give him 'just the facts, ma'am.'"

Regardless, *kruszkies* were jumping around in my stomach.

The wildest things that ever happened at my suburban Oak Forest police station was when the town drunk was hauled in, and nine out of ten times he was in a stupor. Not so in Detective Kelly's Chicago district. This police station buzzed with complainants, lost souls, ladies of the night and a few crazies. I was apprehensive, but enthralled, and already making mental notes for use in a future story.

As I was ushered into the good ol' interrogation room, I hoped the other people brought in for questioning would join me. Good luck with that pipe dream, Samantha, I thought. Passing through the station, I recognized a couple of them from the seminar seated by detectives' desks.

Hmm, lucky me. I get Detective Kelly in a room all by myself. Damn, I should've worn slacks. My skirt was too short. Sitting, I wouldn't be able to keep my knees covered. And the stupid blouse. The material barely overlapped enough to cover my bra. So much for planning a conservative wardrobe. What was I thinking to have worn this outfit?

When Detective Kelly entered, he gave me a brisk "Good morning," and an even brisker head-to-toe look. No need to avoid his baby blues because he was too busy avoiding my emerald greens. The devil in me wanted to be frisky and ask, "And where are you taking me for lunch," but I behaved myself.

Detective Kelly brusquely inquired, "Were you aware of a cooking class going on in the building where your writing seminar was held?"

I was dumbfounded. "A cooking class?"

"Yeah. You know. Where food is prepared. Where a stove heats up soups and sauces. Where meat is broiled, fried, baked. Where vegetables are micro-waved. Where desserts are conjured up. A *cooking class.*"

Why the hell was he so hyped? His sarcastic tone got my American dander up. Before I could spit out a few sharp words of my own, he rose from his chair and stormed out of the office, slamming the door behind him.

Hey, I was the one who should be acting nasty. I steamed as I sat and awaited the return of my inquisitor.

The door flew open. Detective Kelly thrust a plastic bundle onto the desk in front of me. I jumped as though gamma rays shot out of it. Two big ol' knives were encased in separate bags.

"Since the last time we spoke, new developments have unfolded. Do you recognize these knives? They came from the cooking class being held on the second floor of the Unique World building. Did you see anyone enter or exit that room?"

"I wasn't even aware of a cooking class being held." The instructor must've been working with sushi or cold foods. I recalled no smells permeating the hallway or stairwells. "And I didn't see anyone go in or out of any other room except the one I was in. I certainly would've noticed a person carrying a knife!"

"For supposedly being a writer, you certainly don't observe things going on around you, Ms. Lisowski, do you? You also hadn't noticed that a woman was stabbed to death."

His caustic tone continued to irritate me. In fact I was almost fuming. I opened my mouth to heave some scathing remarks at him, but was saved by the bell. Well, actually by the door being opened by a burly detective. Just like in a *Law and Order* episode, Detective Kelly was beckoned to leave the room. He ordered me to stay put.

I almost saluted and said, "Yes, *mein Fuhrer.*"

After two cups of lousy coffee and a stale sweet roll a female officer brought me, my interrogator returned. This time he tossed a folder onto the table and opened it. I literally jumped an inch out of my seat. I stared at an eight-by-ten glossy of a dead woman decked out with a knife in her chest and splattered with so much blood, I couldn't make out the color of her blouse. Her long black hair was matted and in wild disarray.

"Recognize her, Ms. Lisowski?"

Saliva had dried up in my mouth. I didn't think I could answer him. But I was also upset that he didn't warn me ahead of time about the gruesome photo. I asked for a drink of water. He heaved a big sigh, told me I might want to look at the other photos in the folder while he was gone and once again left the room.

Cautiously I leafed through the rest of the glossy prints and got the third shock of the morning. I knew this woman!

Detective Kelly reentered with a paper cup and bottled water. He noticed my distress as he poured me a glassful.

"What's the matter? Are you going to faint?"

"No, I'm not ready to swoon into your arms." He quickly looked up at me but let the remark go. "I know this woman. I mean, I don't *know* her, but I've seen her. She passed by the building a couple of times that Saturday and even tried to talk to me when I was behind the police line."

I remembered her long stringy hair, those big black Elvis-like glasses and her weird outfit. Who could forget her extremely short skirt that sprouted one bare leg while a white opaque stocking adorned the other? I recalled how she wobbled on her spiked heels and sang to herself.

"What was her name?" I whispered.

"His given name was Zachary Wilson but everyone called him by his stage moniker, Long Tall Sally. He used to be a female impersonator who was no longer content remaining a female copycat."

I had sensed at the time that there was something extremely strange about that person. Nonetheless, this information bamboozled me.

"Mr. Wilson pursued a complete gender overhaul," Detective Kelly continued. "Unfortunately, a few botched sex-change procedures affected his mind, as well as his body."

What a bizarre situation. I wished I had never become involved in any of this. How could a writing seminar go so wrong?

Detective Kelly had more to tell me. He added that Mr. Wilson eventually ended up the neighborhood eccentric, harmless, but inclined to meander into buildings and nose around.

"Most people tolerated him. Others would become annoyed. They'd call us, and we'd escort him to the community mental facility. As soon as he was released, Zachary'd be up to his old ways."

I swallowed a couple of times. This information was too much and coming at me way too fast. I finally realized the seriousness and danger of the situation in which I was involved. I yearned for the water glass in front of me to change into a strong martini. My eyes began to tear.

"Are you okay, Saman — Ms. Lisowski?" I actually heard warmth and concern creep into Detective Kelly's voice. "Maybe I was too rough on you, throwing those photos and that knife practically in your lap. Can I get you anything?"

"No, I'm all right." I felt wretched. I looked up and forgot my rule. Baby greens and baby blues collided. We both quickly looked away. "Just give me a few moments," I said, in a voice I didn't recognize.

Detective Kelly nodded and turned his back to me, busying himself with other folders in his possession. I sternly reprimanded myself for being a weeping willow and admonished myself to get my act together. When he turned to face me again, I told him I was up to questioning.

"Can you tell me again under what circumstances you saw Zachary Wilson? Where and when?" His voice seemed human and sympathetic. "What did he say to you?"

I told Detective Kelly about her confusing words to me as I was behind the police tape barrier. Then I told him about our wordless encounters, once on my way to lunch and the second time after lunch when I ran out of the building looking for help. Each time, Long Tall Sally seemed happy, smiling and humming a tune.

"I wondered to myself if that's what 'she' did all day, wander aimlessly around the block. I feel so sorry for her, I mean him. Are the murders connected?"

"At this point, we think Mr. Wilson may have stumbled onto the person who stole the knife from the cooking class. He conceivably could have seen the murder and was deemed a threat to the killer. We are concerned that some of the others in your class may have spotted the murderer as well."

"Well, I didn't," I told him. "No one was in sight as I ran from the seminar room, and I certainly didn't pass anyone in the stairwell or hallways. In fact, I thought the place was deserted." I hesitated. "That's all I can tell you, but I feel I should mention that I got a creepy call two nights ago around midnight. I was home alone. An eerie voice on the other end kinda breathed, 'I'm watching you. It's such a pleasure watching you.' It spooked me."

I still wasn't positive the phone call hadn't come from him. Looking very closely at Detective Kelly, I thought his reaction seemed normal. If he felt guilty about being the party at the other end of the line that night, he hid it well. I saw no embarrassment or reddened cheeks. He asked why I didn't punch in star sixty-nine so as to identify the caller. I explained that I didn't have the service.

"You probably do but are unaware of it. You might want to check that out. Also, I want you to contact me if similar calls occur or anything else odd happens. We are dealing with a dangerous person. Here's my card with the phone number where I can be reached day or night."

He placed the card in my palm and wrapped his fingers around my hand. "Samantha. Please forgive me for my unprofessional behavior on your porch. I'd had a couple of drinks and was feeling lonely and sorry for myself. Because of my conduct that day, I felt uncomfortable around you this morning. I know I treated you roughly. I'm sorry. Thank you for not filing a complaint."

My heart immediately melted. Imagine — a man who apologized!

"Forget it, Detective," I answered with a dazzling smile. "In the past, I've said a lot of things under the influence that I certainly shouldn't have said. If it makes you feel any better, I was kind of flattered."

"Well, for what it's worth, I'm sorry you're married."

His baby blues nearly made me swoon. I forced my rubbery legs to leave his office before I said something that I couldn't blame on the wicked firewater.

Chapter 12

By the time I returned from the police station, Harry had gone to work. He had left a note for me on the kitchen table stating that he wished I had awakened him before I left that morning.

The last part of the message blew me away:

I'm sorry I was such an unfeeling jerk toward you. We'll discuss whatever you want when I get home from work. I hope everything turned out okay for you at police headquarters.

Love, Harry

Was I in the twilight zone? Apologies from two men in one day? I'd have to look this up in the *Guinness Book of World Records*. And *"Love, Harry?"* Was Darling hitting the bottle early in the morning? He never left me notes, and certainly wouldn't sign them that way if he did. Maybe he found out that I had some deadly disease and was trying to make my last moments in life enjoyable. If I had found flowers on the dining room table, I'd have dropped dead!

I jumped on the phone to bring Reenee up to date. She had been almost as stressed about the morning encounter with Detective Kelly as I was. I also was dying to tell her about Harry's note.

"So you chickened out of a rendezvous, huh, Sammy?" she teased, after I gave her the details of the sunrise meeting.

"Yeah, but wait. I haven't told you everything yet. Harry left an note of apology for me about his poor behavior and signed it 'with love.'"

"Oh, my God, Sam! He's having an affair."

"Harry? Are you nuts? He's too satisfied with life to complicate it by taking a lover. I'd expect to hear that the pope was engaged in an illicit relationship before I'd believe Harry was having one."

"Well, if you find a box of candy on the dresser or an expensive piece of jewelry on your bed, that will clinch the affair thing. Remember how we smirked whenever we saw a man buying flowers or a luxurious gift for his wife? Didn't we always assume he had a guilty conscience about some serious screw-up?"

"That's because we're both so cynical. This is Harry we're talking about."

"All the same, I'd make him a nice candlelight dinner and trade your Donald Duck PJs tonight for a Frederick's of Hollywood special."

"You are too funny, Reenee. I gotta go. If you hear that Harry's had a heart attack, you'll know I followed your advice."

Without going into lurid sexual escapades, or perhaps the better phrase would be boring details, Harry and I made nice before retiring. He really was a sensible man and put my mind at ease about several of my concerns. I fell asleep at peace with the world.

The phone rang around midnight.

I shook Harry awake.

"What's the matter?" he mumbled.

"The phone's ringing."

"Well, answer it."

"Harry!"

"Okay, okay." He grumbled out some vivid words.

By the time he yawned and stretched and yawned some more, the answering machine had kicked in. The caller left no message.

"Must've been a wrong number."

"Wrong number, my *dupa*," I snapped. "You don't think a murderer is gonna leave a message on the answering machine. . .?"

The phone interrupted my sentence.

I grabbed the receiver and turned it over to Harry.

"Who the hell is this and why are you calling so friggin' late?" Harry looked at the receiver in disgust. "He hung up. Must've been your secret creep-o killer."

"Hurry! Dial star sixty-nine to see who it was."

Before Harry could follow my instructions, the phone rang again.

"Who is this?" he asked again into the receiver, using a firm tone. He listened for a second and then banged the phone down. "He says he's watching you."

"Watching me? Where? When?" I was on my knees bouncing on the mattress in anticipation. "Did he say anything else, Harry — was it a man's voice?"

"Stop jumping on the bed. Act your age." Harry turned his annoyance toward me. "He or she just repeated, 'I'm watching her all the time.' We have to do something, Samantha. This is no longer funny. "

"No one said it was funny in the first place," I said, as I slowed down my calisthenics. On top of everything else, I was getting seasick. "Just dial star sixty-nine before he calls again."

But we had no luck. The code revealed no information regarding the midnight creepy-caller.

The telephone rang. Cursing, Harry picked it up, listened, slammed the receiver down and took it off the hook. "I can't believe this! Whoever heard of a murderer leaving messages?"

"What, huh? Like what? Like what?" I was ready to pull the words out of Harry's mouth. He can be so slow and infuriating.

"He wants you to answer the phone from now on. He misses your voice."

"What? That's ridiculous! Why would a murderer miss my voice? You must've misunderstood that message. I've been telling you for weeks to make a doctor's appointment to clean out that wax build-up in your ears."

"Don't start, Samantha. My ears are okay. I know what I heard. But I agree with you. The remarks were bizarre. This person must be a pervert besides being a murderer."

Harry sounded disgusted, but the caller was getting on my last nerve. "I'm calling Detective Kelly right now. He told me to let him know if I received any more calls. I have a number I can use, day or night."

"Go to bed, Samantha. We'll deal with this in the morning. Screw Detective Kelly."

Wow, did he actually give me permission?

Returning from the bathroom, I noticed that Harry already was gently snoring away. He'd fall asleep even if an atomic bomb blew up in the backyard, saying that he'd handle the catastrophe in the morning. His philosophy has always been: "Don't do it today 'cuz by tomorrow it may be taken care of by someone else."

But I was hyped up. Being a well-balanced Libra woman, I forced myself into serenity. Sleep, however, eluded me as I relived the episode in my fertile brain. Nuts, I thought. Might as well start on the article due next month.

I put on my robe and quietly made my way to the computer room. I booted up the PC and started to write my story for the magazine, exaggerating the events of my last couple of days:

The Note
I had left the house that morning with strained feelings between Eddie, my husband of too many years to count, and myself. Upon returning from shopping, I was bowled over to see that he'd left a note of apology for his behavior. . . .

As I finished the article, I glanced at the clock and was shocked to discover the hour. Time goes by when you're having fun, and even when you're not. I could almost hear the rooster crowing, or might have if we'd lived on a farm, which we didn't, and even if we did I probably wouldn't hear crowing anyway because I sleep like a dead person, and why am I rambling?

I figured I was slaphappy. So I went to bed.

Chapter 13

The next morning, I slept late. Harry already left for work. I either dreamt, or he told me while I was in a zombie state, to call Detective Kelly as soon as I woke up. Being the ever-obedient housewife and subservient spouse, my first call was to Reenee.

"Got more creepy phone calls last night, girlfriend," I burst out as soon as she answered the phone. I told her the rest of the story with expletives every time I mentioned Harry's casual reactions to the calls.

"Be careful, Sammy. If Harry hears you, you'll be in the dog house again."

"Not to worry. The enemy is not here. He usually doesn't go into the office on Fridays, but he told me last night that he had a few loose ends to handle."

"Uh-huh," she answered in a knowing voice. "Loose ends being blond and statuesque."

"Don't start that again," I said with a laugh. "Harry is not having an affair. Besides, if he did, it'd be with a dark-haired woman. He likes brunettes better than blondes. Enough about Harry. Why do you suppose the killer misses my voice? What's that all about?"

"Weird, Sammy, weird. Are you sure it's the killer calling you? Could it be just coincidental, you getting those phone calls at this time? Maybe it's a secret admirer."

"Yeah. At my age, a secret admirer. If so, he'd probably be an old codger with false teeth, bald head, and Coke bottle lenses for glasses. The days of secret admirers are gone for me."

Reenee laughed, then added, "Detective Kelly thinks you're still hot stuff. Why couldn't there be someone else around as well? We're getting up there in age, but we're not exactly dumpy-looking old broads."

"You're too much, Reenee. Maybe he's got a buddy for you; next time he calls I'll give him your number. Don't get me started in this silly talk. I'm eager to call blue eyes, so I'll talk to you later."

No sooner had I hung up than the phone rang. If that's the midnight caller, I told myself, I'm gonna really rag him out. Bright sunshine made me braver than the former stormy, black nights.

I answered, heart racing, fully armed for battle.

"Hi, Sam. It's Khara."

Whew. I calmed down so that I could chitchat with her in a normal voice, *sans* racing pulse.

"You told me to find out more about the Morrow family. My sister's friend's Aunt Aggie built up quite a friendship with Frances over the years. They've shared their life histories. Aggie knows a lot about the family and their more interesting highlights."

"That's great, Khara. I'm anxious for any news you can pass on."

"Well, I was told that Frances used to be a marvelous cook. Aggie said that friends and acquaintances treasured invitations to the Morrow dinner parties. Frances seemed to have enjoyed experimenting with recipes from around the world. Aggie said that she tried Frances' famed rocky road fudge and insisted it rivaled Godiva's and Fannie May's."

"Didn't you also tell me that famous writers and movie stars attended the Morrows' parties?"

"Yep. From what I've gathered, she and her husband must've been quite the entertainers. Truman Capote, Sinatra, Sophia Loren. They all graced her table through the years. I heard that her shindigs were the talk of the town. Hey, you could find out more about the Morrows and their parties by going online."

"Thanks. Why didn't I think of that? I'm still not comfortable around a computer, but I'll certainly investigate. What about the devastating disease that incapacitated their daughter? Did you find out what the girl contracted?"

"Uh-huh. Lori's condition is called — wait a minute, I've got it written down: bacterial meningitis caused by the Haemophilus influenzae, type b. Back in the '70s the condition wasn't always determined early enough for effective treatment. Five-year-old Lori was already burdened with childhood diabetes, and somehow the diagnosis of her new affliction wasn't correctly made for some time, which further complicated matters." Khara stopped talking and spelled out the affliction for me, then continued. "Look up that type b stuff while you're on the Internet. It's really scary to read about."

We commiserated for a while and agreed how unfortunate some people were. I thanked her, and she promised to keep in touch with any further news.

After running upstairs and booting up my computer. I intended to search for information about the Morrows on the Internet later. For now, I was anxious to find out about the disease.

What I read was very disturbing. Meningitis caused by the type b bacteria is an extremely infectious condition. Immediate treatment and monitoring are absolutely necessary. If an early diagnosis, or treatment, is delayed, the person contracting bacterial meningitis could develop seizures lasting a lifetime. More importantly, the lack of early treatment can cause brain damage, paralysis, deafness, mental impairment, or even death. Because of serums developed since the 1970s, early diagnosis and the intravenous administration of drugs could make the results less severe nowadays and stabilize the disease to a certain extent.

From what I'd learned from Khara, Frances' daughter contracted the disease in the '70s and was not diagnosed correctly until several weeks passed. Her childhood diabetes made her more susceptible to side effects of the disease. Khara also stated that Lori's condition unfortunately ran the full gamut of the bacteria's devastating, life-altering maladies.

No wonder Frances walked around with a scowl on her face. I wish I'd known about her predicament when we were in class together. I would've tried to be a bit friendly toward her, killer-look or not. That poor woman. I wondered whether I'd be able to handle the misfortunes she'd suffered. I grew crabby and impatient nursemaiding Harry's bouts with a simple cold or a light touch of the flu.

I phoned Reenee again, and we hashed out the latest information. Both of us were appalled by the thought that anyone at any time could be rubbing elbows with a person in the early stages of that highly contagious disease.

Contagion, I learned, resulted from bacteria released into the air on droplets of mucus from sneezes and coughs. As teachers, we had close contact with many families. Also, our students were always coughing and sneezing on us.

The disease transmits through bodily fluids, even if the person is being successfully treated at the time. Reenee and I were horrified by the thought of how easily we could have contracted bacterial meningitis and passed this disease along to our sons. Taking advantage of the 50+ Retirement Plan offered by the Chicago Board of Education turned out to be a godsend.

"Good grief," I told Reenee. "I'm so upset by this talk of doom and gloom, I forgot that I had to call Detective Kelly. Good-bye, girlfriend. Later."

Chapter 14

I left a message for Detective Kelly to contact me ASAP. Only eleven and a half minutes elapsed before he returned my call, but who's counting?

"I'm sorry I wasn't available when you called, Ms. Lisowski. Things can get hectic around here. Is there a problem?"

"Yes. I wish you'd call me Samantha, like you have a couple of times in the past. Ms. Lisowski makes me feel like my mom-in-law, dear that she is."

I could hear the smile in his voice. "Only when no one's around, Samantha. I hope that's your only complaint?"

"Deal. And, no, that's not my only complaint. The murderer called four times last night. My husband, Harry, answered each call and was actually told by that sicko to have me answer the phone the next time, that he missed hearing my voice! Don't you think that's bizarre? Why would a murderer say something like that? This lunatic is driving me goofy. I'm no longer scared; I'm angry."

"Did you try to determine the caller's ID by punching in star sixty-nine?"

"I'd like to punch him to the stars, and, yes, we tried but weren't successful."

"Well, he either had a block on his number or used a cell or throw-away phone."

"So now what do I do? Can you put a trace on my phone or a tap or what?"

"I can initiate steps to identify the caller, but don't get your hopes up too high."

I couldn't believe what I was hearing. We can put a zillion songs on I-pods, pay bills over the Internet, rocket to the moon, microwave a complete dinner in three minutes, but we can't identify an unhinged caller?

I listened impatiently as Detective Kelly went on to explain that with a tap on my land phone for a set amount of weeks, I'd have to list the days and times of the weird calls so that the initiator could be tracked. Not only would the police be involved in this process, but also the state attorney's office.

"As far as cell phones are concerned," he continued, "they are difficult to track down, and the criminals know it. I would advise you to change your phone number and keep it unlisted."

I wasn't buying that. I read in crime novels and in the newspaper how these crackpots get frustrated when they can't get through by phone. The caller then turns into a stalker. I'm out at night by myself a lot. I didn't want a maniac sticking a knife in me on the way to my car.

"I'm not changing my phone number, Detective."

"Well, then, I advise you to be very careful and vigilant, especially at night. Whenever possible, walk to your car with someone, but if you are alone, be aware of your surroundings. It never hurts to ask a security guard from a mall to accompany you to the parking lot."

"Yeah," I said. "With my luck, the guard'll turn out to be my caller, or worse. You will hurry and solve this case, yes? If the murderer is frustrated enough to be making these calls, he must feel I am a threat to him." I paused for a moment as reality hit me. "I really have to be extra cautious."

"Absolutely, Samantha. Just keep your senses active. If something feels wrong, it probably is. And be sure to look inside and around your car before getting in. Beware of vans and SUVs. Criminals have been known to hide beneath them or suddenly pull open a door and yank an unsuspecting person inside."

After listening to Detective Kelly, I probably would never go out again by myself for the rest of my life. There had to be a better way.

"You certainly didn't make my day, Detective. I'm more worried than ever. And what about the caller missing my voice? Murderers don't talk like that, do they? Please don't tell me this guy is also a sexual deviant."

Teardrops began to fall from my eyes, amazing me. I'm tough and usually don't let things get me down. But it seemed I couldn't get a handle on my situation. Maybe I should hire a personal bodyguard, I thought. Something had to give.

"I won't lie to you, Samantha. The caller's remarks are unusual, which might complicate matters. Sounds like he has more than one issue with you. Have you considered the possibility that the caller and the killer are unrelated?"

"Please, please. My head is spinning enough, Detective. I can't absorb any more. The thought that I have a killer, or a maniac, or both after me, is too much to handle. I feel as though I'm one of those furry animals scurrying around in a wheel, getting nowhere and hoping no one catches up with me."

"I'm sorry to bring up the possibility, Samantha, but I want you to know what you might be up against. I'll keep in touch, and you do, also. I'm going to notify your Oak Forest police chief. I'll ask him to contact you."

"Oh. Chief Nick Vincetti. I know him fairly well." I took a deep breath and tried to keep the trembling out of my voice. "Thank you for following through for me."

"I wish I could do more. Don't think circumstances like yours don't thwart us detectives as well. You'll be hearing from me." His voice level dropped and warmth crept in. "You know you're one of my favorite people."

I must've really been upset. Even the implication in Detective Kelly's voice didn't lift my spirits. After I hung up, I shivered and decided to have a long talk with Harry. He'd have to decide on a more active role in my social life, or start investigating funeral homes.

I hoped it wouldn't be a hard decision for him.

Later that afternoon, Police Chief Nick Vincetti called me. He asked if I could come into the Oak Forest police station that day since his calendar was miraculously clear for a while. I left Harry a note as to my whereabouts in case he came home early, and went on my way.

"So, Samantha." Chief Vincetti welcomed me into his office and pointed to a comfortable-looking chair. The surroundings were already more soothing than the cold Chicago district interrogation room which unfortunately had become familiar to me. "I was concerned to hear about your problem."

He made me relate my whole story, from leaving home for the writing seminar to the present day, only interrupting me when he needed to clarify or enlarge upon my account of the situation. Just as the last few words poured out from my thinning lips, Harry was issued into the room.

"Good Lord!" I exclaimed. "Now what's wrong? Did something happen to the boys? Is the house on fire? Are you. . .?"

"Settle down, Sam. Everything's okay. I read your note when I got home and figured I should be here with you."

Oh, my God! I screeched inwardly; Reenee was right. He's having an affair! He feels guilty about it and is being considerate toward me as penance.

I peered closely at him. Harry seemed worried and even animated. Was I in one of my stories? Was I losing contact with reality? Had he put his arm around me at that moment, I would've fainted dead away!

"What can we do about this problem of Sam's, Chief?" Harry asked as he kept looking sideways at me. The intense looks I was giving him probably made him think I was losing control of myself.

"Well, besides the excellent advice that Detective Kelly has given Sam, I'm going to add some of my own. If this person calls again, continue to hang up on him. Whatever you do, don't get into a conversation or a confrontation. If your caller is not the killer but a person who admires you in a sick way, arguing with him will make him feel that you are leading him on. It will only encourage him. Detective Kelly and I both agree," the chief went on to say, giving me an uneasy look, "that your caller may be unrelated to the murder."

I looked around. I had the sensation of being Alice in Wonderland. How can I be in this mess? There's Harry. There's the Chief. Out the window, there's Central Avenue. But what in God's name am I hearing?

"If you are unwilling to change your phone number," the chief continued, "I'd suggest that each time he calls you yell loudly into the phone, 'Stop calling here!' and bang down the receiver. Or use the high-frequency whistle that I'm going to give you, Samantha. Blow it as loudly as you can right into the receiver and hang up."

"Maybe we should consider changing our number, Sam, and keep it unlisted."

I looked at Harry in exasperation. "Right. So the caller can get more perturbed and start stalking me instead. Isn't that a possibility, Chief?"

"You never can tell what a person with psychological problems, or a murderer who feels threatened, might do. He might drop his contact with you altogether, or he may well become a stalker. Remember Detective Kelly's advice about being aware of your surroundings, even if you do decide to change your number."

Chief Vincetti opened his bottom desk drawer and brought out a canister. "I've just come from a luncheon with the Oak Forest senior citizens where I spoke about protecting oneself with pepper spray," he said. "I'm going to give you a can. Keep it with you at all times, but be careful when using it. Don't point the arrow toward yourself."

The chief showed me how to maneuver the spray. I didn't even like holding the damned thing. My brain was skipping around like water on a hot griddle. This couldn't be happening to me, a *normal* person, could it?

Chief Vincetti also told us that he would issue an order for a drive-by several times during the day and night to discourage any loiterers around our home. He reiterated that we should call him if any further problems arose, and that he would keep in contact with Detective Kelly. Harry and I thanked him for his help, and left his office lost in our own thoughts.

The session with Chief Vincetti exhausted me emotionally, but the martini Harry made for me once we got home was wonderful. He also brought me a pillow and settled me into his favorite lounge chair. His concern made me teary. I sternly told myself that I cried more these past few days than I had in my entire married life. I worried that I was becoming soft and compliant, with all the babying and comforting I was getting lately.

C'mon, Samantha, I thought. Are you nuts or what? This was Harry. No doubt he'd return to his indifferent senses by morning.

Ah, what the hell. I'd just enjoy the pampered evening, phone firmly off the hook.

The next day, I called Jeff, and then Glen, to share my latest dilemma. Both of our sons are sensible, and I valued their opinions. Besides expressing their concern, they both encouraged me to change the home phone number.

"If you're worried about this guy turning into a stalker because he's frustrated that you switched to an unlisted number, leaving the receiver off the hook will have the same effect on him," Glen told me. "See what Dad says. He always gets to the core of a situation. I think you should consider his advice."

And when I talked the problem over with Jeff, he cautioned me that not only would the weirdo caller be unable to contact me if the phone was off the hook, but also no one else would be able to get through. "What if Gramps called with a health crisis, or Glen or I were in a car accident, or some other family emergency arose?" he asked. "I know you never keep your cell on; do you even know how to retrieve its messages?"

"Ah," I sighed, after hanging up. We all come to the time of life when the children/parent roles reverse. My sons were right.

I threw up my hands in exasperation. "So, I'll change the friggin' phone number," I yelled to the empty room.

Giving myself no time to change my mind, I got on the phone and called AT&T Customer Service. I was shocked to hear that I'd have the new unlisted phone number set up almost immediately. I thought it would take days, weeks, with workers coming in and out of the house poking holes in the walls and laying cables and wires. I'm as bad as Harry when it comes to new-fangled processes.

Although the rest of the day was quiet and peaceful, the thought of informing my relatives and multitudes of friends about the new number exhausted me. A further idea popped into my head. "Please, please, don't let Midnight Caller be an acquaintance of mine," I declared to the bedroom walls. They stared back at me with no advice or comfort, standing strong and upright in their carefree world, unconcerned about their desperate need of a paint job.

For the hell of it, I didn't disconnect the phone that evening.

No one called.

I figured the unlisted number already kicked in or the killer/stalker, or whoever the hell it was, didn't *work* on Saturdays.

Chapter 15

Sunday, Harry and I spent most of the day at a polka dance. Enjoying this kind of music, and workouts at the Riviera Country Club, were two of the few interests we still had in common and that we shared together. I had such a good time dancing the Polish hop that phone callers, murderers, and possible stalkers were the farthest things from my mind. It felt good to relax and forget the last few days.

On Monday, my first call with the spanking new unlisted phone number was to Detective Kelly.

"I'm glad you've made this decision, Samantha," he told me. "I have some news for you, as well. We've checked the phone records of Frances Morrow and the other people we questioned. No listings of your phone number were on any of their billing statements."

Wondering whether that was good news or bad, I asked, "So none of the persons of interest made the calls?"

"Not unless they used a throw-away phone, making identification of the caller virtually impossible."

Detective Kelly mentioned that type of phone once before, but I was too tired at the time to ask for an explanation. My knowledge of telecommunication technology on a scale of one to ten is minus zero. "What in the hell is a throw-away phone?" I asked. "No, don't tell me. I'll just get more frustrated. I'll take your word for it."

I hesitated for a moment and then pursued another thought. "Are you able to tell me if more information has been uncovered regarding the murders? Is your department any closer to solving the crimes?"

"We're pursuing a couple of different leads and investigating a few lines of thought, but, unfortunately, we haven't been able to make much headway. Our chief concern is that you writers could still be in danger. Just remember to stay aware of your surroundings."

Detective Kelly also assured me that I'd be informed if and when an arrest was made, and that I'd be asked to view the suspect. He reiterated his point about keeping vigilant and informing him of unusual episodes. I told him I hoped there wouldn't be any, especially regarding the now frustrated Midnight Caller who, please, God help me, hasn't progressed into the Samantha Stalker.

Next, I called Reenee and announced that she had the honor of being the second person I called with my new number.

She asked who was the first. When I told her it was Detective Kelly, she said, "Uh-huh. That's what's known as a Freudian slip."

"I don't wear slips, Freudian or otherwise," I countered, but I could feel that smirk of hers over the phone. "Anyway, he said the calls weren't coming from the home or cell phones of any of the persons of interest. But that doesn't leave me with a comfortable feeling, because he told me the caller could be using an innovative throw-away gizmo."

"I just heard about those on TV. It seems that criminals love them because they are practically untraceable. But, y'know, I've been thinking."

Oh, lord, we were in trouble now. When Reenee starts *thinking*, I start shuddering. She can come up with the most far-fetched scenarios for her and me to worry about. With her fertile mind, I think she should be the one to pursue a writing career. That wild ride to my house at three in the morning during a vicious downpour a few days back was a result of one of her brainstorms.

I recalled that, not long ago, Reenee had us both hyped up about how her hearing was getting worse. She brought up weird situations for days about how awful the effect upon her life would be when she'd eventually be stone deaf. My soul mate worked both of us into a nervous frenzy. When she finally went to her doctor, Reenee was told she had a build-up of wax in her ears. After two minutes of flushing those tender attachments, the doctor cleared up her hearing problem. I was the one left with a giant earache — and a headache, as well.

Now Reenee was *thinking* again. I braced myself. What new idea had she conjured up to further jumble my mind?

"It's a thought we touched upon the other day. Did you ever consider," Reenee asked, "that maybe the caller is some pervert who watches your TV program and wants to do nasty things to you? Maybe he's a psycho who likes the way you look and no longer wants to be a secret admirer?"

The idea left me speechless. Then I shook myself and said, "I've told you before, Reenee, I'm not some hot young chick someone out there is yearning over."

"C'mon, Sam. We're both striking-looking babes and you know it. Lotsa younger men nowadays are fascinated by older women. Cougars, and all that stuff. And remember when you first started your TV show? You got a call from some guy who said that you had great legs and he'd like to see you show them off more on the program?"

Reenee's   mind was like Ms. Claus' Significant Other. She remembers everything about everybody and doesn't have to write it down in a *Naughty or Nice* book like you-know-who.

I   completely forgot about that anonymous caller. Although I never felt threatened by his words, I wore slack outfits on the show for months afterwards. I also remembered using a little more caution at the time when I came home alone at night. He must've   tired waiting for the "Great Legs Exposure of Community Television," because he never called again. Maybe slimy thoughts festered in his sick mind since then? Could he be back in earnest, harassing me?

See, this is what I mean about Reenee. She sets my mind in action, thinking up wild scenarios to worry about.

But, of course, she had a valid point. Upon further consideration, I suggested to Reenee that a trip to Detective Kelly's area station was in order. This possibility was too involved to discuss with him over the phone.

Before she could comment, I said, "And, no, I have no ulterior motive." But I could feel that smirk of hers again, coming over the phone lines.

I picked Reenee up within the hour, and we were on our way. I figured Detective Kelly was still at work serving and protecting, so I didn't call to let him know we were coming.

"Don't breathe a word about the lunatic-fan-on-the-loose idea to Wally, and certainly not to Harry," I cautioned my girlfriend. "If Harry found out I might be getting calls from a crazy fan, he'd hound me to give up my TV program. You know I'd rather sacrifice my left *kruszkie* than give up the show."

Reenee suffered through my tirade and then sighed. "Do you really think you had to tell me this, Sam? We never enlightened either of our husbands about our past escapades: not even our harrowing, perilous time in New York. Why'd you think I'd start telling them everything we do now?"

She was right. "That was dumb of me," I said. "I'm sorry. As usual, my mouth is working faster than my brain."

We reached the Chicago police district in record time because of light traffic on the expressway and Reenee, my Super Navigator. We didn't make one wrong turn. I considered hiring her as a chauffeur.

As soon as she and I made our way into the police station, we noticed the cool scenery. During past visits, I was so engrossed with other concerns that I never observed the handsome officers and plainclothes men walking around. Reenee and I kept poking each other and rolling our eyes. Harry would've been disgusted by my adolescent behavior.

"I think we should've gone into law enforcement, Sam, instead of teaching," she whispered. "Did you ever see so many good-looking men in one place?"

"Sa — Ms. Lisowski, what brings you here? I hope nothing's wrong?" Detective Kelly suddenly appeared and interrupted our ogling. He looked from Reenee to me with concern.

"This is my friend, Reenee Solinski. Reenee, Detective Kelly."

If my pal hadn't erased her silly grin or held onto Kelly's hand any longer, I would've kicked her.

"We were visiting one of our friends on the Northside," I lied, "and decided to stop in to discuss a new idea that popped into our minds."

I guessed the infamous interrogation room had a serial killer in it, because Detective Kelly led us to the break room instead. He offered us beverages and rolls. I was probably now listed as a line item in the district's budget because of all the stuff I ate there.

After we were settled, he asked, "Now, ladies, what's the new thought?"

I explained the isolated phone call I received after the first airing of my TV program and how nothing came of it. Secretly, I also had to pinch Reenee a couple of times to keep her from staring at Detective Kelly with speculative eyes.

After he listened to my story and conjectures, he said, "You certainly raise an interesting idea. This may clarify why you are the only one of the group getting phone calls."

"If that's so, won't it even be more likely that my caller will become my stalker, not being able to reach me by phone anymore?" I asked. "This turn of events is like going from Jack the Ripper to the Big Bad Wolf. How many psychos can one girl hope for in a lifetime?"

Detective Kelly advised me to remain cautious and to inform Chief Vincetti about the possibility of my TV caller having begun calling again. This new situation would come under Oak Forest jurisdiction, but that didn't mean Kelly would stop his investigation regarding the calls. He believed it was still possible they could be connected to the murders. We made some small talk. Then Reenee and I thanked him and left.

"Better keep Harry from seeing your detective," Reenee remarked on our way to the parking lot. "I felt a lot of electricity between the two of you. I was going to ask to use the ladies' room so you two could have a few minutes alone."

"You're goofy, Reenee."

"Well, he sure is a sexy, good-looking man."

"Gee," I asked in my most sarcastic voice. "Did you really notice?

Chapter 16

The following morning I phoned Chief Vincetti and explained why I thought Midnight Caller could be a lunatic fan of my TV show. He strongly advised that I carry the pepper spray with me at all times, reiterated the need for vigilance, and cautioned me about not being alone when out at night.

Humph, I thought. Two police departments involved, loads of advice dumped on me, but no tangible help. I had to look to myself for protection against this telephonic weirdo. I wondered if Pierce Brosnan would be available for bodyguard work, now that he no longer played 007 in the movies.

I spent a good portion that day investigating the Morrows on the Internet. Surfing relayed much information about the couple, but I didn't see how any of it would help solve my problem.

My phone buddy, Khara, was right. In their glory days the Morrows were social butterflies. Pictures displayed two vibrant, good-looking people and an absolutely beautiful little girl. I could understand why Lori's debilitating disease made the parents sick at heart and totally devastated them. If I were in her mother's place, I probably never would smile again, either.

I also learned about Frances' former position. It made me wonder why she attended the fatal writing workshop. After all, she was one of the youngest vice-presidents of a major publishing house in the last century. She handled their public relations and entertainment events. Her social circle included world famous writers, best-selling authors, and ghostwriters for actors and actresses who wanted to *pen their own* books. No wonder she was known as the Pearl Mesta of her time. Her husband, John, had a seat on the stock exchange; his philanthropy was amazing to read.

The Morrows' public life ceased in the late 1970s. Brief mention was made of their retirement from the social scene due to their child's illness, then, abruptly, news about the couple dried up altogether. I figured Lori would be near forty by now, her parents in their late-seventies, early eighties. What a dreadful amount of time to be besieged with an illness that had no cure and offered no future hope for a better life. What an existence the Morrows must be enduring due to their daughter's incapacity.

No sooner was I off the computer than Khara called. We joked about becoming phone pals, although I wasn't in the laughing mood after what I'd read. Khara told me that lately none of the neighbors saw either of the adult Morrows at the grocery market or enjoying fresh air with Lori in their backyard.

"The last couple of times when my sister's friend's Aunt Aggie called Frances to ask whether she'd like some company, she got turned down. She said Frances sounded older and more despondent each time they talked. Things must have gone from bad to horrendous for the Morrows."

After we batted that idea around for a while, Khara told me she had to go and would call back if anything new developed.

"Nuts," I said out loud and called Reenee. "Can you come over tomorrow?" I asked her. "We're going to do some snooping on our own."

"It's about time, Sam. I've wondered when I'd get this kind of call from you. I'll be there by nine."

I distracted myself the rest of the day, reflecting upon a plan of action. I busied myself cooking a full-course dinner. When Harry got home from work and smelled a hot meal in progress, he asked who was coming over. I didn't even answer him sarcastically.

We ate in peace, comfort and comparative joy, although Harry complained that I dirtied up every dish, pot and pan when I prepared food, just like our younger son did when he whipped up a meal. I let that remark go as well, because I knew Darling wasn't happy unless he was complaining about something.

When he asked me if I was feeling more at ease since we changed to an unlisted number, I didn't lie. "Not really," I told him. "I seem to be on edge when I'm out. I'm so aware of that pepper spray in my purse. Although it's a small container, it feels like it weighs a ton. I don't know whether I'd be able to use it if necessary. How long is this shit gonna last, Harry?"

That was the wrong question to ask. Darling began reprimanding me, making me feel like his child instead of his mostly faithful companion. He told me I needed to adjust my lifestyle and then made suggestions on how to do it.

I answered abstractly. Harry probably didn't notice, because when he's in his lecture mode, he's really not interested in my responses. I tuned him out, kept a silly smile on my face and nodded, hoping I said "umm" in the right places.

Someone looking into the kitchen window would've thought that we were two newlyweds smiling at each other, happy as lovebirds. The scenario would change drastically if Love Bird #2 even got a whiff of what Love Bird #1 had in mind for the next day.

Chapter 17

"'Mornin', secret agent," I greeted my partner-in-crime. With perfect timing, Reenee arrived the next day as Mr. Coffee was ready to treat us to a caffeine jolt — which we didn't need. We were both hyped up and could've rumbled without the brew.

"Harry would probably start divorce proceedings if he got a hint of our upcoming jaunt this morning." With a mischievous grin I added, "Well, maybe I should've told him — no, no, no, what'm I thinking?"

"Oh, Sammy, you are too funny. I love you!"

Besides keeping our surreptitious plan from our husbands, we decided not to seek Detective Kelly's or Chief Vincetti's advice either, because we knew they'd strongly discourage us. They'd warn us not to interfere in police business. Both would probably sympathize with our husbands if Harry and Wally decided to lock us up in our homes' crawl spaces until this whole business was over.

Reenee and I spent an hour or so ironing the kinks out of my plan and picturing what we would or would not do or say. Then we jumped into my car for our daring short trip.

Both of us had the *kruszkies*.

Twenty minutes later we arrived at our destination. I parked the car in the driveway, and we boldly walked up to the front door. We gave each other an encouraging look and took a deep breath. This was it. We were actually going to confront Killer-look Woman.

I rang the doorbell.

Not knowing what to expect, we were nevertheless surprised by the woman in a nurse's uniform who answered the door.

"Yes," she said. "Are you from the church?"

After a brief, puzzling silence I answered, "N-no. We came to see Frances. I know her from a seminar we took together."

The nurse invited us into the den, which was to the right of the foyer, and asked who we were. I told her that Frances probably wouldn't recognize my name, but that I'd like to have a few moments of her time. We were told to wait in the den as the nurse left for an inner room.

Reenee and I looked at each other, a bit panicked. This already wasn't going according to Plan A, B or Q. Frances was expecting church people? We both took an audible swallow and squeezed each other's hands for courage as we surveyed our surroundings.

Framed photographs of famous people from yesteryear decorated the den's walls. Warm sentiments with flourishing autographs adorned each photo. The pictures dated back to the era when the Morrows were the lavish hosts of the in-crowd.

Pictures of the Morrows' daughter, from infancy through childhood, took up a good section of the opposite wall. What a beautiful little girl Lori was. Her soft blond locks framed an angelic face; her warm smile was enchanting. We could see the intelligence in her eyes. Her photos abruptly ended at ages six or seven.

"I guess that's when Lori contracted bacterial meningitis," I whispered to Reenee.

We turned as Frances came into the room and looked from one of us to the other. We could almost see the question mark and anxiety on her weary face. She appeared haggard, like she was forcing her legs to move. I noticed she lost tons of weight and seemed years older than only weeks before when I last saw her.

"Oh, my." Frances broke the silence as her hand trembled to her throat. "You're one of the women from the writing seminar. You were on TV about what happened that day."

I gave Frances the most comforting smile I had in stock and used what I hoped was a soothing tone. "Yes, I'm Samantha Lisowski. And this is my friend, Reenee Solinski. We don't mean to intrude. Is this a bad time for you?"

"Lately, there is no good time." Frances appeared apprehensive. In fact, she seemed jittery, wired up, ready to scream any second. She didn't ask us to sit down. "May I help you with something?"

"I hoped we could discuss a few things with you." Could I put this poor woman through more anguish? C'mon, Samantha, I told myself. Just come out with it.

Bluntly, but with a small smile and using my nicest tone of voice, I said, "I'd like to know why you were giving me such hateful looks at the seminar. And then, when I saw you in church during our lunch break, you seemed to be crying and laughing at the same time. I. . . ."

Frances let out a moan. Her hands shook. We reached for her and helped her to a chair as her knees weakened.

I damned myself. Now look what you've done. This woman has collapsed because of your insensitive directness.

"Shall I call for your nurse?" I asked. I was shaking myself and noticed that Reenee was very upset as well. This trip was turning out to be the worst idea I ever had.

"No, no. I'll be okay. Remembering that day always upsets me." Frances began sobbing quietly. She seemed to be falling apart right before our eyes. "I care for a disabled daughter, and now a husband with deteriorating health. I'm so overwhelmed. Please forgive my outburst."

"Please forgive us, Mrs. Morrow," Reenee and I said, practically in unison.

"We know from acquaintances about your daughter. We should never have come," I added. "We'll just leave."

Reenee and I looked at each other as Frances tried to compose herself. After a few uncomfortable moments, she said, "No. Please, maybe I'll be able to handle things better if I talk them over with someone who was at that writing seminar with me."

The atmosphere relaxed a little.

She invited us to be seated and asked if we'd like some coffee or tea. As we both felt we were intruding enough upon this poor woman's troubles, we declined her offer.

"Mrs. Morrow," I began.

"Please. Call me Frances."

I smiled and began again. "Frances, I'm only here because since I found Jean Thorpe's murdered body, I became one of the suspects. I'm no longer under suspicion, but there's been another murder, and

I've been harassed by a weird phone caller who may or may not be the killer."

"Oh, my God!" she cried out. "That can't be possible. You think the killer is calling you and that you're in danger?" She began wringing her hands, then pulling on her hair. "No, no, that cannot be. Oh, my God."

Frances began rocking and staring into space. This time we didn't ask if she needed the nurse. Reenee went to find her while I put my arms around the poor woman's shoulder, trying to comfort her.

"What is it, Frances. What's wrong? I'm so, so sorry to keep upsetting you."

She didn't respond. When the nurse entered the room, Frances allowed herself to be led from the den. We found our way out the front door by ourselves.

"Wow, Reenee. Was that the stupidest idea of the millennium?" We were both uneasy and angry with ourselves as we got into the car. "I hope Frances is going to be all right. Pray we didn't cause her to have a nervous breakdown!"

My nerves were jangling like Mexican jumping beans. I was mentally kicking myself for being so tactless. What sounded like a good idea in my warm kitchen next to my best friend turned into a disaster. We'd brought more tension and anxiety into that poor woman's already stressful life. I expected to find a cold person with a frozen, hateful look about her. Instead we barged in upon a desolate soul almost at her wits' end.

When we reached my place, I pulled out the wine bottle. We had a few sips to calm our nerves.

"Sam," Reenee whispered. "I'm so miserable. We never gave a thought about the callousness of that plan of ours. What's wrong with us? We dumped even more worries on poor Frances."

We looked at each other in distress. "I feel awful about my behavior," I said. "I became so embroiled in my own fears and problems that I didn't give a thought as to how my directness might upset Frances. I'm also ashamed of myself for pulling you into this wild scheme of mine."

"You didn't put a gun to my head, Sam. I'm feeling guilty as well."

I brought out our favorite comfort food, filling the table with everything chocolate that I could find. We silently ate ourselves out of our funk.

After a while we tried to sort out what we had experienced. On paper we listed our statements in sequential order and Frances' reactions to them.

"Frances didn't seem to mind my questions about the hateful looks she sent my way, right? Or about that episode in the church? She seemed to have had herself under control until I mentioned the phone calls. Didn't her reaction seem overly strong to you? "

"You bet it did. Why do you suppose Frances got so distressed about those phone calls? Does she know who could be making them? It seemed she was more upset over them than the murders. Like she was resigned to the fact of the two homicides."

"I wish we could've asked her if she knew either victim, Carole Langley or Long Tall Sally. I think we goofed royally, Reenee. We handled the circumstances poorly. I need another drink."

"Not me, Sam. I gotta drive home. I'll be stuck in rush hour traffic as it is. I sure wish we lived closer."

We hugged each other and commiserated a bit more about the catastrophe we seemed to have worsened. "I hope Frances has calmed down and is feeling as well as possible," I told my pal. "How about I give the Morrow household a call later this evening to see if her situation has improved?"

Reenee agreed. "But don't be surprised if Frances or her husband slams the receiver down in your ear."

"I'd probably feel better if that happened, like some deserved punishment. Drive carefully, Reenee. Call me tonight if you can't fall asleep. I know I'll have a hard time sleeping as well."

Later that evening I debated with myself about whether or not to call the Morrow home to ask about Frances. I figured I couldn't make things worse by calling — but I was wrong.

Chapter 18

I was surprised that I had such a good night's sleep, considering my faux pas at the Morrows. No dreams of trudging through slushy mud without getting anywhere, no nightmares of masked men chasing me with sabers while lions bit at my *dupa* as I danced. Ever since I took a class on dream interpretation and discovered the key to understanding my dreams, my subconscious stopped me from remembering most of them. My loss. Many dreams of the past included Old Blue Eyes or that sexy country singer Alan Jackson serenading me. Now I merely awaken with good ol' Harry snoring by my side — and not in tune, either.

I barely finished my morning coffee and a couple of chapters of *Song of the Rails*, by Helen Osterman, one of my favorite authors, when the phone rang. I answered the call and felt the pleasure of knowing it wouldn't be the psycho murderer/stalker.

"Sam." Khara sounded breathless and excited. "I figured you'd want to know. An ambulance was at the Morrow house during the wee hours of the morning. John was rushed to Palos Hospital. That Aunt Aggie I told you about is there now with him and his wife."

"Oh, my God, Khara. What happened?"

"As I heard it from my sister, who heard it through the grapevine from her friend's Aunt Aggie, who heard it from Lori's nurse, a chain of events was started by two women who visited the Morrow home yesterday. Then, later in the evening, after a phone call of apology from one of them, Frances turned into a shrieking banshee. She began verbally and physically attacking her husband!"

I couldn't catch my breath. Dear lord, I thought. What did Reenee and I do?

"Frances kept yelling incoherently at John throughout the onslaught," Khara continued, "something about phone calls and another murder. Neither the nurse nor the housekeeper knew what was happening. They finally subdued her as John fell to the floor, gasping for breath."

"A heart attack or a stroke, or what?" I choked out. "And what about the daughter? Is she okay?"

"I don't know, Sam. The nurse thought that John suffered a stress attack, which would be bad enough. I'll try to learn more. But isn't this awful? As if the Morrows don't have enough troubles."

I couldn't talk any longer without dialing for the paramedics for myself. As soon as I could, I ended our conversation and called Reenee.

"Oh, lord, girlfriend, we screwed up," I moaned into her ear. "John Morrow is in the hospital and Frances is beyond consolation. And it appears that you and I caused this mess."

Heading off her questions, I suggested we meet at Hannah's Hutch, a restaurant we frequented, halfway between her home and mine. I needed her face-to-face to be able to tackle our latest dilemma.

On my way to the restaurant I prayed like hell for the Morrows. I begged God to punish me for my stupidity, not the unfortunate couple.

But common-sense thoughts also churned in my mind. By the time I reached the restaurant, I already sorted out a few possibilities.

Pulling into the parking lot, I noticed Reenee was already there. As I entered the restaurant and approached her booth, I was grateful that she had a cup of coffee on the table waiting for me. But the way I felt, a Hannah's Hutch Chocolate Martini would've been much better.

"I can't believe I got here without getting into an accident," Reenee said as she hugged me hello. "What've we caused? What're we going to do?"

"What we're not going to do is blow our responsibility out of proportion over this chaos." I used the twenty-minute ride to the restaurant for prayer and reflection and concluded that events would probably come to a head with or without our intervention. Although it sounded coldhearted, I decided we simply speeded things up.

I told Reenee everything I knew from Khara's phone call. We examined our feelings and thoughts. My dear friend's hands were shaking each time she sipped her coffee. I mentally kicked myself for bringing her into my scheme.

After I finished relating the unfortunate news, I said, "I think we need to look at this turn of events objectively, Reenee. In simple terms, we paid Frances a visit, our conversation disturbed her, and she later over-reacted by attacking her husband, who's been distressed about their plight for decades. They've both been stroke victims waiting to happen."

"How can you be so callous and detached, Samantha?"

I took Reenee's hand in mine and squeezed it. "Stop! Right now! There's something strange going on with the Morrows regarding the murders, and possibly the phone calls. We seemed to have been the catalyst, stirring up dark secrets about this case. John is somehow involved, or he and Frances know something they haven't shared with the police."

Reenee took a deep breath and looked steadily into my eyes. I could feel her stress slowly ebbing, as I knew it would. Like me, she's resilient and tough. Her returning composure was evident to me when she said with a deep sigh, "My brain's spinning like a rap star's butt on the dance floor. Where do we go from here, girlfriend?"

"I'm wondering if we should let Detective Kelly into the loop." I looked at her to see her reaction.

"I don't see how we can keep this from him, Sam. Maybe you should give him a call once you get home?"

We discussed that idea and others as we finally ordered lunch. Unfortunately, no catastrophes seemed to ruin our appetites.

I realized, however, that Reenee wasn't completely back to her old self. When Rick, the hunky owner of the restaurant, sat down at our table, she didn't flirt with him as she usually did. So I figured that unpleasant job was up to me.

The task made my patty burger on rye taste even better.

"You, what?" I could feel Detective Kelly's blood pressure rise over the phone. "This is a police matter, Samantha. You are not to interfere with an on-going investigation. Leave this Morrow business to us." He sounded very angry, even as he went on to say, "Did you consider the risk to you and your friend? I want you to promise that you'll stay away from that family and their home. Serious repercussions could result from your interference."

Hell, Detective Kelly's tone and vocabulary sounded more and more like Harry's.

In my meekest voice I said, "I won't contact the Morrows again. I promise to keep my nose out of police business." Little was he aware that I had my fingers crossed, which, as anybody over fifty knows, means the promise doesn't count.

When Detective Kelly asked how Reenee and I were handling the chaos emerging from our ill-timed visit to the Morrows, I assured Chicago's finest that we were okay. After telling me he'd be in touch and for me to keep extra vigilant, he added, "You're too lovely a woman to have anything happen to you." His warm concern brought immediate tears from the new leaky faucets dubbed Samantha's Teary Greens.

With a deep sigh I hung up the phone. I felt *Lost*, worse than Kate and Sawyer and Locke in that recently-popular TV series. With a zillion thoughts I didn't want to tackle zooming through my mind, I decided instead to see whether the postman rung twice.

The first letter arrived with the afternoon mail.

Chapter 19

I opened the envelope with no return address or stamp on it. One quick look was all I needed as I riffled through the printed sheet and pages of pictures. The note and its contents fluttered out of my trembling hands. My mouth felt gaggingly dry. My breath came in spurts. *Kruszkies* started jumping around so furiously in my stomach that I thought one would pop right out of my mouth. "Oh my God; oh, my God," I whispered, hugging myself.

I took a deep breath and sort of pulled myself together. Gingerly, I picked up the spilled contents. My hands shook as I read the creepy message, words blurring on the paper:

NEW PHONE NUMBER? NOT NICE, SAMANTHA
BAD, BAD GIRL NEEDS A SPANKING!
YOU'D LOOK SO SEXY IN THESE OUTFITS
SEE YOU – ALL OF YOU – SOON

I threw the repulsive papers to the floor. I don't know how long I stood there, trying to decide whether I should scream or faint. Too many shocks attacked my nervous system already, and the week was still young. I was so unnerved that I would've 'fessed up to Harry about everything had he been home.

Gasping, I mentally yelled at myself to get a grip on my nerves. Forcing myself to calm down, I took a couple of deep breaths before examining the legal-sized envelope. It was addressed to me in block letters. The message itself was printed in purple ink on plain, unlined paper.

But worse than the letter were the enclosed pictures. Through my teaching years, I confiscated porno publications from my students, but these pictures were even beyond *Hustler* magazine's raunchiness. I never saw such grossly disgusting poses in my life. The *clothes* on the women were nothing more than a string or a sequin here and there, and not in strategic places either. No insides of private body parts were left to the imagination. I felt my cheeks burning.

Heart beating one-hundred-twenty miles an hour, I tried in vain to phone Reenee and then Detective Kelly. My call to Chief Vincetti was successful.

"Chief, he was here. At my house. This morning — I was out. No stamp on envelope. Must've dropped the note in my mailbox — horrible note. In purple ink! How does he know that's my favorite color? And pictures —." I tried rattling off the entire incident to him in one minute flat.

"Slow down, Samantha," the chief interrupted. "Are you in danger?"

"I don't think so. I don't see anybody in the yard or hanging around. I'm nervous but getting madder by the second. How dare he come to my house! How dare he use my mailbox for his own nasty purposes!"

Chief Vincetti asked whether I felt calm enough to drive to the police station or if he should send an officer to pick me up. Taking a deep breath, I told him I could manage on my own. He said to wait for a squad car to accompany me.

"While you are waiting, Samantha, get your kitchen tongs and carefully lift all the material. Put everything into a plastic bag."

When I tried to follow his advice, my hands were shaking so badly that it took me three tries just to open the Ziploc baggie.

From Chief Vincetti's grimaces as he read the note and looked at the pictures, I knew I was in for further ghastly news.

"What a sick-o we have here, Samantha. I know you don't want to hear this, but there'll probably be more notes to come. This type of person usually takes great sexual pleasure in writing and sending messages like this. He romanticizes about his prey reading the letter and becoming stimulated or infatuated with him."

"Now my problem has sexual overtones," I moaned. "Are you telling me that I've made my situation worse by changing my phone number?"

"You're not to blame for any of this. The writer is psychologically unbalanced. He fantasizes about you for his own sick reasons."

Great! That made me feel *so* much better.

But I settled down enough to think more clearly. It dawned on me the wording of the note seemed to be written by a psycho-watcher and not a psycho-murderer. I brought this idea to the Chief's attention, and he said he tended to agree with me.

"I want you to follow my instructions the next time you get mail from him," he went on to say. "Handle whatever he sends you very carefully. Touch only the edges and immediately bag it. We might be able to get fingerprints off the paper."

What? I did a double-take. Although I know this happens on the *CSI* television program, I couldn't believe that the Oak Forest Police Department was going to run this person's fingerprints through state and FBI records just for me. No major crime had been committed. Even though the message scared the hell out of me, I knew that, to the police, this was simply a harassment problem. At least for now.

"If we can lift fingerprints," the chief explained further, "we'll keep them on file. It's possible that this person could be stopped for driving under the influence of alcohol or drugs, or commit a burglary, or assault someone, and we'd get a match."

Although this sounded rather far-fetched to me, it seemed to be the best I could hope for. "What do I do now?" I asked. "Just wait for the next letter?"

"Unfortunately, that's all you can do. We'll keep a drive-by order on your house. As you talk this over with your husband. . . ."

I stiffened and moved to the edge of my chair. "Uh, Chief, that's the other thing. I'd rather not let Harry know about this note. And I'd appreciate if you didn't mention it to him."

Chief Vincetti looked piercingly at me. "I highly recommend you tell him about this, Samantha. You're going to need moral support and probably a change in your lifestyle. Mr. Lisowski's always impressed me as being a sensible, realistic man."

Uh-huh. Sensible and realistic, but not reasonable or empathetic toward me.

"I don't want him to know just yet, Chief." I had to talk the situation over with Reenee first. She'd understand that Harry would eventually blame everything on me. More importantly, he'd hound me to give up my TV show if this sick-o turned out to be a fan. No. Although I was spooked, I wasn't spooked enough to tell Harry just yet.

Chief Vincetti shook his head. "I think you're making a mistake, but it's your decision at this point. Will you promise at least to think about changing your mind?"

I told him I could do that, without crossed fingers this time, and thanked him for his time and concern. He said he'd pass on the new development to Detective Kelly. But when I got home, I called the hunk myself.

"Your predicament is disturbing, Samantha. After you relax a little, I want you to think hard about who could possibly be harassing you. Go over any encounters you've had lately that might have left you with a funny feeling. Don't get paranoid, but consider any unnerving looks someone might have been giving you in the past few months. Or a stranger who's turned up wherever you seem to be."

Detective Kelly's compassion brought out old Ms. Dewy Eyes again. What was it with this man that brought out the tears? I got a grip and said, "Yeah, I know the old joke. Just because you're paranoid, doesn't mean you're not being followed."

Detective Kelly laughed but ended with the same advice as the Chief's: Tell Harry everything.

I knew when I called Reenee, she'd agree with me: Tell the enemy nothing!

Chapter 20

The following day, Reenee and I discussed the whole episode again and again over breakfast at Hannah's Hutch. I thought she feared for my safety more than I did. We both agreed that a murderer was not after me. That, instead, the phone caller/letter writer was some sick person who fantasized about me as he watched my television show. We also agreed to keep our husbands in the dark about this dilemma for the time being.

Promising Reenee that I'd be extra careful, especially when I was alone at night or when pulling into my driveway or garage, I reluctantly left her. Again I wished we lived closer to each other, to have her nearby during this stressful time. She understood me so well and was always unconditionally supportive.

On my way home, I thought I'd stop at a local mall to get a few birthday and anniversary cards, hoping that a little shopping would take my mind off my predicament. Paying only forty-nine cents for a card at the Factory Card Outlet, instead of three dollars and up at a regular store, would give my conservative soul a lift.

I parked my Grand Am and dutifully observed my surroundings. No nefarious-looking characters seemed to be lurking, so I exited, locked up, and went on my merry way to the card shop.

I love looking at greeting cards. I could linger for hours just reading all the funny ones. The rare times Harry drives me to the Factory Card Outlet, he drops me off and waits in the car.

"Fifteen minutes and I'll be right out," I tell him. "I need only two cards."

An hour later he comes looking for me with the sourest puss you ever saw on a human being. I could never figure out why he is so irritated. He should know after all our years of marriage what fifteen minutes means in Samantha time.

So here I was, at one of my favorite stores, enjoying all the fun cards. I immediately became engrossed in searching for the right greetings, finding several I'd consider buying. Cards in hand, I quickly turned and bumped my foot on an opened drawer below the display case, stumbling into a young guy, his cards and mine flying into the air.

"I'm so sorry," I said. "I wasn't watching where I was going." I lifted my foot and rubbed my ankle.

"Entirely my fault. Are you all right? Seems to me you bumped yourself pretty hard." He began picking up the greeting cards. He handed me my bunch and smiled. "Have a nice day, miss."

"How satisfying to see there are polite young men in the world," commented the stylish woman standing next to me. "Don't see many of those around nowadays."

"And one who calls me *miss* at my tender age!" We both smiled and proceeded to the check-out register.

The woman stood behind me in line. She asked, "I hope you don't mind, but what scent are you wearing? Your perfume has a fantastic fragrance."

"Oh, thank you! The scent is Rare Pearls, and you can purchase it from your friendly Avon lady. Not expensive at all." The perfume was really Fay-Tel, self-named, my own personal blend and very expensive. I conjured it up myself at a skin therapy and spa place in Orland Park where you can mix your own scent. But when asked about the perfume I always lie and say it's Avon's because I have stock in that company. Besides, I love Avon's Rare Pearls cologne, as well, and use it frequently.

The woman thanked me for the information, and I left the store. On the way to my car, my ankle began to ache in earnest. As I opened the door and looked up, the young guy from the card store was entering his car a few spaces down. He smiled and waved to me. I smiled and waved back — wait a minute, was I nuts? He could be the psycho, and here I was encouraging him! I quickly got into my car, locked all the doors, and waited until he left the parking lot.

I began sweating, and it wasn't due to the heat or humidity. As I drove away, I kept watching my rearview mirror to be sure he wasn't following me. If I saw a car that even remotely looked like his, I was going to drive straight to the Oak Forest police station and yell like hell.

Arriving home safely, but with a pounding heart, I turned on my answering machine. Khara left me another message with an update on the Morrows. John was released from the hospital and Frances calmed down. But no sooner had the Morrows returned home than their daughter suffered a severe seizure, and she had to be hospitalized. As a result, John had a relapse, and Frances totally shut down. The household was in complete chaos.

My brain began to spin, my head throbbed, and my heart pounded even harder. I felt like a boxer who'd gone all ten rounds. I took a deep breath, cranked the air up high, guzzled down a glass of cold water, and plopped down onto the sofa. Grabbing the phone, I called Reenee, before I dared to check my mailbox.

My dear friend was very upset with me after I gave her the low-down on my experience at the card shop and the latest occurrences at the Morrow household.

"Dammit, Samantha, forget the friggin' Morrows. You've got bigger problems. You promised me you'd be alert and focused on your surroundings," she scolded. "You're not taking this screwball seriously enough. I can't believe you put yourself in danger the minute you left the restaurant."

Why was everyone beginning to sound like Harry?

"Okay, okay, Reenee. I got it. I'm not worrying about the Morrows or speaking to any men, young or otherwise."

"Repeat after me. And I'm going to be aware of people around me at all times."

"And I'm going to be aware of people around me at all times. I am sorry for my sins and ask for absolution. What's my penance, Father?"

"Don't be a smart ass, Samantha. I'm worried about you."

"I hear you. I'm worried about me, too."

We rehashed a few other things. Then I told her to hold on while I checked my mail. The walk to my mailbox was like struggling down death row. The phrase "Dead Man Walking" kept flitting through my mind. I held my breath as I pulled out the ridiculous amount of correspondence left by the postman, cautiously flipping through the letters, praying that there was no envelope addressed to me in purple ink.

My heart returned to its normal beat. I was relieved to find only six thousand pieces of unthreatening junk mail and three bills. After I told Reenee, who was also waiting with bated breath, we both prayed out loud that the pervert fulfilled his sordid desires by contacting me just that one time by post.

If only that were true!

Chapter 21

Regardless of all the hoopla happening in my life, I had to get ready for the taping of *Straight from the Forest*, my monthly community television show. Although I'd already contacted the people whom I'd be interviewing, I had to call them again to finalize odds and ends.

Each month, *Straight from the Forest* was taped at a different restaurant in the viewing area; then that hour-long program repeatedly broadcasted each week in that month.

Even though I previously scheduled the restaurant, I learned over time that the owner always needed a reminder from me. Also, I had to figure out my script, the guest host's, the questions for the interviews, and the time schedule, as well as the order of segments within the show. And I still had to submit next month's article to the magazine. I wanted it to be an especially good vignette, because the editors would soon make a decision about whether I'd have a permanent job with the publication.

I sighed a loud one. Just looking at all the work I needed to do within the week made *me* weak. I sorted the pertinent material by forming piles of paper on the floor of my home office.

"Good grief," Harry said, poking his head into the room. "I bet Bill O'Reilly doesn't make a mess like this or take as long to prepare his TV show as you do. You always manage to find a job for yourself that requires hours of work and no pay."

"It's called volunteer work, Harry. You ought to try it someday." I gave Darling my Samantha look. If my face ever froze that way — squinted eyes, lips pinched tightly, eyebrows stretched up to my hairline — I'd never again have to wear a scary mask for Halloween.

"I've told you a million times: sarcasm does not become you."

Harry went on with his pontification. "If you have all this time to spare, you should volunteer at a hospital or nursing home; do something worthwhile for people."

I sighed an even bigger one. "The show is worthwhile for people," I told him. "I bump into fans all the time. They tell me that they'd miss a lot of cool events in their communities if it weren't for my program. They say that *Straight from the Forest* is a welcome break from all the crime and mayhem going on in the world." I glanced at Harry to see if he was listening to me, since he seems to have a very short attention span when I'm speaking. "Fans enjoy the trivia and my wise-cracks. You should watch the show once in a while and see what it's all about."

We've had this conversation so many times that I felt I should print out my retort so I could hand it to Darling every time the subject came up. Harry soon lost interest in annoying me, no doubt to go watch his cable news programs. It's amazing that his chair in the den hasn't grown roots to the television set.

I went back to getting the show organized. Wal-Mart should give me a commission for all the markers I bought there to write out my script. I make a 16-font computerized script for my guest host, but for myself I print in large, black marker print. My sons tease me about the letters being so big that they can read the words while watching the show, even though the script is upside down to them. The print needed to be huge so I can refer to my notes on the show *sans* those friggin' eyeglasses.

I became entrenched in preparation. Three hours later, thankfully without being disturbed by disparaging remarks from Harry, I took a break. The phone rang.

"Hi, Sammy. It's just me." Reenee's voice came across a bit stressed and breathless. "I'm getting a little scared about being your guest host Saturday. Why did I think this was a good idea?"

"Relax, girlfriend. It'll be a snap. You'll do good." Reenee had a gift of gab, like me, and I wasn't a bit worried that she would bomb. "You know I'll lead you along. Just be yourself, and we'll have fun and wow the audience."

"Easy for you to say; you're a natural. I'll probably make a fool of myself."

"You will not, Reenee. I'm e-mailing the script to you as soon as we get off the phone, so you can acquaint yourself with the information. The only material I won't send is when we get to chitchat because I like spontaneous responses for that segment."

"What if I get tongue-tied, or my brain blanks out?"

"None of that'll happen, so stop making up scenarios that won't play out." Reenee tended to worry about what might and might not happen in the future. I'm content to take what comes hour by hour or day by day. That's one of the reasons we make a dynamic duo.

"Most of the time you'll just sit next to the person on camera and smile and look pretty," I told her. "Each individual wants to get his or her message across, so you won't have to say much. You've seen the show a million times. You'll know how to handle things." We talked a little more about the program and then switched topics to my dilemma.

"I'm worried that you haven't gotten any more notes from that nut-o, Sammy. It's like he's gearing up for some sickening next step. Are you being careful when you're out by yourself?"

"Yes, my dear friend. My eyes are open wide and my Mace is near at hand. No lectures, please. I get enough of them from Harry. And now I've really gotta go and tie up loose ends for the show. See you Saturday around noon at Hannah's Hutch."

Reenee sighed. "At least we'll be taping the program at a restaurant I know and love," she said.

The rest of the week flew by without incident. My stalker must've given up on me or was taking a mini-vacation. I hoped it was the former. I was actually starting to relax a little.

Saturday came around filled with sunshine and warmth. All systems were "go" for *Straight from the Forest*.

I arrived at Hannah's Hutch earlier than the rest of the staff, because I liked to get organized at the restaurant before everyone else came in and things got hectic. My main worry was that the segments I scheduled wouldn't stay within the time limits I allowed. As program director, besides being the show's host, I had fifty-nine minutes to use up for the show, and I always had the allotment timed to the last second. If a guest used up more time than I planned for an interview, or a guest didn't show up, my *kruszkies* started bouncing in my brain as I frantically adjusted and juggled the time crunch. Besides that worry, I had to focus on my own time on camera.

It ain't easy being a big star.

Rick, the hunky owner of Hannah's Hutch, graciously gave us carte blanche at his restaurant. Most owners of other restaurants where we previously taped programs were equally cooperative. *Straight from the Forest* repeats each week during the month. Restaurant owners were grateful for the weekly TV exposure in over eighty surrounding communities at no charge to them. Being able to eat the food that the owner talked about during his or her portion of the program, and compliments about the show from our viewers, were our only *pay*.

Reenee arrived, gorgeous in her turquoise blue dress. Her jewelry was exquisite, her makeup perfect. She looked ready for *Fox Network News*.

"Wow," she said after we carefully hugged each other, not wanting to mess up our hair or makeup. "Don't you look fantastic, Sammy, in that magenta outfit! Are those new earrings? Long and lovely, as usual."

"'Wow' back to you, Reenee. I can already hear Hollywood calling for a screen test. That color is dyn-o-mite on you! We are going to look fantastic on camera sitting next to each other."

Our Mutual Admiration Society conversation completed, we squeezed hands and air-kissed again to keep ourselves intact. *Straight from the Forest* was a low budget endeavor; in fact we had no budget at all! We couldn't yell out, "Makeup," and have fourteen people run out to adjust our eyeliner, throw a powder puff at us, or pout up our lips. We were on our own.

When the small crew arrived at Hannah's Hutch, it was like a party. We all hugged and kissed each other and caught up on news because, although *Straight from the Forest* was in reruns weekly, we only taped a new show once a month. The guys got busy rearranging the tables and chairs, and the director selected the optimal place for taping the program, light and décor-wise. Rick brought out beverages and a couple of wonderful-looking appetizers for us. The food looked marvelous, but I never could eat before or during a show. The excitement and anticipation in the air were enough for me and my *kruszkies.*

Happily the interviewees showed up, and I was able to keep their interviews within the anticipated time limits. The regulars, reporting community news from Oak Forest, Tinley Park, Midlothian and Worth, as well as our three local high school student reporters who presented updates of their schools' events — all did their segments right on time. Our genius director, Ron, who was also our editor and a frequent participant in the show, would put the segments together later into a finished, smooth-looking program. People who watched the taping from the restaurants told us how amazed they were to see the disjointed bits and pieces turned into professionally finished TV programs.

I breathed a sigh of relief. Sliding a little more gloss on my lips, I checked myself out in my compact mirror. Now it was Reenee's and my turn to open the show, introducing the segments in the order I previously set up. We also needed to chitchat, be funny and seem natural through it all

Like I said, it ain't easy being a big star!

Chapter 22

Hearty applause erupted at the end of the show. I felt it had been lively, witty and informative. I gave Reenee a big hug, not concerned with makeup or hair anymore. She did an astounding job as my guest host. I was sure this month's show would be a winner.

Reenee and I grabbed some plates and silverware that the wait staff brought to the table. We filled up our plates with a little portion from every dish that Rick selected to show our TV viewers during his interview segment. Although the completed show is an hour long, it takes between three to four hours to tape it, so we were all hungry. We attacked the various items like vultures, even though most of the food was already getting cold. Rick brought around more beverages and even offered alcoholic ones. Reenee and I took advantage of that perk.

We took our drinks and food to sit down at one of the tables. I noticed a couple of black roses on the table wrapped in lilac tissue paper. A note was stapled to the paper with my name printed in purple marker and *Lookin' hot, babe* scrawled in capitals. With a smile on my face, I caught Rick's eye and motioned him over.

"Thank you, you sweetheart!" I exclaimed, giving the hunk a big hug and a smooch on his cheek.

"Nonsense," he said. "I was happy to have you guys here; the food and drinks were the least I could do."

"Well," I said, giving him my sassy Samantha look, "the flowers certainly were not necessary. What a nice touch! They are absolutely beautiful."

Rick looked at me nonplussed and then down at the table.

"Flowers? I didn't bring you these roses, although the idea's a great one. Sorry I didn't think of it."

I was embarrassed at my faux pas. Reenee, seeing my discomfiture, came to my rescue. "Looks like you have a secret admirer, Sammy."

"Besides me, that is," Rick said, also trying to put me at ease.

We laughed, joked around a little, and then Rick left us, saying he hadn't noticed who placed the roses on the table, but would ask around.

Reenee and I peered at one another, the same thought crossing our minds. I don't know why I hadn't become apprehensive sooner. Probably because I was still in the glow from taping a superb program. A shudder went through me The food I just ate seemed to congeal in my stomach.

"The stalker," Reenee whispered. She looked ready to gag as well.

We quickly glanced around, but noticed no one giving us special attention.

"Black roses — just like at the Bears training camp, Sammy. We were wrong at the time to think the flower on your windshield was a joke from one of the Bear players. I'm getting more spooked by the minute."

A couple of the staff crew, plates laden with food, interrupted our nervous chatter. They remarked how jam-packed the program had seemed and congratulated us on a job well done. Spotting the flowers, they made a few teasing remarks about them.

"Secret admirer, ladies?" Ron, our mastermind director/editor, glanced at the roses and cocked an eyebrow at us.

"Did anyone notice who left the flowers, or are you going to tell us they're from all of you?" Reenee asked, covering up her anxiety well. "Nice to know someone appreciates our good looks."

That best friend of mine is a jewel. I knew she had a lump in her throat as big as mine, but she nicely put the kibosh on a dragged-out explanation about our stalker predicament. We previously agreed that the fewer people who knew about my situation, the better.

Everyone laughed at Reenee's remark, but claimed no knowledge about the person who left the flowers. Being busy with their various jobs during the taping, no one noticed who might have been near the table. The subject was dropped, and we all went back to talking about the program. My eyes, however, remained vigilant, checking out the other people in the restaurant.

After everyone had their fill and left the table to pack up the cameras, lights, microphones and such, I carefully wrapped the note and then the roses in napkins.

Reenee agreed to speak with the wait staff and bartender, to ask them if they noticed a customer coming in with the roses or hanging around the table. But Saturdays were always hectic for the restaurant. Staff was too busy serving drinks and food to notice flower-bearers. They weren't any help.

Reenee and I shook our heads. I felt crushed. Again we missed our chance of getting a glimpse of my screwed-up admirer.

The stalker had to be cunning or mad to pull off a stunt like today's. The thought made me even more on edge.

I took a big breath to calm myself and told Reenee that I'd drop the flowers off for Chief Vincetti at the Oak Forest police station on my way home. She wanted to come along, but I nixed the idea. I'd be poor company, as I still had details of the show to deal with. I wouldn't be able to spend any quality time with her for at least a couple of hours.

The biggest monster I faced was the forwarding, via the computer, of the programming schedule, as well as the names of the participants for our director/editor, Ron. Although I gave him a hand-written copy of this information at the taping, he also liked to have one on the computer as well, to load in or boot in — or whatever the hell the proper term is. I am absolutely illiterate when it comes to his genius performance of getting the show lined up and running smoothly from segment to segment. So by the time I'd be ready to *party*, Reenee would be sound asleep on one of my couches.

A couple of the guys helped me carry my stuff to the car. Reenee followed close behind. After they left, she grabbed my hands and made me promise to be careful on my way home.

"Be sure you keep an eye out for any cars tailing you. Look around when you take those flowers to the police station, and then again when you pull into your driveway. I am so worried about you, I can't think straight."

"What a lousy way to end a great afternoon, huh, Reenee? You did a fantastic job as guest host. We were both on a high, and then that bastard had to leave his calling card — again. You be careful driving home, too. God only knows what that sick-o is planning next. All I need is to have you in danger as well."

We looked at each other, no other words needed.

"Keep the faith, girlfriend," Reenee said, as she left for her car.

I waited for her to get in. We glanced at each other making sure our cars started. We waved, and I mouthed "Call me." We wanted to hash over the taping of the show in detail later that evening.

After all, stalker or no stalker, black roses or no black roses, today we were Stars.

Chapter 23

Since it was a Saturday, Chief Vincetti had no office hours, according to the officer at the Oak Forest police station front desk.

What? Do crooks take off for the weekend, too? Since when do cops have nine to five hours?

The officer referred me to Sgt. D'Antino. Thankfully, she was acquainted with my case. She led me to the evidence room, placed the flowers and the note in evidence bags, dated both, and then marked the bags with the case number and my name. Next, we moved to the interrogation room where Sgt. D'Antino took my statement, had it typed up, showed me where to sign, and said the data would be brought to the chief's attention on Monday. It appeared I wasn't a high priority on the Oak Forest crime investigation list.

I supposed I could've demanded that the sergeant call Chief Vincetti at home. After all, I'm a tax-paying citizen of Oak Forest, but I figured if the police could forget about it till Monday, so could I.

"Do you want an escort home, Ms. Lisowski?" Sgt. D'Antino asked.

"No, that's okay, but thank you for the offer. I've driven over twenty miles to get here; I guess I'll be okay the next three blocks on my own." I tried to keep the sarcasm out of my voice. I was a teeny, teeny bit peeved that the sergeant showed only lip-service concern to my problem. But then I figured, what more could she really do?

"I'm sure the Chief will be in touch with you Monday morning," she repeated.

And I supposed if I were attacked on the short drive home, it'd be my fault, according to Harry, for not accepting the police accompaniment.

I just couldn't win lately!

Although I was emotionally exhausted when I arrived home, I was also hyped up. After each taping of the TV show, I empathized with rock stars and famous personalities. I could see how they needed drugs or alcohol to either keep up that euphoria or come down from it. Usually I just came home, sent Director/Editor Ron the necessary information, then scrubbed the bathrooms or cleaned out the refrigerator to work off my nervous energy.

But then, one day, I asked myself as I grabbed the bottle of Lysol, does Oprah swab down toilets after her show, hose down her garage, clean out her cabinets? No way!

So I tried, instead, to convince Harry to take me out.

"Harry," I used to say. "I'm on a high. Let's go out for a couple of drinks or something."

"Y'know, Samantha," he answered, "you never have enough. You're gone all afternoon with that stupid show of yours, and you still want to go out. Why didn't you eat more at the restaurant? I can't believe you're still hungry."

"I'm not hungry. I get the *kruszkies* after taping a show. Does Beyonce go home after a concert and settle down to watch TV? Does Lady Ga-Ga grab a broom and sweep down her basement after a video performance? Does Oprah. . . ."

"What the hell are you talking about now? Sometimes I think you're nuts. Go out if you want. All I want is a sandwich and to watch that special on Tea Party organizations." He'd give me the look that meant *here comes another sermon.* "You should listen to the program as well. Get yourself involved in something worthwhile instead of all that fluffy volunteer work you sign up for."

Never end a sentence with a preposition, I almost told him but controlled myself. As for his remarks, Harry, who volunteered for nothing, didn't realize there's no fluffiness in volunteer work. He never appreciated the value of the organizations in which I was a member. He pooh-poohed my trustee position on the library board and the chairmanship of the cable commission. He rolled his eyes at my involvement in the book discussion club and my writing group. He resented the time I spent with the adult literacy program. Fluffiness. Hah!

Harry couldn't begin to understand the let-down feeling I suffered after each taping of the show. So, I have learned to come home, sit down at the computer, send the info off to Ron, clean out something or other to lessen my *kruszkies*, and let the rest of the world go by. But I'd feel unsettled and on edge the rest of the night.

One of these days, I promised myself, I would go out, and Harry might be sorry about the outcome; but, then again, he just might not care.

Hmm, maybe I would try out this idea tonight. I was still dressed up from the show, I had nothing to do — the bathrooms could wait. I wondered what the fine Detective Kelly was doing this evening — oh, hell.

I went to change clothes and then to see what might need some touching up around the house or maybe just watch TV, when the phone rang. It was Reenee.

"Now, Samantha, I don't want you to get upset or anything . . . ."

"Why? What happened? What's the matter. . . ?"

"Wait a sec, Sammy. I'm okay. I just had a little episode on the way home."

"What kind of episode? Were you in an accident? Are you hurt? You're not calling from a hospital, are you?" The words got louder and shot out of my mouth faster than I could think of them. "Where are you? I'll be right there."

"Relax, Sammy. Take a deep breath and hear me out, okay? You sound like you're hyperventilating."

I took her advice, toned down my words a couple of decibels, took a deep breath, then said, "Okay, okay. What happened?"

"I was on my merry way home when — now don't get excited again — I was sideswiped by someone in a white car."

"What?" I screeched. "The stalker? . . . oh my God. . . ."

"Take another breath, kiddo, and sit down. Put Harry on the phone."

"No, no, Reenee. I'm okay." Easy for me to say. Not! I think I *was* close to hyperventilating. I took a monstrously deep breath, shivered it out and sat down. "Really. I can handle it, girlfriend."

"All right. It happened on that lonely, narrow stretch of road, you know, right before my subdivision? Good thing I wasn't going fast. Obeying that twenty miles per hour speed zone there really helped me keep control of the car."

Although Reenee was playing it cool, I could hear the tremor in her voice. She must be more shaken up than she admitted.

"I can't believe what you're telling me, Reenee. Did you call the police? You didn't need an ambulance did you?"

"I called the police, and an ambulance came along as well. The paramedic insisted that he check me over. Although I had a nasty bump on my head, he did not suspect a concussion. I have a few scratches and a couple of bruises beginning to blossom, but. . . ."

"That friggin' stalker! I'll kill him if I catch up with him! Are you resting now? What did Wally say?"

"I called Wally from the accident site. He drove over to where I was, then called the insurance company and a tow truck. When the car was pulled out of the ditch . . . ."

"What ditch? You didn't mention any friggin' ditch!" I had been screeching so much through the whole conversation that Harry unloosened himself from the TV and came upstairs to investigate the noise I was making. His scowl was already in place.

"What the hell are you yelling about now, Samantha? Did a spider drop into your hair or . . . ."

"Harry, Reenee was sideswiped into a ditch on her way home!"

"What did you say?" He looked dumbfounded. "Reenee? Is she okay? What happened?"

I put up my hand to stop his questions and went back to my conversation with Reenee. I had to let her know that she shouldn't mention anything about stalkers because uninformed Harry was around.

"Harry just came upstairs, Reenee. I'm going to have him lift the extension in the other room. Wait a second till he gets there."

A couple of moments later Harry told us he was on the line. Reenee started her rendition from the beginning, with Harry telling me to stop interrupting her with my choicest expletives.

"Were you able to describe the car or give the police a license number, or a few letters off the plate?" Harry asked. "Did you get a look at the driver?"

"I was too busy trying to keep the car from hitting a tree," Reenee said. "The bastard just kept going. Couldn't be bothered to stop to see if I was hurt, or if the car would explode . . . ."

Evidently, reliving the dangerous scene was too much for her. She began to sob.

Wally took over the phone. "Reenee's shaken and upset. I want her to take a couple of aspirins and go lie down. I think the car is in better shape than she is. She'll call you tomorrow."

I could hear Reenee trying to get back on the phone, but Wally remained firm, then hung up.

Thank God she was all right, but I was crazy with worry. Was Reenee a victim of my predicament? Was the accident related to my problem? I also wanted to know what she told the police, and Wally — if she mentioned the possibility of the driver being my stalker. This gigantic mess of mine might now be dangerous for my precious friend, as well as for me. My head began to pound, and a couple aspirins sounded good to me, too. Was this nightmare never going to end?

I also became upset with Harry. One would think, wouldn't one, that he'd kind of talk a little about Reenee's predicament with me? Or offer me some comfort and say that she'd be okay. But no. He simply caught my eye, shook his head, sighed and went back downstairs to his beloved television. Ugh. Sometimes I could choke him.

I calmed down and decided to wash the gooky makeup off my face. Then, as I began brushing my teeth, my cell phone rang. I was surprised that I still had it turned on. Had I never shut it off since I discovered the murdered woman? How long does the battery last before conking out? And why was I wondering these things instead of just answering the damned phone?

"Please," I whispered a prayer to Whomever was listening up there, "not more trouble." The screen displayed Reenee's cell phone number. I quickly pressed the keypad.

"Reenee!"

"I can't talk long," she whispered into the phone. "Wally will be right back; just want you to know I didn't mention the stalker to him or the police. I'll call you tomorrow."

I shut off the phone and looked at my exasperated image in the bedroom mirror. Now I'm making my best friend lie to the police. I scowled at my reflection and chastised my soul.

How much more danger would Reenee be forced into just for being my steadfast, unbeatable, priceless friend?

And then it dawned on me what either of us had not yet addressed: was it the stalker, or could it have been the murderer, who sideswiped her? Was it possible that both those deranged criminals had some beef with my friend? That sounded ridiculous. My brain started conjuring up scenarios faster than speeding bullets at a shooting gallery.

I'd need more than a couple of aspirins to fall asleep this night.

Chapter 24

Though I slept peacefully through the night, I awoke with a headache and a feeling of doom. My body matched the scorching, humid Sunday. I splashed water on my face, took two aspirins, and put my polka CD into the player. Rosemary, the singer from Casey Homel's Honkiest Polka Band, was going to help me chase away the blues. I put my mat on the bedroom floor and started my exercises to the polka beat. After one song my mood changed for the better, and I got all my juices flowing for the next forty-five minutes. There's nothing like lively music played by the world's honkiest polka band to make me feel happy and snappy.

Wiping the sweat off my face as Rosemary and I finished the workout in unison, I jumped into the shower. I let the refreshing cold water blast over my clammy, sweltering skin.

Hearing a knock on the bathroom door followed by muted words, I happily ignored the intrusion and finished my shower.

Harry was posted near the door when I came out. "You had the water flow so forceful and high-powered that you couldn't even hear me yelling for you to lower it," he said. "Your sons must've learned how to turn faucets on full force from you. They always used to run up the water bill with their long showers." His complaint agenda was not yet over. "What takes you so long to shower anyway?"

"Well," I answered, now feeling pretty good and totally refreshed, "first I wash this little toe and then that little toe and...."

"I refuse to talk to you when you get absurd." He took himself and his disgusted look back downstairs.

Ah, I figured, another wonderful start to another wonderful day.

How could I have thought, those many pre-marriage years ago, that nothing bothered Harry? That he could take problems and mishaps in stride and keep everything pleasantly under control? Now he gets upset because I run the water with too much force?

What happened to us, Harry?

The phone interrupted my thoughts.

Reenee was on the other end. "Can you talk, or is the enemy around?" she asked.

"He's downstairs. I've been dying to hear from you." I could feel my body temperature rise. I should've waited to shower until after my conversation with Reenee. I knew our talk was going to get me riled up again.

"I couldn't call until Wally left for the gas station to fill up the Beamer," she said. "We're going to have to use his company car for a while. Mine will be out of commission with the repairs it needs."

"Nuts about the cars, girlfriend. How are you? Did you sleep well? Do you ache this morning?"

"My back and my shoulders have been better, but I'm like you, Sammy. Nothing seems to disturb my sleep or, unfortunately, my appetite."

"Evidently keeping things from the police doesn't bother us either. I'm growing more concerned that you didn't give the police the whole story yesterday."

"How could I, Sam? Neither Wally nor Harry knows about your stalker. How could I mention that problem at the accident site with Wally standing there next to me? I figured you and I needed to talk before I made any further statements." Reenee caught her breath. "You don't think I could be put in jail or fined or something for withholding evidence, do you?"

"Good lord, I hope not!" I thought a moment, then said, "Maybe you could explain that the bump on your head made you woozy and forgetful or confused — bewildered. But I don't think you should wait too long to set the record straight. Maybe you could call the police while Wally is still out and revise your story."

"Good idea, Sammy."

"Don't hold anything back on my account. Be sure to tell the detective in charge that Chief Vincetti of the Oak Forest police is aware of the stalking situation. I'll leave a message of my own for the chief as well."

"Wait, wait. The police from my village will probably contact you, too. How are you going to cover that up with Harry?"

Damn. My head spun with all the possible ramifications of Reenee's telling the cops everything. Maybe it was time to confess to Harry about the stalker. If he demanded that I give up *Straight from the Forest*, I'd just hold my ground and refuse to do it. I'd locked horns before with Harry in other circumstances, then continued to do my own thing. Didn't I get my way about the trip to Vegas with Reenee, about housing our younger son's two damned cats until his college graduation, about eating most of our meals in restaurants? Each accomplishment had entailed a battle, but in the end, I'd won. Why was I so stressed about confronting him with this situation?

"I'll worry about the cover-up when and if the time comes, Reenee. If worse comes to even worse, I'll just have to tell Harry the whole story. Now call the police, and then let me know how you made out, okay?"

"Are you gonna tell the hunk, too?"

"Why would I tell Rick about your accident?"

"Rick? Who's Rick — oh — Hannah's Hutch Rick? No, I meant the other hunk, the one with the badge and the disturbing baby blues."

"It'll be a terrible inconvenience for me to call the fine detective, but somebody's gotta do it." Reenee and I both started to giggle. I was glad we were still able to make wisecracks.

We chatted a little longer, comforting each other and keeping the rest of our conversation light and frivolous. Reenee promised to call me when she straightened out her situation with the police.

"I'm surprised you're not off and running to see Reenee after her accident," Harry said to me later in the day.

We were at one of his favorite Chinese buffets in neighboring Tinley Park. The menu always made Harry mellow and put him in an excellent mood. Today was no exception. He became talkative and even smiled once in a while. Maybe this would be a good time to tell him that a certain way I look on television had won me a stalker who lately was getting more intense.

I figured I'd take it one step at a time. "Reenee seems to be feeling okay and with Wally babying her, I don't want to horn in. His job keeps him on the road so much. I'm sure they're both glad to spend a day alone with each other."

"We haven't spent much time together either, Sam." Harry gave me a sad look. "You always seem to be running off to some meeting or outing or event, or you're on that damned computer writing the world's greatest novel."

I cut a glance at Harry. Was he complaining as usual, or was he reaching out to me? It had been so long since he'd tried the latter, I couldn't be sure. I gave him the benefit of my doubt.

"I guess I have been gone a lot lately, huh? I really wish you'd come with me once in a while. I don't think you'd find every event I attend boring. And as for the hours on the computer," I said, speaking in the warmest tone I could muster, "I'm just trying to get the job as an assigned writer to that magazine. The great American novel will come later." I smiled at Harry, hoping he wouldn't think I was being sarcastic again.

"You know, Samantha, you never show me any of the articles you send in. I have no idea what they're even about."

His interest so surprised me that the egg drop soup I had just been swallowing detoured up my nose instead. "What?" I said and began to cough. Was Harry showing me a concerned side? The egg roll rolled off my plate, duck sauce slopping over my white slacks.

Little feet attached to the sweet young Chinese waitress came scurrying over to our table. She looked distraught and began to speak in her native tongue. People at surrounding tables stopped eating and stared at our booth.

"I'm okay," I said to the audience. I'd spoken too soon. My cough increased and all kinds of little Chinese *krushkies* spewed out of my mouth. Embarrassed to astronomical proportions, I covered my mouth with a napkin and headed for the ladies' room.

Harry could deal with the disaster zone.

"Didn't your mother ever tell you never to talk with your mouth full?" Harry asked me when I returned to our booth, smiling to people who caught my eye along the way. "You okay?"

"My mother never told me anything." Except to think twice about marrying you, my alter ego whispered to me. I had to push my lips together with my fingertips to keep the words from escaping. I knew they'd be construed as sarcastic, not humorous.

"What's the matter? Did you bite your lips during your coughing spell?"

"No, no — everything's fine. Was that embarrassing or what!"

"You always like to be in the limelight, so the situation shouldn't be too awful for you." Harry seemed to be back to his scathing remarks, as a smile or a little affectionate touch did not accompany his words. "Should we go to the buffet table for seconds, or do you want to go home?"

Sadly realizing that "our moment" had passed, and just too tired to reopen our conversation about my articles, I got up in my sassy way and headed for the feeding trough.

Chapter 25

When we returned home, Harry headed upstairs for bed. Since he had gorged himself with MSG, desserts and caffeine-free coke, he was ready for sleep. I stayed downstairs and called my pal.

"I tried you earlier on your cell, Sammy," Reenee said, answering the phone, "but I didn't leave a message because I knew you still can't retrieve voicemail. I really should write down the simple procedure for you, step by step."

"I'd probably just lose the instructions, kiddo. Don't bother. How'd you make out with the police?"

"You sound down in the dumps. What's wrong?"

"Nothing, really; just tired from dealing with Harry. Our relationship continues to deteriorate. I'll tell you all about it tomorrow. I'm just too lethargic after a big Chinese feast to go into it now. So, you went to the police and —?"

"Everything went fine. I convinced Wally not to come with me, so I was free to bare my soul to the cops. I'm not being fined or thrown in jail. I explained my lapse of memory — blamed it on my confusion after the accident, as we discussed. A Detective Witkowski — hey, Sammy, a countryman — will contact your chief and you, too." Her tone changed, became more serious. "Witkowski warned me that I may be in danger — duh — like I didn't know that already? He told me to be vigilant — his word — and advised me to carry a can of pepper spray in my purse. Sound familiar?"

It seemed to me that if the police forces involved put as much energy in searching for the stalker and the murderer as they put into giving victims advice, my problems would be over.

"At least," Reenee went on to say, "Harry will probably be at work tomorrow when you receive a call from Witkowski, right?"

"Hmm — I almost confessed tonight, Reenee."

"To your pastor, the pope, God? Certainly not to Harry!"

"Oh, girlfriend, you are so funny. I can always count on you to raise my spirits. Let me tell you what happened after all."

Harry was surprised to see me up early the next morning and setting a semblance of breakfast on the table. Regardless of how I complained about him, he never begrudged my sleeping in every morning. He realized that I was not a morning person and that he generally already had almost four hours of sleep in by the time I called it a night.

"This French toast is really good, Samantha. Do I taste vanilla, or cinnamon? Watching Rachael Ray lately?"

"Oh, yes, you know me, Harry. Feverishly writing down every new recipe she rattles off. Not. The only thing she and I have in common is eating too much."

"Time to go," he said, drinking down the last drop of decaf. "This was really nice having breakfast together this morning."

I am in the Twilight Zone, I thought. Maybe his lifted spirits were the lingering effects of too much MSG. If he kissed me goodbye, I'd either faint or go screeching insanely out of the house.

What was coming over Harry?

"Won't be hungry tonight, so soup and a sandwich will be okay by me. Got a lunch meeting at P. F. Chang's. Humpf, as if I didn't have enough Oriental food yesterday." Harry got up and stretched. "Going to see Reenee?"

I couldn't tell him that I wasn't going to see Reenee nor was she coming by to see me until this horrendous stalking business was over. I had put my girlfriend in enough danger already. If we stayed away from each other, the stalker might leave her alone, thinking, in his screwed-up mind, that she was no longer part of my world.

A stray thought almost made me jump. What about Harry? Wouldn't the stalker want him out of my life? I really needed to come clean about the mess I was in and warn him that he might be in danger. No time like the present.

"Harry," I said. "I think we have to do some serious talking. Maybe you can go into work a little later today?"

"Do you not listen when I speak, Samantha?" His face began to heat up, and he looked disgusted. "I told you I have a very important meeting at lunchtime, and I have to finalize things for it this morning. Can you tell me real fast what's so important?"

Harry never fails to get my American, liberated-woman dander up. The egg fu young he ate last night had worn off. How could I think he was changing — could ever change — or that I would change and accept him as he was?

"Never mind. Better leave; newscasts are filled with warnings about especially busy rush-hour traffic."

With no further ado, Harry grabbed his newspaper, briefcase and was on his way, barely saying good-bye.

I had another couple of cups of decaf while finishing the latest mystery thriller by Sherry Scarpaci. *Lullaby* was engrossing and made me forget my worries for a while. Then I washed up the few breakfast dishes and called Chief Vincetti. He was indeed up-to-date on the latest episodes of black roses, notes and Reenee's sideswiping incident. But I got the same old story: nothing new on the case, I should be careful, inform Harry about what was going on . . . yada, yada, yada.

I comforted myself with the thought that I had made an attempt with Harry at breakfast to take the latter advice, but it didn't work out. Right now, I needed to inform Detective Kelly about Reenee's hit-and-run and to see if there were any further developments to complicate my life.

Well, really for other reasons, too.

He answered his phone immediately. "Samantha! I was just thinking about you."

Good lord, could his voice sound any sexier than it already did? Thinking about me? As a friend or a sexy siren? Please, Lord, don't let these stray Samantha-isms tumble out of my mouth. Stick to the problem, girl.

"I hope you're not calling with bad news?" he asked.

"Yes, unfortunately. More bad news. My friend, Reenee, was sideswiped on her way home Saturday from the restaurant where we taped my TV show." Once I started explaining, the words flowed quickly and intensely. By the time I finished my story, my cheeks were burning and a fine sweat had broken out near my temples.

"Take it easy, Samantha. You sound panic-stricken. Get yourself some water; I'll wait."

This seemed a good idea to me. I went into the kitchen, thinking how different Harry's response to my rant would've been. He'd probably have just said, "Slow down, for chrissake, and stop being dramatic."

I took a deep breath and enjoyed the coolness of the ice-cold H2O. I put the glass to my forehead, then to my cheeks and chest. Rejuvenated, I returned to the hunk on the phone.

"I'm better now, Detective. I need to thrash out some concerns with you, the biggest being about the car that sideswiped Reenee. Isn't it possible the driver might have been the murderer and not the stalker — or maybe the driver is coincidental to my problem. But either way, things are escalating, right?"

"I don't think your anxieties are off base. If the driver was the stalker, he, in his sick mind, might be jealous of anyone around you, male or female. The killer, on the other hand, could be trying to discourage you from being any further help with our police inquiries."

"Those thoughts happen to be foremost in my mind, Detective." I again began to get flustered. "I can't go around in a vacuum; I have loads of friends — and two sons and my dad and a sort-of husband."

The last remark brought a lull in the conversation, but the hunk didn't pick up on it. Instead he said, "I can only advise that you continue being careful, and for the duration, keep your loved ones away from you as much as possible. First of all, tell Harry about the stalker, so he's aware of the danger to himself. Your sons know, don't they?"

Ideas were flying around in my mind as if my brain were a pinball machine. I was quiet for so long that Detective Kelly probably thought I had hung up.

"Samantha?"

"Yeah, I'm okay. I hear ya. I'm dumbfounded with goofy, scary thoughts — yes, my boys know; they don't come over that often anyway — busy enjoying the summer with their near-Northside pals. My dad's on an extended trip to his sister's place in California, and Reenee knows to keep away from me." I sighed deeply and shook my head in frustration. "That leaves Harry. I'm wondering why the stalker didn't knock him off the road instead of Reenee? Wouldn't that be more logical? Will this wacko, and then that killer on the loose, ever be caught, Detective!"

"Yours is a frustrating and difficult situation, Samantha. I'm going to contact the Burr Ridge detective who's handling Reenee's case. Do you know his name? I'll be sure to get a hold of Chief Vincetti, too."

I gave the information to Detective Kelly. He told me to hang tough and that he'd be in touch.

Then he said something as he hung up.

Something that shouldn't be said to a woman long into an indifferent, loveless marriage.

Something a woman cherishes to hear and to remember on cold lonely nights — and hot, humid ones, too.

His low, sexy voice gave my sizzling body more *kruszkies* than it could handle.

Yikes!

I couldn't wait to call Reenee.

Chapter 26

I awoke the next day determined to file away Detective Kelly's steamy remarks in a compartment of my brain for later assessment. I probably misread his tone of voice; no doubt he was just kidding or flirting to see my response. Anyway that's what Reenee and I had decided last night after hashing over his torrid words. We both agreed I should stay focused on my dangerous problems and lay the hunk's comments aside for a while. Maybe he'd had a little too much to drink again; I knew how that could cause diarrhea of the mouth.

Harry was up and had read half the newspaper even though he didn't have to leave for work until the afternoon. He probably thought I was gonna cook a Samantha Special for him, but as I came downstairs in full make-up, he figured a home-cooked meal was not in the running. I might have mentioned I hated to cook? He and I left for *The Egg and I* and breakfast.

At the restaurant, I had hoped Harry, as usual, would bury himself in the paper while we ate so that I could plan my course of action for the day. Instead he said, "I've been thinking, Sam. Why do you suppose the caller hasn't found another way to contact you?"

Yikes. I gagged on the grits I was savoring and gulped down some pineapple juice too quickly, the liquid bubbling simultaneously through my mouth and nose. I felt dizzy with *deja vu*. Hadn't this just happened at the Chinese buffet a couple days ago?

This spectacular display of bodily dysfunction was being witnessed by people in the restaurant who recognized me from the TV program. I had noticed several people looking my way when I came in. Now they had a front seat for a different kind of show.

Harry began patting me on the back and I kept trying to get him to stop while at the same time mopping my face, my blouse and the table. I knocked over both our glasses of water. A waitress and a couple of busboys hurried to our aid but made matters worse by accidentally overturning the coffee carafe. Spilled hot coffee completed the buffet on my slacks. I yelled out a few not-so-nice words. Now we had all the customers' attention. The scene was like a Three Stooges' production.

Harry added to the melee with his "comforting" remarks. "How many times have I told you, Samantha? You eat too fast, and you always keep your coffee cup or glass where you can easily knock it over."

Because I felt guilty about keeping him out of the loop, I bit back a Samantha retort. Was I becoming a wimp?

The distraction also sidetracked Harry's line of thought. After we wiped up the mess as best we could, I told him that I'd like to finish our breakfast without talking about the caller and then get home to change my messed-up clothes. Darling agreed, and for the rest of the meal he treated me to the fascinating world of "The Financial Development of the Lisowski Portfolio."

He began to talk about roll-overs. Whatever the hell that meant! I can't even teach the damned cats to roll-over.

Leaving the restaurant, I again apologized to the staff for creating such a mess. They were all smiles and a-twitter, telling me it was a pleasure to serve the local TV celebrity.

Walking to where our car was parked I busied my mind trying to figure out why people became flustered and giggly, like the wait staff, when they recognized me from the TV show. It continued to amaze me and . . . .

"What the hell?" Harry's outcry interrupted my thoughts. He looked around in confusion. "This is your car, isn't it, Samantha?"

On the hood of my beautiful red Grand Am, a bunch of black roses in a cellophane bag was secured under the windshield wiper. Harry reached for the accompanying card. In purple block letters, large enough for me to see without my glasses, it read:

Love those legs. And everything else!

I frantically started waving my hands at Harry and yelling, "Don't touch anything! Leave it alone. Oh, God!"

"What?"

"Fingerprints," I shrieked.

Harry looked at me as if I were a green-skinned alien from outer space with three eyes and an antenna sticking out of my ear. Catching my reflection in the side-view mirror I realized I actually looked as pale as a vampire who had missed her weekly blood feast.

"Stop screaming. What's wrong with you?" Harry studied me like a bug under a microscope. "Okay, Samantha," he said. "Let's have it."

I panicked. I'm screwed, I thought. I had to come up with a reasonable explanation in ten seconds or tell Harry the truth. I opted for the truth, the whole truth and nothing but the truth. Well, sort of.

Harry wanted details. I was trying to think faster than he could ask questions, but he was an interrogation wizard. He would've been The Golden Boy of the Spanish Inquisition. Our tender conversation accumulated quite a busybody crowd.

Him: "What previous note?"

Me: "Through the mail."

"What? When?"

"A couple of days ago."

"Why wasn't I told?"

"Told Chief Vincetti."

"What's he doing about it?"

"Can't do much."

"The hell he can't!"

Bystanders looked like spectators at a tennis match, shifting their heads from Harry to me and back again.

Darling gave the masses an all-encompassing dirty look and, almost gently, steered me into the front seat of the car where our conversation continued in earnest. I almost thought he'd take out an easel and outline the points he wanted explained. From the scowl on his face and the irritation in his probing voice, I knew I was in for an award-winning lecture. The only props missing were a mountain and a stone tablet. A lesser woman would've started bawling; good thing I'm not a lesser woman.

Instead, my heart was beating like mixer blades swirling around in mashed potatoes. In fact I was getting crazy mad. Enough is enough,

I thought. I got out of the car and slammed the door. Too bad Harry's fingers, or an even better part of his body, weren't in the way. I used my keys to pop the trunk and took out a roll of Bounty. Carefully I took the bouquet off the windshield, wrapped it and gingerly placed it on the back seat. I got back into the car and then turned to face the Love of My Life.

Harry looked back in exasperation. "When were you going to tell me about this fiasco, Sam? After the situation escalated into an attack? Would I first hear about it from your hospital bed?"

"Well, I'm telling you now," I answered in my coldest voice. Why couldn't Harry just get mad without using hundred dollar words like "fiasco" and "escalating?" Who talks like that when they're angry?

"Settle down, settle down." His voice returned to a normal decibel. One good thing about Harry is that when he's through venting, he doesn't stay angry. "Are you okay? Seeing those black flowers on the windshield must've scared the hell out of you, huh?"

So I also mellowed a little and said, "I am settled down, Harry. Let's just get these flowers to Chief Vincetti and call it a day. I don't know if I'm more angry or more scared."

We remained silent as we drove to the police station. Harry had not as yet declared an edict about the value of giving up my TV show, and I didn't want to give him an opportunity to do so until I rearmed myself for a power struggle.

It took the rest of the afternoon to sort out the latest incident with Chief Vincetti.

"So," I said to Harry on the way home, "the bottom line is that unless I am raped, murdered or hacked into a million pieces, the police can't do anything about my situation."

"Don't get dramatic, Sam. You brought a lot of this upon yourself by not confiding in me from Day One."

Bullshit, I thought. That's the stupidest thing Harry had said in a long time. How in the hell would telling him sooner have made a difference? The only difference I could figure it would have made was that I'd have had to listen to accusations and lectures for a longer time. Since I was worn out, I merely nodded and kept my trap shut.

The red light was blinking on the telephone pad when we walked into the house. Skimming through the messages I discovered they were all from Khara, but I disregarded them. I didn't want to hear about any further problems of the Morrows. I had plenty of my own.

Harry wanted to plot a course of action for us to pursue, but I'd had it. I went upstairs, called Reenee and then remained there the rest of the evening. Harry stayed downstairs.

My stomach was in knots even after discussing the whole miserable day with my pal, so I didn't even venture out of the bedroom to eat. I took out my emergency stash of World's Greatest Chocolate candy and called it supper. Darling must've made himself a sandwich or something. I didn't know, and I didn't care. When I hit the pillow around eleven o'clock, black roses, not sugarplums danced around in my head. Whether Harry came up to sleep or stayed downstairs, I didn't know, and again I didn't care.

Samantha's best advice for a long pseudo-successful marriage: buy a multi-leveled house — so when things get tough, the tough stays on her own level.

Chapter 27

Harry wanted to stay home with me the next day. Reenee wanted to spend the entire day babysitting me. I told them both that I had a Gazebo Commission meeting in the morning at Oak Forest City Hall and would be surrounded by friendly faces. They cautioned me to be aware of everyone in the building, parking lot and around the house.

"Yes, Ms. Harry," I said to Reenee.

"Yes, Father," I said to Harry.

Both accused me of being a smart-ass.

Before I left for the meeting, Detective Kelly called. I caught my breath, leery that he'd get my cheeks burning again with sexy remarks. But he was all business.

"I'll be in your neighborhood this afternoon," he said. "I'm leaving the precinct shortly for Tinley Park to further question the Morrows. If it's not inconvenient, I'd like to stop by your house afterwards to clear up a few loose ends in this murder case."

I didn't know if I appreciated being called a loose end, but I figured, hell, why not? The more police around me, the better I'd like it. I assumed my Drew Carey's *The Price Is Right* voice and hollered, "Detective Kelly, come on down!"

"Samantha!" Khara, the phone buddy who'd been keeping me informed about the Morrows, confronted me as soon as I stepped into City Hall where the Gazebo Commission meeting was being held. "I left you a bunch of calls on your answering machine. How come you haven't called me back?" She seemed in a tizzy, her hands and fingers accentuating her every statement. "Why didn't you tell me you were one of the visitors at the Morrow house the day that all hell broke loose there? What's going on with you?"

Wow, what's with *her*? I thought. Imagine getting so upset over unanswered phone calls. She should try my stressed-out life.

I tried to keep my voice calm and conciliatory. "I've had such a lousy couple of days, Khara, that I really didn't want to hear about anybody else's problems. I'm sorry I didn't at least touch base with you. And I didn't tell you I was one of Frances' visitors because I was embarrassed and felt guilty about being there."

I didn't want to tell her the real reason. Khara was kind of the neighborhood gossip. I knew she'd grill me for details and then exaggerate my situation to anyone who'd listen. "I should've clued you in. But what's up now? As I said, I haven't listened to your messages yet."

My telephone buddy looked miffed. "I wasn't aware that I was bothering you by leaving information you wanted," she said with a toss of her head. "I thought I was doing you a favor. I thought you wanted to know about the Morrows."

"I do, I do, Khara. I'm ashamed of myself. You've been very kind about keeping me informed. Are matters much worse at the household?"

"All that I know is on your machine. Maybe you should listen to the messages and then call me if you can spare the time." Khara turned sharply on her heels and walked away in a huff.

I wanted to apologize further, but the meeting was called to order. Our most important agenda item was to plan the last entertainment event of the summer to be held in front of the gazebo on City Hall grounds. The suggestions offered were concise and to the point, and sub-committees were formed to implement them. We settled all our plans in two hours flat.

Once things were wrapped up, I persuaded Khara to join me at the beverage and dessert table so I could make nice. We sipped our coffee and munched on the sweet rolls as I apologized again. Khara accepted my act of contrition, then said, her voice snippy with glacial overtones, "When my sister heard the names from her pal of the visitors at the Morrows' house, she recalled that you and I were acquaintances. When this information trickled down to Frances, she asked for your phone number. I know you want to protect your unlisted number, so I'm asking you for permission to give it to my sister so she can pass it on."

I hesitated. Although I was almost a hundred percent sure no one from the Morrow household was my stalker, I strongly believed that the couple had something to do with the murders. And didn't Detective Kelly tell me just this morning that he was going there today to investigate further?

Khara took my reluctance as more evidence of my secrecy and inconsideration toward her. "Forget it, Samantha. I'm sure you have your reasons. I'll see you at the gazebo event." She tossed her head and again walked away in a huff.

Why is everyone being so testy lately — although I could see Khara's point. I'm sure she had better things to do than gather up information about the Morrows for me. I put my phone pal in a back compartment of my mind. I'd deal with restoring our relationship at a better time and headed for home, determined to listen to the messages she had left me.

I returned home on high, in spite of the run-in with Khara, because the Gazebo Commission meeting had been a success. Miraculously, all of us opinionated women were on the same page, which was quite a feat. The last program would be a spectacular culmination to the city's summer season's entertainment events.

It was a bit stuffy in the house, so I went to open the patio door in the den before keeping my promises to call Reenee and Harry and to listen to Khara's messages. As I opened the sliding door, a piece of paper fell to the ground. I picked it up but immediately dropped it. A glance at the purple capital letters was enough for me. My stomach churned and I broke into a sweat. Stumbling up the stairs to the kitchen I pulled a Bounty off the roll. Still in my high heels, I almost killed myself getting back to the patio. I gingerly picked up the note with the paper towel.

Through blurry eyes, I read:

YOU LOOK EVEN SEXIER IN PERSON

YOUR SCENT LINGERS
I CAN SMELL YOU EVEN NOW

God, he'd been here again, at my house — in my backyard!

I quickly double-locked the patio door. I felt dizzy as I ran to the bathroom where my sparkling clean toilet bowl accepted my morning meal. I rinsed my mouth and sat down on the seat cover to catch my breath. Taking a few deep breaths I calmed down, then hurried to the phone to call the police.

The front door bell rang.

I froze. My knees gave out and I plopped into the La-Z-Boy. My heart was beating like a metronome keeping time to a Chicago-style Polish hop. I was also in a quandary. The Tiger or the Lady? First open the door or first call the police?

Oh, I suddenly thought. Detective Kelly! He said he'd be stopping by after talking to the Morrows. I'd certainly welcome *him* with open arms.

But what if it wasn't the hunk?

I cautiously approached the front door, then stopped and took a breath.

"Who's there?" I called out in a shaky voice.

"Who's there?" I asked a little louder. Getting no answer I rushed to the front window so I could see the driveway. A white car was erratically backing out into the street. In vain I tried to focus in on the driver as the vehicle sped away. I was too scared to see clearly, even had I had my glasses on.

I rushed to the front door and slowly opened it. Cautiously I took a few steps out and stumbled over something. I looked down and saw a small bundle. Catching my breath, I kicked the package into the house and quickly slammed the door and locked it. My hands were shaking and my knees were weak with no Elvis Presley around to supply the music.

I booted the package into the kitchen. Gingerly I picked it up with the metal tongs and sheets of Bounty. At this rate I was gonna run out of paper towels. I got a pair of rubber gloves out of the sink cabinet, so I could open the bundle, when the doorbell rang again. I dropped the gloves and held onto the table for support.

He can't be coming back, I thought. I didn't know what to do.

Taking the phone with me in case I had to dial 9-1-1, I stumbled to the front room window and peeked out at the driveway. I was ecstatic to see a dark sedan with a blue light on its dashboard. The tension in my body suddenly gone, I started laughing like a maniac, ran to the door, opened it and threw myself into the arms of Detective Kelly.

My chaotic situation didn't keep me from being oblivious of his sexy after-shave lotion or his warm, great-feeling chest.

Chapter 28

Detective Kelly treated me like a guest in his house instead of the other way around. He led me into my prehistoric kitchen and rummaged through the cabinets for the Folger's. He made the coffee in no time at all.

Oh, God, I sighed, he can cook, too!

I settled down — in some ways more than others. I don't think I have to explain that statement, but I'm going to anyway. This detective in my life soothed me mentally. But emotionally and physically — well, that was a different story. He was anything but soothing in those areas. I laid my feelings in another back compartment of my mind for scrutiny later with Reenee. If this case wasn't solved soon, I was gonna run out of compartments.

I drank my coffee and reached into the cookie jar, stuffing about a zillion Oreo's into my mouth. I must've looked like a cow chewing her cud as I chomped away and related my story. Detective Kelly listened without interruption and put a comforting hand on my arm when he felt it was necessary. It crossed my mind how different his technique was from Harry's third degree.

When I finished, the hunk asked if talking about the occurrence made me feel better. I wanted to say *he* made me feel better, but I bit my tongue and just nodded, as I mentally washed out nasty thoughts about him with a bar of soap. My emotions were too high to be blurting out admissions that I couldn't shove back into my mouth at a saner time.

"Let's take a look at the package," he said. "Or aren't you up to it yet?"

"I'm all right, I think." I sighed a big one. "I want to get this over with."

Detective Kelly said he had to get a few things from his car. I held on to his arm all the way to the front door. "Don't worry, I'm coming right back," he said. The memory of his great smile kept me company for the few minutes he was gone.

When he returned, he had an evidence bag with him. He pulled out a pair of latex gloves from his pocket and put them on. Carefully he picked up the small bundle. He inserted it into the bag and labeled it with the time, date and my name and address.

"Aren't you going to open it?" I asked.

"This is Chief Vincetti's case, Samantha. I'm going to bring this evidence to him and let him proceed from there."

"Well, don't think you're leaving me here alone! I'm coming with you."

"Wouldn't you rather call your husband to come home? I'll wait till he gets here, if you wish."

Of course that was the sensible thing to do. But I've never been accused of having the quality of sense. Besides, I wasn't ready for Harry's reaction and bullshit. I was going along to the Oak Forest police station even if I had to run after Detective Kelly's car.

Chief Vincetti led us immediately into his office. He told the detective that it was a pleasure to finally meet him. Until now they had only spoken by phone.

"Did you travel all the way from the Chicago Northside to help Samantha?" He tried to keep a professional tone, but I could almost feel his brain clicking "aha, well, well . . . ."

"No. I drove into Tinley Park this morning to make a few inquiries of Frances and John Morrow, who are persons of interest in the murders under my investigation. My partner and I uncovered a few relationships worthy of note that I wanted to discuss with them. As I'd be in the area, I called Samantha to let her know I'd be stopping by. I wanted her to review that day in light of the new information. We never got around to it because of this latest intrusion of the stalker into Ms. Lisowski's life."

Maybe we should pull out a couple of bottles of beer, toe off our shoes and relax with mundane conversation, I thought, and just forget about the package, *which was boring a hole in my head*. I was ready to explode while the two policemen held a chit-chat cop session. Both men must've felt my body waves ready to implode the room, because they abruptly said they'd discuss the Morrows later.

The chief then listened intently as I related the morning's incident. By the time of this second retelling, my eyes were no longer glassy or as big as flying saucers. In fact, I felt as though I was talking about somebody else — a friend of mine, maybe a person I'd read about in a book or a character in one of my short stories. But I also felt a wild desire to scream, tear out my hair, kick something. Determined not to lose it in front of two good-looking men, I mentally tightened my resolve and continued to speak as calmly as possible.

When I finished, Chief Vincetti wanted to know if I recognized the car or caught a glimpse of the driver who'd delivered the package.

"All I know is that the white car was new and — oh, my God, Reenee was sideswiped by a driver in a white car!" I began seeing double and suddenly got weak in the knees. I sank into the chair that thankfully was behind me.

"Let me get you some water," Chief Vincetti said. "You just rest there for a minute."

As soon as he left the room, Detective Kelly took both my hands into his. That sure got my heart pumping again. "You're not going to fall apart, *Ms. Lisowski*," he said, as he winked at me. "You're doing fine."

He might have said more, but the chief returned with water and a cool, wet washcloth, both of which I gratefully used.

"Can we get back to that white car, Samantha?"

"Yes, Chief. I'm okay now. I have no idea of its make. I didn't even think to look at the license plate, not that I could've read it anyway without my glasses. The driver was a complete blur."

Chief Vincetti must've noticed that I still wasn't myself. He looked meaningfully at Detective Kelly. "I think it's best if we have a female officer take Samantha home. Patrolwoman Zahara can stay with her until her husband returns from work. She doesn't need to be here when we unwrap the package. I can call her later."

I perked up immediately, straightening my spine. "Oh, no! I'm not going home." I was going to duct tape myself to the chair if necessary. "Don't either of you think you're going to get rid of me. I want to see what's in that bundle." My voice began to quiver and my eyes became teary. "You owe me that much."

Detective Kelly spoke up for me. "We really do owe her, Chief. She's been through a lot and we know the tough times are not over for her. Ms. Lisowski will have to be told about the contents either way. She'll probably handle the situation better by staying here."

Chief Vincetti gave me that "women are so difficult" look and reluctantly agreed to let me stay.

The chief led us to the evidence room. He was quite proud of it. *Kruszkies* were popping around in my stomach like balls in a bingo cage as he chatted away about the room's purpose, its contents and the government grant that made it possible. I was in no mood for a tour and dissertation about my taxes at work. Midway through his explanation, I was ready to tear open that package with my teeth.

The chief and Detective Kelly finally donned latex gloves. Good thing, because the top of my head felt like Mount St. Helens ready to explode.

Containers, scissors, box knives, labels, opaque and transparent evidence envelopes and marking pens were already on the metal table. Slowly and carefully, Chief Vincetti cut the string on the bundle and unwrapped the paper. He unfolded some kind of clothing. Photos, wrapped into the folds, and a note, fell to the floor.

"Oh, my God," I whispered. A chill skittered down my spine. I gaped at the apparel and the spilled contents in stunned silence, gripping the edge of the table as the room began to spin.

Chapter 29

The vertigo lessened as I continued to stare at the spilled photographs, wishing they'd change into something else. I couldn't make out clear images or read the note on the floor because I wasn't wearing my glasses. I knew they were bad though, by the grim expressions on the men's faces. I swallowed hard to control my mounting panic.

Detective Kelly put his arm around me and led me to a chair, softly urging me to be strong. I sat down in a daze, but his comforting gesture and words toughened me up. He remained at my side and did not remove his reassuring embrace.

Although Chief Vincetti didn't raise an eyebrow over the familiarity, he did give us a furtive glance as he carefully picked up the note and the photos and put them on a pile. Then he separated the rest of the items, not that there was much to separate. He put the two flimsy bras and the two pairs of transparent crotchless panties next to each other. They were identical except for color, one being black and the other a brilliant red. A couple of paste-on glittery stars and ankle bracelets completed the outfits.

As I stared at the items, my breath was barely trickling in and out. Several times Detective Kelly whispered for me to take a couple of deep breaths, which I did and which kept me from feeling dizzy. I couldn't believe I was involved in this horrendous mess.

The chief looked through the pile of photos, then read the note. He avoided looking at me. "Detective, could I see you outside for a minute?"

"No, you can't see him outside for a minute. Show me those photos and the note and talk to me!" My shaky voice was so angry and cold, even I didn't recognize it.

But Detective Kelly gave my shoulders a reassuring squeeze and, no longer pretending to call me Ms. Lisowski, said, "Don't worry, Samantha, I promise we won't hold anything back from you." He smiled. "Be a good girl, don't touch anything and we'll be right back."

They took the photos and note with them and left, but I couldn't sit still. I ignored the directive of the detective, laughing inwardly like a crazy person over the alliteration. How could I have these extraneous thoughts? Was I going mad?

Shaking irrelevant stuff from my mind, I got up to look at the scanty items on the table. I figured I wouldn't destroy any evidence if I put on a pair of latex gloves to browse through them.

The outfits were a whole level beyond Victoria's Secret or Frederick's of Hollywood. There were no tags to identify the manufacturer or the store from which they were purchased. The total weight of the items couldn't have been more than three ounces. I felt funny touching them, even through latex gloves. They made my skin crawl. How could the photos or the note possibly be worse than this vulgar attire? I wondered. And what the hell was taking those guys so long?

I took off the gloves and sat down again. Then it hit me. Oh, my God, I thought, I haven't called Reenee or Harry! I was supposed to phone them as soon as I got back from the morning meeting. Reenee would've sent out the National Guard by now, and Harry's ears must be erupting with steam and lava.

I took out my cell phone and called my friend. She was so relieved to hear from me that she began to cry. I felt like a dirty rat. I apologized for not calling her sooner, promising her another call with details as soon as possible because I couldn't go into full explanations right now.

Reenee pulled herself together. She was tough all right. She used the same word for me. "I know things must be tough, Sammy, but you're tougher. Hang strong. My spirit's there with you. Call me as soon as you can. I'm not moving from the phone till I hear from you."

Harry's office phone was on "leave a message" mode, so I tried his cell.

"Dammit, Samantha. It's about time you called. I've been leaving messages for you on our home answering machine all afternoon. And I can't get through on your cell. Don't you ever keep that friggin' phone on?" His voice was blasting into my ear. "Where the hell are you? I'm on my way home; I should be there in less than a half hour."

"Please, I'm sorry, Harry. I know I should've called." I gave him a shorter run-down of what had happened than I'd given Reenee. He kept shouting "What?" in disbelief after every sentence I uttered. He was furious with me. I hoped his anger stemmed from his fear that I was in harm's way, but I was inclined to believe it was due to my supposed thoughtlessness and inconsideration toward him. He wanted to go into details but I said that Chief Vincetti and Detective Kelly were coming back into the room and. . . .

"Detective Kelly? Of the Chicago Police Department? *That* Detective Kelly? He came all the way from the Northside of the city to accompany you to the Oak Forest station? You mean you called him for moral support instead of me? Is something going on here that I should know about, Samantha? I'm angry as hell that you don't tell me anything until it gets out of hand. I'll bet Reenee's been kept up-to-date. "

I don't need this, I thought. "Harry, please. I can't go into it now. I'll explain everything when you get home. I've got to hang up." I made my voice as cold and sarcastic as I could. "And in case you're interested, I'm holding up fairly well." I disconnected and shut off my cell. He could call the police station if he wanted to harass me further. Why couldn't he be sympathetic and comforting like Detective Kelly? Why did he always make me feel like I was the cause of the trouble?

But he was good for one thing. Harry took my mind off my immediate problem and got me angry enough to face whatever the next shock would bring. And good thing, too, because it turned out to be a zinger.

When the men returned, they eyed me guardedly. Chief Vincetti mumbled something under his breath and shook his head. Detective Kelly came and sat down next to me. They looked like Doom and Gloom, ready to predict an end of the world, Ka-Boom.

I couldn't stand the tension any longer. "Well," I said, "who's brave enough to tell me what's going on?"

The chief cleared his throat. "First, we want you to look at the photos, Samantha." His demeanor was grim. "They are repulsive, but we want you to be brave and scrutinize them. See if you recognize anybody." He gave me three pictures encased in transparent evidence bags, withholding the fourth.

I put on my glasses and gasped. The photos were foul. The first one portrayed two naked women, locked in a disgusting sexual pose. The other pictures were worse, involving what looked like an orgy between three nude women. Little was left to the imagination.

I closed my eyes and shuddered. I could see the sordid pictures as if they'd been imprinted on my eyelids. I'd never forget those scenes. Who could send something so hideous?

"Do you recognize any of the women?" the chief asked. "Look at them again, Samantha."

I didn't need to. Their faces were already etched into my brain for all eternity. "None are even faintly familiar to me." I swallowed hard. "Could I please have something to drink?"

Chief Vincetti did the honors. He took a bottle of water out of the small refrigerator in the room and poured me a glassful. The water was like nectar of the gods, returning saliva to my dry mouth.

"Okay." I braced myself and asked, "What else? Show me that last picture you're holding, Chief. How can it be any worse than the ones I've seen? And what does the note say?"

Detective Kelly squeezed my shoulder. "Take it easy, Samantha. You're doing great." He took my hand and gently pressed the note that was in a transparent evidence bag into my palm. The thing seemed to burn my skin. I tightly shut and opened my eyes a couple of times. I put my glasses back on and warily examined the purple-inked printing. I gawked at the message; I read it a couple of times. My breath seemed to leave my body.

I looked at Detective Kelly in a daze. "This can't be," I said. "Oh, my God! This can only mean that my stalker is. . . ."

Chapter 30

"A woman. My stalker is a *woman*?"

Even though I had my glasses on, I reread the note to assure myself that I wasn't mistaken:

> Would you like to do some of these things with me
> ~~*Samantha* ~~
> Only another woman knows how to really love you

Suddenly, as strange as it sounds, I felt better, freer, less scared. A woman? Why should I be afraid of a woman? It was ludicrous, laughable. In fact, I started giggling. Who's afraid of Virginia Woolf?

I looked at Chief Vincetti and chortled some more. Then I looked into the soothing blue eyes of Detective Kelly, and the giggling fit changed into a crying jag. The sobering thought of how my tears would mess up my eye makeup and make me look horrible in front of the hunk stopped the flow. I rummaged in my purse for a Kleenex. "I'm sorry for that display," I said. "I'm usually not such a cry-baby."

"No need to apologize, Samantha. You're holding up better than Detective Kelly and I could've hoped for. But you have to hang in a little longer. I have this last photo for you to see."

I furtively glanced at the picture in its protective plastic evidence bag, and then looked again more closely. No, please, I thought. That can't be a picture of me with Reenee, smiling over a meal in a restaurant! I had on my glasses so it had to be so. But how *could* it be?

"Turn it over," Detective Kelly whispered to me.

On the back, in the same bold purple ink were the words:

MAYBE YOUR GIRLFRIEND
CAN JOIN US FOR A THREESOME

"I can't take any more of this," I whispered. "You will *not* tell me that my dearest friend is now in this mess with me. I won't have it; I won't!" I wanted to rip the photo and the note and all the other stuff into shreds. I wanted to sock someone. I took a swing at Detective Kelly. He gently held my arms together and pulled me to his chest.

And wouldn't you know — Harry took this moment to burst into the room, escorted by a patrolman.

No one spoke for a long moment. We were like kids in that statue game we used to play long ago where everyone had to stand still or be "out." Then, before the silence became even more uncomfortable, we all started talking at once. I talked a little louder than the rest and approached Harry.

"You've no idea . . . I've been through hell . . . wanted to punch somebody . . . took it out on Detective Kelly . . . had to restrain me."

No one looked directly at anyone else. Then Detective Kelly cut through the tension in the room and extended his hand to Harry. "We've never met, but I want you to know you have one brave and feisty woman!"

Harry hesitated before he reluctantly shook hands. His tone exuded sarcasm. "Oh, she's feisty all right. I'm sure the sexual innuendos she tosses around when she interviews men on her TV program started all this stalking mess. She never could resist a cute comeback line. No wonder she's being hounded." He clenched his jaw, gritted his teeth and shot me a look that almost burned off my eyebrows.

Chief Vincetti cut in. "Uh, now let's calm down, Mr. Lisowski. Samantha's not to blame. You've got to understand that she is being pursued by a crazed, emotionally unsound woman. Who knows what set her off?"

"What —'her?' Are we talking about a *female* stalker here?" Harry glared at me as though the latest news was another nail I had driven into his crucified hand. "I want to know everything, Samantha, and right now. We're going home."

The chief again intervened. "I'm afraid that's not possible, sir. I've got several more issues I need to discuss with Samantha before she leaves. And Detective Kelly wants to speak to her about new information uncovered in the murder he's investigating. How about I have someone take you to my office where you can relax and have a cup of coffee, watch the news on TV?"

Harry bored a hole right between my eyes. "Don't bother. She can stay here all night if she wants. I'm leaving."

The men looked at me for direction, but I knew it was useless to talk to Harry until he calmed down. He'd be better off at home alone for a while to sort through his thoughts. He'd probably have a plan of action for me to follow spread all over the dining room table by the time I returned to our happy abode. With no further comment, he stormed out, slamming the door behind him.

The awkward atmosphere still filled the room. "Well!" Chief Vincetti said, as Detective Kelly made a negligible sound, and I fought making eye-contact with either.

"I'm sure your husband will figure out that you're not responsible for your situation by the time you get home, Samantha," the chief said. "I think we could all use a break."

I left first for the women's lounge, which I had noticed was in the hallway next to the evidence room. Thankfully no one was in there. I looked at myself in the mirror. The bags under my eyes appeared baggier and my skin looked droopy. My makeup had all but disappeared. The fluorescent lighting didn't help the image staring back at me. I feared putting on my glasses and really taking a good look at myself. All I needed was for my circumstances to age me. I'd then for sure stalk the stalker and kill the killer, whom I'd almost forgotten about, but suddenly felt lurking somewhere out there, waiting for his turn to put my life in more danger.

"All right now," Chief Vincetti said after we reconvened in the evidence room. "I hope you're feeling a bit less stressed, Samantha?"

The break had restored my spirit. "I'll be relaxed when this friggin' woman gets caught and you hang her up by her pasties!" I said. I was angry at everybody and especially ready to confront the stalker head-on.

Both men grunted a little chuckle. Detective Kelly gave me a smile and a "thumbs up."

The chief again handed me the photo of Reenee and me. "I want you to think back to when and where this picture was taken. Maybe at a restaurant or some sort of event? Take a close look at the food on the table and the décor around you."

Even though the background was fuzzy, I knew exactly where the photo had been taken because of what I was wearing. I had worn that outfit the last time I met with Reenee at Hannah's Hutch, a couple of weeks before the taping of my show there. That stalker-witch, with a capital B, must've been following me for some time. How could I be so unaware of her? But, of course, I was expecting to see the same *man* popping up wherever I went, not the same woman.

"Try to recall that day, Samantha," Chief Vincetti said. "Picture who might have been around you, who might've smiled or said a few words to you, or a woman whom you caught staring your way. One who looked a bit familiar from your having seen her in other places."

"A lot of people smile at me because they recognize me from my TV program even though they don't stop or say anything. I never wear my glasses in public, so no one is in focus until they're practically on top of me." My brain was on overload. I needed some time to rejuvenate. "I'll have to think about this later when my mind clears up. I'll talk to Reenee. See if she remembers anything unusual. Can this wait till tomorrow?"

Chief Vincetti agreed that sleeping on it was a good idea. He advised me to write down any bits of memory that might pop into my mind and to have my friend do the same. "We are dealing with a psychologically unstable woman who is getting bolder in her approaches to you. She feels immense pleasure from escalating her actions. Your situation fits a pattern. I must warn you that personal contact is not out of the question. Don't think you're in any less danger because your stalker is possibly a woman."

Well, wasn't that a lovely speech? I thought. Out loud I said, "So? Do I hire a bodyguard . . . wear a wig . . . change my hair color . . . walk around in disguises? Do I bury myself in my basement . . . take a vacation . . . move . . . get out of town?" I felt my voice rising as I spurted out each alternative.

"Take it easy, Samantha." The steadfastness in Detective Kelly's voice kept me from getting too panicky. "We're only trying to make you aware of the seriousness of your situation, that you must remain constantly alert. We don't want you to brush this aside because the stalker is quite possibly a woman. A female can be as vicious and dangerous as a man, maybe more so."

"Would both of you please stop saying 'possibly a woman?' Why is there any doubt that the stalker is female? Doesn't the evidence prove it?"

"Although the odds are that it's a 'she,' we need to investigate further to be absolutely sure," the chief said.

"Some male fanatic, in his twisted psyche, may have his own purposes in wanting to appear as a female fan. The chief and I don't want to overlook any possibility."

My spirit oozed out of me. I was spent. "Then what do I do in the meantime?" I asked, practically dropping into a chair.

"Taking a vacation might not be a bad idea," Chief Vincetti said. "You have no job commitments. Maybe you should think about it."

"Can you assure me that when I return, this sick-o broad will no longer be interested in me? That she'll have moved on to someone else?"

The chief and detective exchanged guarded glances. As Mama always said, "Actions speak louder than words." I had my answer. Their expressions told me everything I needed to know.

"Is it possible that Susie Sick-o will attack me?" I asked.

Both men avoided looking at me and shuffled their feet. "You want to be in the company of another person as much as possible," Detective Kelly said. "Hopefully the stalker's next move will be to approach you in public so that you can get a good look at her."

"And also hopefully, she won't be toting a weapon. I guess I'd better wear my glasses all the time now so I can make out the features of people around me. I hope the women I'll be scrutinizing won't think I'm making a move on them."

Detective Kelly gave me a warm smile. "That's the spirit. You're beginning to sound like your old self."

My old self? Were we getting to know each other well enough for him to make that statement about me? God, he looked so handsome standing there, with his boyish grin and aura of concern. Maybe I could hire *him* to be my bodyguard.

Chief Vincetti interrupted my speculative thoughts and brought me back to my predicament. "I'll have the drive-bys increased, but, to reiterate, your job is to be sensitive to your surroundings, and for the duration, don't go anywhere alone. We'll investigate the manufacturer of these sleazy outfits, and find stores where they can be purchased, and explore a few possibilities regarding the photos and ankle bracelets. I'll keep in touch with you. Any further concerns right now?"

I shook my head. "Thank you, Chief, for your help. Your police doing drive-bys make me feel a little less anxious. I hope they'll be *close* by the next time she decides to contact me."

He smiled and added a bit more advice. "When you're on the road, be aware of white cars in your vicinity. Keep paper and pencil available and copy license numbers of cars that seem to be following you." He wished me luck getting things straightened out with Harry and turned me over to Detective Kelly, saying, "You'll probably be more comfortable in the staff meeting room." He accompanied us there and had an officer bring us some coffee.

"I'll leave you two alone. If I can be of any further help, just use the phone and press pound-one. That's my direct extension. I'll stick around the office until you both leave. Let me know when you're through here."

"Are you sure you're up to more questioning?" Detective Kelly asked me after the chief left. "We can do this another day. You must be tired, and hungry, too."

"As long as I'm not slaphappy yet, I'd like to keep going. My stomach has so many *kruszkies* in it right now, a glass of water couldn't slide down my throat. What do you want to know?"

He pulled out a photo from his breast pocket and showed it to me. "Do you recognize this man?"

I put on my glasses. The picture portrayed an older, handsome gentleman with a great smile and a mane of beautiful white hair.

"Never saw him in my life. Who is he?"

"Are you sure? Take a good, long look at him."

"If I look at him for seven thousand minutes, I still won't know who he is. So, who is he?"

"Are you positive you didn't see him hanging around the area where that writing seminar was held? Perhaps in the church where you stopped to visit during your lunch hour and found Frances Morrow in an emotional state? Or maybe on your walk back from the restaurant where you had lunch?"

"Are you telling me that this is Long Tall Sally out of drag? The guy/woman who was also stabbed dead that week?" My mind's eye recalled the bizarre fashion and manner of the female impersonator as she passed me on my way to lunch and then later at the crime scene. "No way. Impossible," I told him.

"No, not Long Tall Sally. This is a picture of John Morrow, Frances' husband."

Well, well, I thought. The plot thickens. "What does he have to do with the murders? Oh, lord, are you telling me that *he's* the suspected killer?" I didn't want to know all this stuff. It'd just make me more crazy. I had enough on my shoulders with Susie Stalker.

"We've found a connection between the Morrows and Carole Langley, the murdered woman. Carole, Frances and John were very close friends during the Morrows' hey-day. They were practically inseparable, even to the point of spending vacations together."

"Wow! Neither woman acknowledged the other at the seminar. Isn't that interesting? Oh . . . wait. That's who Frances was shooting her killer-looks toward — Carole." I had been sitting next to the soon-to-be victim. I mistakenly thought the looks were directed at me. "Is that why you visited the Morrows today? To question them about their relationship with the victim? To ask Frances why she wasn't forthcoming with this information at the onset of the investigation?"

I was on a roll. What a mouthful. Harry had nothing on me when it came to interrogation skills. I was even using big words like he did. "What was the reaction of the Morrows? What did they say?" I was spending so much time lately around the boys in blue that I was beginning to sound like one.

"Although I personally think you have a right to know, I really can't divulge any more information. I've probably told you more than

I should have. All I can say is that John is a person of interest, and so is his wife."

Thoughts were bouncing around in my brain like tennis balls being swatted against a brick wall. My mind was a Jaguar, a Jag-U-R, racing along the Samantha Highway two hundred miles an hour.

I figured that, so far, the police had the murder weapons and sufficient evidence to suspect that either Frances or John Morrow had the opportunity to kill Carole and Long Tall Sally. I've read a zillion detective books and watched an equal number of police TV programs in my lifetime, so I knew the only thing left was to determine their motive for the crime, then tie up loose ends well enough to bring the criminals to justice. I was sure the hunk wouldn't take much longer to figure out motive.

I chewed over what I knew and gave my deductions a try. Hercule Poirot had nothing on me; his little gray cells weren't the only ones that could click fast and furiously.

I made a bet with myself that John Morrow stabbed both Carole Langley and Long Tall Sally, and that Frances knew and was covering up for her husband or had a hand in the actual murders as well. Their motive probably stemmed back to some trouble with the Langley woman in the past.

Hah! There. I had it. Samantha Lisowski and Agatha Christie's Miss Marple: Sisters-Under-The-Skin.

I tossed my ideas out to Detective Kelly. He stared at me as though I might have read his official reports when he wasn't looking. "You're keeping information from me after all, aren't you, Samantha?" His voice and manner returned to official interrogation style.

Where, oh, where did my sensitive, caring detective go? A Dr. Jekyll and Mr. Hyde transformation had taken place right before my very eyes.

"No, honest to God. I've told you everything." I got feminine on him and conjured up a shaky voice. I didn't have to conjure up the tears rolling down my cheek. They surprised me with their sudden appearance. "What I just told you were simply thoughts spinning around in my brain."

The hunk did not look pleased with me. He let out an exasperated sigh and shook his head. Hours seemed to pass by as I waited for his reply.

"What in the world am I going to do about you, Samantha?" Then he suddenly smiled, took my face in his hands and gently kissed me.

My body betrayed me as I responded. Then I froze. I didn't know what to do. I couldn't ignore the kiss, but I didn't want to comment on it either. I hoped I had a compartment left in my brain to store this sizzling surprise.

I avoided his eyes and looked down at my clenched hands. I swallowed hard, wondering what to say next.

The phone rang, startling us both.

"In the nick of time," Detective Kelly quipped with a lopsided smile. He looked as uneasy as I felt.

The caller wanted to know whether to order food for us, as dinnertime was creeping up. I shook my head to the request. The way I felt, a hotel room would've been more apropos.

Stop, Samantha. Just stop. A harmless kiss of compassion. This is not teenage nonsense.

I controlled myself and shyly smiled at the hunk. I continued my story as if nothing happened, as if my body were not on fire. "Frances probably knows where I live by now, thanks to my phone pal, Khara's, generosity with my personal information." The full force of my worries brought down my body temperature. "What if John thinks that I have upset his wife for all eternity because of my stupid visit to their home? What if he's crazed by that idea and now will come after me? Some people win the lotto; all I win is a stalker *and* a murderer in my life. How lucky can one girl get?"

Detective Kelly took my hand in his. His soft voice was reassuring. "John Morrow has enough to worry about. It's unlikely that he will come after you. I'm asking you to be vigilant on the off-chance that he might." He looked at me closely. "I want to believe you that you are not planning another confrontation with him or his wife. I hope you know it's in your best interest to be truthful with me. This is no time for amateur detective work."

I squeezed his arm and looked directly into his eyes. "I wish I could be more helpful, but I know nothing further about your murder case. Please. Believe me." Tears again formed in my eyes.

He dried my face with his handkerchief, and I could see his baby blues soften. A fleeting thought slipped into my head. What color were Harry's eyes? Brown? Did I even care? Whatever color they were, his look hadn't been this warm and responsive to me in a long time. I could tell Detective Kelly, as well, was making the best of an uncomfortable moment. He returned the squeeze, making it feel more like a caress.

"Okay. I'll take you at your word, Samantha. Forget the Morrows unless you hear something in the neighborhood about them that I should know about." He stood and gathered up his things. "I think we're through here. Let me tell Chief Vincetti that we're done. He won't need to get a squad to follow you home; I can do that."

Home. Harry. Hell. The three H's hit me square in the gut. My tender moment with the detective faded in the background as I steeled myself for Harry's confrontation.

I figured that if I got mad enough, I'd give Kelly a hug, a fourth H, when we pulled into my driveway, hoping Harry'd see us and get even more of his dander up. But being a Libra, I knew I'd handle things in a balanced way and control my wicked, devilish side. One innocent kiss was enough for the little lady today, thank you. Besides, I really had been unfair to Harry since this turmoil began. See, the Libra in me was already kicking in.

Detective Kelly and I both put our impractical encounter on hold during the short drive to my house. He said he'd be in touch, and I didn't linger in the car.

I entered my house, prepared for Harry's onslaught.

All right, Samantha Ann Mary Toczolowski Lisowski, put on your big girl panties and deal with it.

Watch out, Harry, here I come.

Upward and onward, and may the pieces of my life fall where they may. Just hopefully not on my blond head.

Chapter 31

The house was as silent as the gray roots oozing out of my head. Graphs and charts explaining my moves for the next hundred years were not spread all over the dining room table as I expected. That's another thing about Harry. Every time I think I have him figured out, he changes courses on me.

Timidly, I toured the first and second levels of the house, expecting Harry to be there waiting for me with a look on his face intense enough to uncurl my hair. But he wasn't around. While climbing the steps to the bedrooms, I heard music.

Aha. Always a good sign. Music soothes my savage beast. Harry must be lying on the bed listening to his CDs. He loves polka music, which usually puts him in a good mood for a while. Upon entering the room, I figured he had calmed down.

To my horror, Darling wasn't lying on the bed. Not a good sign, I reflected. He was sitting on the easy chair next to the CD player, legs crossed and his right foot shaking up and down. This quirk of his happens when he is irritated about something I've done (frequently), bored with my conversation (habitually), or was upset like hell with me (regularly.)

I had my story ready and plunged ahead. "Hi. Could I talk to you?"

Harry's foot began to move so fast I thought it would fly off his leg. He didn't lower the volume of the polka music or glance my way. No need to consult a crystal ball to know this time he was both aggravated and infuriated.

I continued in a loud enough voice to be heard over the music. "I've got good news and bad news, and I'm going to tell you the bad news first. I'm having an affair with Detective Kelly."

Bingo! Harry's foot abruptly stopped moving. His jaw dropped as he turned his head to look at me. He appeared stunned. For the first time since we said, "I do," he was speechless.

I let a couple of seconds go by and then in a rush I said, "The good news is that I'm just kidding; I'm not having an affair. I just need to explain why I haven't been up-front with you about the horrible things that have been happening to me."

Harry turned down the music, as I got ready for an explosion of expletives or, at the very least, an Academy Award lecture. Instead, he looked at me and bestowed the papal indulgence to explain away. As I said, Harry shifts gears when I least expect him to and confuses the hell out of me.

Starting with the first note that came in the mail, I summed up the mess as concisely, but completely, as possible. Without trying, my voice wavered and my lips quivered when I came to the end of my tale.

"The bottom line, Harry, is that I've been afraid you'd make me give up my TV program. That's why I didn't want you to know about any of this. I guess I thought I could handle it by myself. That it would all go away. Instead circumstances escalated."

"Humph. I'd rather you had the affair."

This time I looked at *him* with slackened jaw. "Harry! I can't believe you said that. I. . . ."

"Don't get your *kruszkies* in an uproar, Samantha. Sit down and let's figure out, like two sensible people, where we should go from here. Listening to everything that has happened to you, I see that you're in more danger than I realized. I think we should hire a private detective to pursue investigations about the Morrows and your female stalker."

"Maybe we could get Bruce Willis or Josh Holloway as a bodyguard for me."

He rolled his eyes. "See? This is why we can never have a rational conversation. You always have to insert some smart-ass remark. You never take anything seriously enough. Is this still a joke to you?"

"Now don't get *your kruszkies* in an uproar. I'm scared, Harry. Only my sense of humor is keeping me from becoming a nervous wreck. I'm sorry. Tell me about this private detective idea of yours."

Of course I should've known that Harry already had a private eye picked out. He just makes it look as though I get a say in his decisions. But truthfully, I was relieved he was taking charge. I knew the police had to wait until I was physically attacked before they could legally act. I figured a private detective had more options and could take a step or two across that fine line of right or wrong if he felt it was necessary.

"And what made you think I'd hound you to give up your TV show?" he asked. "If I have anything to say about it, no stalker is going to make you discontinue hosting a program you are good at and that makes you happy."

Such contentment and bliss overcame me that I got up and gave Harry one of my biggest hugs and most sensual kisses, then led him to our bed.

Darling was shocked. It wasn't even his birthday.

Laying in bed, I listened to Harry breathing contentedly, as my guilt about enjoying Kelly's kiss troubled my mind. I *was* a closet slut. How could I get hot and bothered by the kiss of one man and then go home to have sex with another? What was wrong with me anyway? I was going to have to think this out clearly . . . soon . . . maybe tomorrow. But right now it was the detective's face that lulled me into dreamland.

The next morning, I crawled out of bed to pick up the ringing phone. I couldn't believe 9:30 displayed on the clock. Where did last night go? I usually heard Harry getting ready for work, but apparently that wasn't the case this morning.

"Hello," I said, still in a stupor.

"Samantha. I couldn't wait any longer. I figured. . . ."

"Oh, God, Reenee!" I slapped my head. "I'm so, so sorry I didn't call you last night. I was absolutely zonked out after the police station thing and explaining stuff to Harry. I can't believe I completely forgot the call I promised you. I just woke up this instant."

"Now *I'm* sorry for awakening you. No need to apologize for not calling. It's okay. I figured when I didn't hear from you last night that you were exhausted or that you couldn't talk in front of Harry. You want to call me later?"

"No, no. I have so much to tell and go over with you."

"Then I have a better idea. Meet me at Hannah's Hutch for breakfast. We can talk the morning away."

"Absolutely not. I told you that you can't be in my company until this crisis of mine is over. I don't want you to be sideswiped again, or worse, by Ms. Psycho."

"*Ms.* Psycho? What? Slow down. What're you saying? The killer is a woman?" Reenee's voice rose an octave with each phrase she uttered. "Then the Morrows aren't involved? The stalker is the murderer? You've got me thoroughly confused. Explain. Explain."

Of course, I thought, mentally whacking my brain. I hadn't brought Reenee up-to-date. She had no idea yet that Ms. Stalker was female and not involved in the murders, or that the Morrows were persons of interest in the homicides. So I slowed down and took Reenee through my entire yesterday.

She was flabbergasted and practically speechless through it all. "Oh, my God!" and "No!" and "Get outta here!" were her only comments dispatched here and there in high decibels.

I wound down my account. "When I saw that photo of you and me, and the stalker's message on the backside that she wanted a threesome with us, I radiated red anger. Out of frustration, I took a sock at Kelly. He restrained me by pulling me to his chest. And that's when Harry decided to burst into the office."

"Oh, my God! This is getting more incredible by the minute," she screeched. "Are you still married, or did Harry move out already?"

"Funny. Not." I finished explaining my further escapades, then said, "I actually ended up giving of the body."

"Shameless! Sex at your age?" Reenee teased, her voice filled with anticipation. "Wow! What did he say this morning? I assume we're talking about Harry and your body, and not Detective Kelly?"

She knew darned well whom I meant, but her remark smoothed out worry wrinkles from my forehead. "Oh, Reenee, you are too much. I intend to live a long time, so you'd better take care of yourself. I want you around when I'm in my hundreds. I absolutely couldn't live without you, my friend. And that's why you are not going to be anywhere near me until this chaos is ended."

Reenee protested, but I won. I was adamant in my resolve to keep her away from me.

"Umm, oh yeah. Kelly kissed me at the police station."

"What?" Her screech could be heard in San Francisco. "The fine detective made a pass? What did you do? What'd you say? Tell, tell."

"It was no big deal; we were both uncomfortable about it. In fact, today I'm embarrassed over the whole situation. I don't think he and I will have the same relationship after this. I'm almost sorry it happened."

"C'mon. Enjoy it for what it was, a weakness of the moment. It's not like you went to bed with him."

"True, but the thought did cross my mind."

"Well, after all, you are human. Don't beat yourself up. You have enough on your plate as it is."

I knew she was right. I turned that part of my brain off and returned to the problems at hand. "Which brings me back to your staying away from me. I promise to call you and e-mail you every day whether anything new happens or not. In the meantime, think over that last time we were at Hannah's Hutch. Maybe it'll dawn on you whether some woman was there with a camera or some babe was looking our way a lot."

"I'm gonna think back over *all* the places you and I've been since this scary business started. Are you finally going to be more careful and alert? Don't you go meandering around alone either, especially at night."

"Well, I'm hoping it'll all soon be over. Harry's hired a private eye. Maybe this guy will be able to bring things to a head in the next couple of days."

"Detective Kelly's gonna be so-o-o-o jealous, Sammy. He wants to be the hero in your life," she teased.

"Good-bye, Reenee," I said firmly, and disconnected before she could say another word. But I laughed as I got dressed to meet the day. That girlfriend of mine was a pistol.

Chapter 32

I threw a dust rag at a few things and shoved stuff into drawers because Harry called almost as soon as I finished talking with Reenee. He said he was coming home around noon with Sam Spade, Private Eye, aka Erwin Tuppence.

"Erwin Tuppence?" I laughed. "What kind of name is that for a private dick? I already have no confidence in him. I want one named Rock Winston or Stone Radcliffe or. . . ."

"Stop it, Samantha. You know I hate it when you talk shit. I told him to join us for lunch. Can you throw something together?"

How long had I been married to this man? Did he not yet know of my hatred for the culinary arts? They'd both be lucky if they got a piece of baloney tossed at them.

"It's too late to prepare pheasant-under-the-glass, but perhaps appetizers like wild mushrooms, greenest of avocados and sultry-marinated chicken would serve up well. Or. . . ."

"Never mind, Samantha, I'll pick up a couple of sandwiches from Pot Belly. Can you manage coffee?"

Many people have misnomers for a name, but not Erwin Tuppence. He lived up to his moniker in height and weight. Although he was puny, he had the deepest voice known to mankind, and womankind, too. He seemed too pleasant to be any kind of detective, private or otherwise. Lunch was enjoyable, with Harry and me learning about Erwin's professional background in cases such as mine. I wondered if we were paying him by the hour. Maybe that's why Tuppence kept the conversation going for so long.

After we were through eating and chatting, we moved to the den. Erwin made himself comfortable and pulled out his recorder, or blackberry or blueberry, or whatever the hell it's called nowadays. As I've said, I'm not hep to 21st century gizmos. My stereo still plays records on a spindle.

Tuppence wanted me to talk about everything that happened, beginning at the writing seminar and running all the way through yesterday's events.

"I really don't see why you want to know about the murder. That has nothing to do with Ms. Stalker and. . . ."

"Samantha!" Harry warned. "Please just do as you're asked for a change. Mr. Tuppence has vast experience in stalking and murder cases. We don't want to waste his time by arguing with him."

"See, Harry. That's your problem. Every time I voice an opinion, you think I'm starting an argument."

"Samantha!"

"Okay, okay, already," I sighed. "It was a hot, humid July day when I started my journey into a life of murder, and persecution from a stalker. I parked my shiny red Grand Am and. . . ."

"Oh for chrissake, Samantha. You're not writing one of those dumb stories of yours. Mr. Tuppence doesn't need background and drama. Simply state the facts for him."

I gave Harry a dirty look and started again, relating the details free of any of my magnificently creative embellishments. Tuppence didn't interrupt me or show any emotion as I went through my spiel. Telling my story, I could hardly believe I was talking about myself. That I was the one who'd lived through these ghastly experiences.

When I finished, Tuppence thanked me and said, "I'll contact Chief Vincetti to find out how the investigation of the items sent to you is coming along. I may also need to contact Detective Kelly."

I did a double-take. "Will they cooperate with you?" I asked. "In the detective books I read, the real cops hated the private dicks and give them a hard time and never want to share anything with them."

"There you go again, Samantha. This is not a book, a TV show, a play. This is real life."

"She's right to a certain extent," Tuppence told Harry, as I stuck my tongue out at my beloved. "I may have some trouble with

Detective Kelly, but I have found that chiefs from smaller departments are more accommodating. It'd probably help, Ms. Lisowski, if you'd call both men and ask that they oblige me."

I agreed to do so and asked if he thought my best friend could be in danger. His opinion backed up my decision not to be near Reenee until the stalking and homicide evils were resolved.

"In addition to jotting down license plate numbers of cars that make you feel uneasy," he went on to say, "take a camera along when you go out. Take photos of the crowds around you and then study the pictures. See if the same face turns up." Tuppence handed me a card. "When you need to get hold of me, you can call my cell phone, night or day."

Wow, I thought. I'm sure getting more than my share of help. But would the criminals cooperate and contact me when surveillance was nearby?

"Now what do I do?" I asked the private dick. "Wait for the stalker and/or the murderer to make the next move?"

Tuppence recited the lecture that by now I knew by heart: be cautious, be sensitive to my surroundings, be aware of people, yada, yada, yada. Private detectives and the police must be required to take the basic course, "How To Advise Stalker & Murder Candidates 101," before they're given their diplomas, or badges, or whatever the hell they're issued.

"From my experience with disturbed people," he continued, "I believe your stalker, at least, has reached the point where personal contact with you is a given. The murderer might just forget about you and worry about his or her own safety. You'll have to brazen this out. Keep your pepper spray handy and scream *Fire* as you're using it. We've found out that *Fire* gets people's attention better than *Help*."

He didn't have to remind me to yell like hell. I got *kruszkies* just thinking about meeting my stalker face to face, let alone the person who had two murders notched onto his or her belt. I kept asking myself if this was really, really happening to me. I kept coming up with the same answer: yes, yes, yes.

"You mean nothing concrete can be done to safeguard my wife from the killer on the loose or this crazed woman?" Harry asked.

"Unfortunately, Mr. Lisowski, the person stalked is usually the one who has to solve her own problem. Ditto regarding the murderer. The lucky ones have security around them when the encounter takes place."

On that note full of hope, happiness and sunshine, papers were signed and our first check handed over.

"I'll keep you both informed about the progress of my investigation," Tuppence said as he gathered his belonging. "Good luck, Ms. Lisowski. Be brave. I haven't had a client succumb to a criminal yet."

"And I don't want me to be the first failure notch on your private-eye belt," I told him as we walked Erwin to the door.

"Do you think this guy is gonna make any difference?" I asked Harry after Tuppence left. The meeting was a real downer for me. "We should have asked him what he's gonna do while I'm running around taking pictures of people and jotting down license plate numbers of white cars that seem to be following mine. It all sounded so hopeless. Basically, I'm on my own. No one can help me."

"We'll tackle this problem together, Samantha. I've put in for some vacation time. You're not going anywhere without me until this situation is over."

Oh, lord, I thought to myself. I'd rather take my chances with the stalker!

Chapter 33

The first twenty-four hours and the following weekend of solitary life, with only Harry around, weren't too bad. Then, on Monday, I finally tackled Khara's voicemail messages about the Morrows. Although I felt very sorry to hear that the Morrows' daughter endured a series of seizures and that Francis remained a mental and physical wreck, I didn't see how I could help their situation. The only family member who seemed to have recuperated was John. After what Detective Kelly told me, he was the one I most feared.

While my mind was figuring out how to quell Khara's annoyance with me at the Gazebo Commission meeting a couple days ago over her unanswered voicemails, I convinced myself to clean the house before I got a letter from the Board of Health stating it had been slated for demolition.

I must've mentioned twelve thousand times already that I hate housework. Using every foul word I knew, and a few known only to sailors, I mopped and waxed and dusted.

"Must you swear when you do housework, Samantha?" Darling asked from the comfort of his chair, in front of his beloved TV screen of stock market results. "Seems to me you'd get a sense of satisfaction to do something constructive like cleaning the house instead of gallivanting around every day as you usually do with that girlfriend of yours."

Humph. This, from a man who doesn't know which end of the broom to use, or a screwdriver, for that matter.

"Any idiot can clean a house, Harry." I got on my soapbox. "My satisfaction comes from having a short story published, winning a writing contest, knowing my TV show is a successful one. I don't get self-satisfaction from cleaning out a toilet. The first thing I'm going to do when I win the lotto, whether you like it or not, is hire a housekeeper."

In fact, we could afford to hire one now, but Harry wouldn't hear of it. We'd had quite a few *discussions* in the past about this subject. Darling thinks I'm healthy enough to do my own housework and that it's good exercise, and how stupid it'd be for me to sit around doing nothing as the cleaning lady tidied up the house.

"I don't know why you're making such a big deal about housework anyway," he told me at the time. "I'll do it, for chrissake!"

And he did. For a couple of weeks. Then he lost interest, and I started to do more and more of the cleaning until I fully re-inherited the entire dreaded job again. I still don't know how Harry tricked me back into that.

"Are you calling the P. I. today?" I asked whizzing the carpet sweeper attachment around his legs. "Maybe he's got the case solved and you can go back to work."

"What? I can't hear you over the noise."

"I asked if you wanted to go upstairs for a quick matinee."

"What? You know it irritates me when you talk while the vacuum cleaner is running and I don't know what you're saying."

I shut it off. "Just making small talk, Harry. Nothing of consequence." I smartly turned and smiled to myself. One takes little victories where one can find them.

Just as I put away the dust rags, the cleaning supplies, the vacuum cleaner, and the rest of the horrible stuff I hate to use, P.I. Tuppence and Chief Vincetti called within minutes of each other. Both told me basically the same thing. The flimsy outfits and trinkets the stalker sent me came from Lover's Lane, a store in neighboring Orland Park that handles scanty clothing and creative sex toys. Unfortunately, the person who bought the items paid in cash. The sales clerk thought the shopper was a woman, but not a steady customer, or she probably would've remembered her better.

Unhappily, nothing else interrupted Samantha's Day in House Cleaning Heaven in Harry's Little Harem on Central Avenue.

Tuesday, with me still being entrenched in another twenty-four hours of solitary confinement, was another story. Having Harry around my neck was worse than the security *kruszkie* around entrepreneur Martha Stewart's ankle when she was under house arrest.

For example, one of Harry's early morning tidbits: "Why do you insist on keeping these shades pulled down when the air's not on, Samantha? Let the sunshine in. Our bedroom looks like a dungeon."

Another little tidbit later in the morning: "Just let the water run while you brush your teeth," Harry shouted, knocking on my bathroom door. "Turning the faucet off and on makes a sound like someone pounding a drum. Next thing you know we'll need a plumber to repair the pipes."

"Good," I hollered back. "While he's here he can fix my shower, which hasn't worked in ten years."

In the afternoon it seemed I couldn't do anything right either. I heated some leftovers in the microwave for a light lunch and Harry, of course, complained. "You never close that oven door after you take something out. If you weren't in such a hurry all the time, you'd notice things like that."

"Did *you* notice that my hands were full?" I said, aggravation creeping into my voice. "Is there something wrong with your hands that you can't shut the door?" I gave an exasperated sigh and plopped the food in front of Harry. This delightful conversation would no doubt have continued if the phone hadn't rung.

"That's got to be the sacred Reenee, or your sons. Who else would bother us during lunchtime?"

"*Our* sons, Harry, our sons," I reminded him, escaping to the den to answer the phone. I didn't want to use the kitchen phone and annoy Darling by giggling or talking too animatedly if it were Reenee on the line.

It was Reenee, and she was breathless.

"Scent, Samantha. Scent!" Her words exploded into my phone ear.

"Sent? What's sent?"

"Not sent. *Scent*. Get it?"

"Are you hitting the bottle this early in the afternoon? What are you talking about? Sent by mail? Who sent what?" Our conversation sounded like an Abbot and Costello comedy routine.

"S-C-E-N-T! SCENT!" Reenee screamed. "That woman. At the

card shop. Behind you in line. Remember? She admired your perfume *scent*."

Click. My brain dropped into gear. "Oh, my God. You're right! And then the next day I get that note from the stalker telling me my scent lingers. Oh, Reenee, you're a genius!"

I worried at the time that the young man who bumped into me at the card store could've been my stalker. But now it seemed it was the woman I spoke to in line that I should've feared.

"Think, Sammy. Think. Do you remember what she looked like, her hair color, her demeanor. Anything?"

I was way ahead of my friend. I already had a mental picture of that babe. She was around my age and height, well-groomed and in an outfit I remembered admiring.

"I gotta hang up and call Vincetti and that private eye guy. Thank you, thank you, Reenee. I'll get back to you as soon as I can."

"Your lunch is getting cold," Darling said as I returned to the kitchen. "Considering all that ridiculous screaming you were doing, I have no doubt that was Reenee on the phone."

With no sarcastic retort, I exclaimed, "The stalker, Harry. The stalker. I know what she looks like!"

After calling Chief Vincetti and P. I. Tuppence, for good measure I gave Detective Kelly a call, too. Nah, not for good measure. I just wanted to talk to him, closet slut that I am. Besides, at my tender age I had to hold on to all the admirers I could find.

The chief asked me to come into the station the next day. He wanted me to describe what Ms. Stalker looked like to a police artist, so he could draw a composite sketch of her. Tuppence said he'd also proceed with a few avenues of investigation from that drawing. And the hunk, well. . . .

My phone calls completed, I finally had time to relax and reflect upon Reenee's *scent* unearthing. I plopped down on the couch in the den and let my fertile mind run through the encounter with my nemesis. Suddenly I perked up.

"Harry," I gasped. "I just had a horrible thought."

Getting no response, I looked over to the easy chair and, sure enough, Darling was snoozing. No doubt watching me cook and then clean up the kitchen made him tired. "Harry!"

"What? What? What the hell's the matter?" He jumped up, the newspaper in his lap flying all over him and the floor. He slipped on one of the sheets of newsprint, but, just in time, caught himself from falling.

I couldn't help but laugh.

Darling didn't see the humor. He scowled. "I dreamt we were being attacked by liberals." But then he laughed, too. "All right. What's the matter now?"

"My card shop stalker was dressed and groomed almost as well as I was. Do you know what that means?"

"Uh, you shop at the same places?"

"Duh. No. It means *she* thinks *she'll* be the female of her imagined twosome and assumes that I'll be the butch! What's wrong with the way I look that she'd think something so horrendous about me, Harry? If she thought *she* was the butch, she'd be dressed in dungarees with a head scarf and a leather jacket, and she'd have a tattoo and no makeup and. . . ."

Harry looked at me like I belonged in a nut house. "Will you stop it, Samantha? How do you come up with this shit? Why are you even worried about what she thinks about you? You get the goofiest ideas of anybody I know."

But I was already off the couch and on my way to call Reenee to discuss this new development. She'd understand. We'd come to some conclusion to make me feel better.

And sure enough, Reenee and I hashed it out.

"I don't know that much about lesbian relationships, Sam. Does one of the women have to look like a butch?"

"I'm not sure, but every time a program airs about homosexual women, that seems to be the case. As if I don't have enough to worry about already, interactions between lesbians will have to be added to my list."

"Well, it's not as though you're ever gonna have an affair with this gal. Maybe Ms. Stalker isn't into the lesbian dress codes. Maybe those were her *going-out clothes*. Besides, if she was huge and ugly and on a motorcycle, you'd probably be more upset about why you'd be attractive to someone like that. Take a couple of aspirins and call it a day. Have sweet dreams about you-know-who."

I yawned. "Good advice, Reenee. I'll talk to you tomorrow."

I was so exhausted after my stressful hours with Harry being home all day and the thought that I'd be taken as the butch in a lesbian relationship, I didn't even watch *Rescue Me* with that sexy Denis Leary. I beat it to bed, hoping my stalker's days were numbered and that the murderer, also, would soon be in jail where he belonged.

Chapter 34

On the third day comes a frost, a killing frost is a line from Shakespeare's *King Henry VIII*. Michael A. Black, a favorite author of mine whom I also happen to call a friend, told me his inspiration for his book *Killing Frost* came from that excerpt.

But for me, the third day of the week made one weak, the one in this case being me.

Harry was even more critical of my behavior beginning at the crack of Wednesday's dawn. Because he doesn't sleep well, he feels that on the days he doesn't work, his faithful companion should be awake also, as he is, when the sun makes its debut. He needed me up and functioning so he could comment on any of my actions that annoyed him.

By the time I was ready to meet with the police artist in the late morning, I was geared up to find Ms. Stalker and plead with her, "Take me. Please take me."

Of course, Harry had to accompany me to the police station. I tried to get away on my own, but he wasn't having any of it. He was in this thing for the long haul. Maybe I could convince Chief Vincetti to stick him in a different room from mine.

Although I wanted to walk because it was a lovely day and the station was only a couple blocks from our house, Harry insisted we drive. He wanted to make a couple of stops afterwards.

I dreaded being the driver with him in the death seat. When he tossed me the keys and said, "You drive," I got ready to be bossed around and criticized for the entire trip.

"Must you always drive fast, Samantha?" he complained in the past, even though I never drove ten miles over the speed limit. Or,

"Why don't you use the rear view mirror when you change lanes? Why do you have to look over your shoulder?" And, "You drive too far away from the median; after all your years of driving I'd think you could judge better."

I'd sigh, suck it up, and usually just ignored his derisive comments. "Reflections on the teacher," I sometimes said, as Harry was the one who taught me to drive in my last year of college. I still remember how long it took before I could coordinate the clutch and the gas pedal on his old Ford. Back in those days few cars had automatic transmissions, and no high schools held driver training classes. Back in those days, Harry was much more patient with me.

My blast from the past ended as we pulled out of our driveway. I couldn't believe my eyes!

A white car slowed down, then picked up speed, and whizzed past.

I yelped.

Harry jumped and swore in surprise as I wheeled my Grand Am baby down the street at break-neck speed.

"What the hell are you doing, Samantha? You know Central Avenue's speed limit is twenty-five. What's wrong with you?"

"The stalker, Harry, the stalker. She's in that white automobile up ahead. Didn't you see her?" I was driving like a maniac. Traffic being nil, the babe didn't stop for the two red lights along the way, so neither did I.

Harry kept yelling for me to slow down, but I ignored him. "Quick. Get the license number when I close in on her. There's a pencil and paper in the armrest."

But Harry kept holding on to the dashboard with both hands. "You're going to get us killed."

"Shit! Where're the cops when you need them? Don't they see two cars speeding and ignoring red lights? You better put on your seat belt, Harry."

"Stop talking and concentrate, Sam, or we'll be decorations on one of these light poles. Watch out, she's turning left on 159th. The traffic on that street is horrendous. You'll never be able to follow her."

"Just watch me," I screeched.

I made a Kamikaze turn as horns blared at me, and no doubt many drivers' fingers flew into the air. Even that female racecar champion couldn't have executed my maneuver better. Danica Patrick, eat your heart out. I laughed out loud like a demented weirdo.

I could see the white car at a considerable distance ahead of me. So many cars between us, I thought. Where in the hell are all these people going? Why aren't the women drivers home baking cookies and these men in their offices chasing secretaries around their desks? This wasn't even rush hour, for God's sake.

I was worried that Harry was right about the traffic on 159th doing me in. If I got stopped by red lights and Ms. Stalker sailed through the green ones, I knew I'd lose her. On the other hand, because it would be too dangerous, neither she nor I could run the traffic signals on this busy street like we had done on Central Avenue. I reached behind my seat, making the Grand Am veer recklessly towards the center lane. I yanked my purse from off the floor, tossing it onto Harry's lap. "Hurry. Pull out my cell phone and call Vincetti," I yelled.

Harry was holding on for dear life. "For chrissake, Samantha. Let her go. How the hell do you turn this thing on?"

I grabbed the phone from Harry and made the call myself, quickly telling the dispatcher my situation and for her to inform Chief Vincetti. I gave her our whereabouts. She told me to stay on the line.

I continued to drive, weaving in and out of lanes with Harry yelling for me to be careful. Like I needed his advice, like I wanted to wreck the car and make us hood ornaments on someone's car.

After a few more blocks, the vehicle was no longer in view. Even with Harry's great eyesight that he was so damned proud of, saying he could see better without his glasses than I could with mine on, we couldn't tell whether the driver turned off somewhere or disappeared into the wild blue yonder.

When I heard the police sirens, I pulled over, got out of the car and told the dispatcher on the open line where I parked. You should've seen the faces of the drivers passing by when five squad cars pulled up in front, on the side and behind us. People must've thought one of America's Top Ten Most Wanted was captured. We created quite a gaper's block.

Chief Vincetti got out of his car and approached us. By the look on his face, I knew he was perturbed because we didn't call him right away and leave the vehicle's pursuit to his boys in blue. Before he could reprimand me, I related our situation as quickly as I could.

In the commotion, I completely forgot about Harry standing next to me. After my crazed rendition accented by my hands and earrings flying around in unison, Harry, in his own off-the-cuff way, calmly added, "I have a letter. O or Q, and one of the numbers of the license plate, Chief. I couldn't get the complete sequence because Samantha was shifting so much from one lane to the other."

Would this man never give me credit for a job well done? I gave Harry a dirty look and fumed. He should be congratulating me on my driving skills. I almost socked him, but with so many police around, I didn't want to be arrested for domestic battery.

Chief Vincetti was pleased with the partial plate ID and dispatched a few squad cars in several directions. He asked if I wanted to put off the appointment for working on the police sketch of the suspected stalker until the next day.

"No, I'm hyped up. I want to do it now."

I looked at Harry to see if he wanted to stick his two cents in, but he just said, "Whatever, Samantha, it's up to you," which almost made me faint right there on the steamy hot, blacktop street.

The sketching of the perp — wow, was I ever getting good with police jargon — was very interesting to watch evolve. I expected a cop with a pencil and a drawing board, but a police specialist using a computer constructed the rough drafts. He was very patient with me. After an hour or so of readjustments to the developing picture, I was satisfied that the likeness of the female on the screen mirrored the woman who spoken to me at the card shop.

"Now what?" I asked the chief.

"We'll want you to look through some books and computerized screens with photos of women who've been arrested, charged with criminal sexual felonies or misdemeanors. We can do this tomorrow. You've probably endured enough for one day."

The chief knew me, but not that well. I'm a Libra. Once I sink my teeth into a project, I don't let go until it's signed, sealed, and delivered. Or maybe I was tired, because I was beginning to think in clichés.

"If there's some reason you want me to tackle that job tomorrow instead of right now, Chief, it's okay with me. But I am quite up to doing it immediately."

"Take your husband and go home, Samantha. Tomorrow's another day. I'll need time to get all the material gathered for you anyway." He then explained how the distribution of the computerized sketch would go out to the cops on the beat, only he used more professional language. He also told me that the police he'd dispatched to scout the community and surrounding areas had spotted no white cars with the letter or license number supplied by Harry.

"Tracking down the partial plate ID will probably prove to be our best lead," the chief went on to say. "We'll have to run it through the computers. Unfortunately, with only one of the numbers and either an O or a Q identified, hundreds of thousands of combinations will no doubt result. In the meantime, don't go around chasing white cars. If you spot one with similar plates, call 9-1-1 immediately, and we'll deal with it."

As I was thoroughly exhausted by now, having come down from the high of the chase, I didn't challenge the chief's remarks. I thanked him and went looking for Harry. As I'd figured, he was in the break room drinking coffee and being charming with the policewomen and staff on break. That's my boy, I thought, as I gestured to him that I was ready to leave.

On the short ride home, I told Harry about the amazing way police use computers to *sketch*, and he related tidbits of his conversation in the coffee room. Never did he say, "Good job, Samantha," or ask if I was dog-tired. On the other hand, he didn't criticize my decision to chase the white car like a bat out of hell. Hmm. Another cliché; I really must be tired. I considered the day a draw and dismissed it from my mind.

My third twenty-four hours with Harry since the week started turned out to be a *killing frost* after all.

Chapter 35

"I thought you were getting up early so that we could make a few stops this morning before my doctor appointment," Harry said. "I'm about ready to leave, and you're still in your pajamas. It'll take you an hour alone to put on your makeup."

Darling was washed, shaved, and dressed, geared up to start another pleasant day of harassing *poor-Samantha-of-confined-to-quarters* fame.

"I really don't want to go along to the barbershop with you, or to the garage to have the car checked out, or to wait for you at the doctor's office," I answered.

"Can't you ever get with the plan, Samantha? I thought we'd stop for lunch afterwards."

The last statement would probably appeal to a lot of women, but lunch with Harry depended upon what discount coupons he found in the local papers. You know, those *two-for-ones*. Harry was happy with a fast food sandwich and no sides. As I eat like a bear getting ready for hibernation, small portions don't do it for me. Invariably, I'd leave the restaurant hungry.

"Well, what're you going to do if you stay home?" he continued. "I figured we'd spend the afternoon at the country club, exercise a little and then get a few rays by the pool. We've hardly been there all summer with this friggin' stalker/murder business going on in your life."

"*Our* lives, Harry, *our* lives. Don't worry about me. Why not spend some time at the Riviera pool by yourself? You enjoy it so much. I can always find some way to keep busy." Like reading in my air-conditioned house without anyone harping that I should enjoy the fresh, sweltering air outside instead. Like drinking a milkshake without snide remarks about that beautiful chocolaty heaven being bad for my cholesterol level. Like enjoying the judges telling people off on Court TV instead of watching the dumb stock market channel. "Take your time coming back. I'll probably clean out the bathrooms and do some dusting."

Yeah, like hell I would.

"Then you'd better be cautious about opening the door to anyone. Be sure you look out the living-room window first and call the police if anything doesn't look right to you. Keep the cell phone by you at all times. And, most importantly, stay home."

I was surprised not to be presented with a printout of further do's and don'ts.

"Yeah, yeah, yeah. Maybe you should have that Tuppence private dick come over and hold my hand while you're gone. What's he doing anyway besides raking in our money?"

"You know I hate it when you make those caustic remarks, Samantha. Tuppence will be over tomorrow to update us on your situation."

"Our situation, Harry, *our* situation." My exasperated sigh almost pushed him out the door. "Good-bye, good luck, and get the hell out of here."

"Hey, you haven't used that phrase for ages." Darling smiled and got a longing look on his face.

Uh-oh, I thought.

"Remember how, after our amorous dates, you'd always say that to me with a wink and a pat on the butt? Brings back warm memories. How about we go upstairs for a while before I leave?"

"Good-bye, Harry." I smiled coquettishly and put the car keys firmly in his hand. I winked and patted his *dupa*. "I promise to repeat that sentence later on tonight."

Heck, I could be magnanimous. I figured that after his busy morning of running around and his afternoon in the sun, he'd fall asleep early tonight and wouldn't remember my promise anyway.

I tenderly pushed him out of the house into the garage.

The last brush of mineral powder on my face and the ringing of the doorbell happened at the same time. *Kruszkies* in my stomach were a close second. Warily I looked through the upstairs bedroom window and didn't know whether to be happy or upset to see Reenee's car in the driveway. I rushed down the stairs to let her in.

"What're you doing here? You were supposed to stay away from me until this business was over. Do you want that nut following you home again?"

"Don't be mad, Sammy. You've been sounding so down and unlike yourself on the phone that I had to chance it and visit you. I didn't call ahead, because I knew you'd tell me to stay put. Let me get a good look at you. You do look a bit haggard."

"Gee, thanks. I'm so glad you've dropped by to lift my spirits." We hugged each other and laughed. "Can you really see more wrinkles?" I asked.

"Of course not. You always look like you're going to a party. I just meant you appear a bit on edge."

"No kiddin'? I wonder why?"

We both laughed again.

"Oh, Reenee, I'm feeling better already. Hey, screw it. Let's go to the mall and do some window shopping and have a fattening, high-cholesterol, zillion calorie lunch!"

"Oh, no, we won't. I don't need any windows, and I certainly don't want Harry to be mad at me for letting you leave the house without him."

"So? We won't tell him. We'll be back before he gets home. Besides, what can he do, kill me? He'd have to take a number and stand in line. I know it's stupid to put myself in danger, but I absolutely have to get out of this house. With the crowds at the mall and restaurant, how much safer from my enemies could I be? And if it makes you feel any better, we'll park close and be extra vigilant in the lot and in the stores."

I started marching around the living room with an imaginary sign in my hands, chanting a World War II patriotic fighting song.

"God, Samantha, you're losing it." My pal started laughing and joined in the march, singing and twirling an imaginary baton. "How old are we anyway?" She giggled.

After we got the silliness out of our systems, we collapsed on the couch. "We're both nuts. I've had more laughs this morning than I've had all week. Let's go, Reenee."

We agreed to stay in sight of each other as we looked around at Macy's, a favorite department store of ours at the Orland Park mall.

Reenee found her way to the jewelry section. I stopped at an adjoining counter to check out Este Lauder's new line of facial cleansing lotions. I looked through the other skin care items as well and became absorbed in the instructions for their use.

A deep, boozy voice startled me. I could feel her breath as she murmured words in my ear. "That scent of yours intoxicates me, Samantha."

Turning around, I nearly bumped noses with the woman at my side. She appeared to be my age and wore a great-looking outfit. She was in full makeup, seemingly enthralled with me. I can't believe now that I noted those details.

I felt her hand work its way from my arm to my cheeks, and I don't mean the ones on my face. I was so stunned, I couldn't call out. Before I could react, an older man appeared on the other side of me, poking me sharply in the ribs with what felt like the tip of a gun. I froze. I wanted to scream or run, but I could do neither. The woman next to me also seemed to freeze. She squeaked out a soft mewing sound. She appeared as confused and scared as I was.

I managed a furtive glance at the gunman and realized with a shock that it was Frances Morrow's husband!

What the hell? I thought. How did John graduate from knife to gun? I thought a criminal always stayed with his same weapon of choice. So much for learning about crime from TV cop shows.

I caught a glimpse of Reenee viewing a video of necklace/earring combinations and chatting with the clerk. I briefly speculated what she'd buy, then more seriously wondered why I was thinking about jewelry when I had a gun stuck in my ribs.

"Don't call out," John said. His tone sounded determined and menacing. "You and your girlfriend next to you, start moving slowly toward the exit. You two have caused such chaos in my life that I'm willing to shoot you right here if I have to."

"She's not my. . . ."

"Shut up," he whispered. "Since you both visited my wife and put ideas in her head about murder and phone calls and stalking, her mind has collapsed. My life has become hell because of you busybodies."

"This woman isn't. . . ."

"I told you to shut up. Start walking, and don't either of you try to be a hero." I could hear the stress and tension in his voice as he poked the gun deeper into my side.

I tried again to tell Morrow that he made a mistake by assuming the other woman was Reenee, but his mission seemed focused on digging the gun harder into my body. I attempted to turn to see if my real friend had caught our exit, but John's rough jab forced me forward. I noticed his free hand had a death-like grip on Ms. Stalker. She walked stiffly, appearing zonked out. A morsel of me, as small as an M & M, felt sorry for her for being entangled in my chaos.

Emotions ran through my body. I knew I could take Morrow. I lifted weights, exercised daily, and polkaed weekly. John was slender, fragile-looking and at least thirty years older than I. I could probably lay a good punch on him or push him down and sit on him. But I also understood that a gun tips the scales toward the guy who's holding it.

I realized we'd be in bigger trouble if Morrow got us away from the shoppers and forced us into his car. I got disgusted with dumb women in books or movies, who meekly allowed madmen to lead them into more danger without a struggle.

"Scream, kick, faint," I yelled at these whimpering women. "Don't let that screwball take you away."

I was quickly finding out that it ain't so simple when you're the victim. . . .

. . . I couldn't scream. My mouth was dry. My throat made unintelligible animal-like sounds that were too soft to do me any good.

. . . I couldn't kick. Morrow kept us walking, and I had no way to lunge at him. Besides, I feared the gun would accidentally go off if I made any sudden moves.

Only fainting was left.
So. . . .
I feigned a faint.

Chapter 36

When I went limp and fell to the floor, Morrow and the other woman lost their balance. I hit my head on the edge of a counter and reinvented the expression *seeing stars*. Ms. Stalker must've hurt herself, because she cried out in pain and tripped over me. John lost his footing and stumbled over us both, the gun falling not far from him. The Keystone Kops couldn't have done a better job.

"Get off me, help, he's got a gun. *Fire, fire!*" I yelled over and over again, flailing my arms and legs around in an effort to untangle myself from various limbs.

Ms. Stalker started crying uncontrollably and reached out to hug me, which didn't make my movements any easier. John seemed to be the only one who could free himself. He jumped up easily for such an old guy, grabbed the gun, and ran toward the exit. Suddenly Ms. Stalker was gone, too. How she managed to disappear from the scene was a mystery to my dizzied-up brain.

Reenee came dashing from the other direction with what looked like store security.

"Oh, my God, Sammy. Are you all right?" Reenee began probing my skin as if she were looking for broken bones. "Someone call an ambulance. Call the police. Call. . . ."

"If you say *Harry*, girlfriend, you're dead meat. I'm okay, I'm okay." I sat up, blinked, and shook my head to clear it, which made the loose parts in that area rattle. "Where's Ms. Stalker? Did security grab Morrow? Have the police been notified. Oh, my achin' head."

Reenee began fussing over me again.

"Just help me stand up, toots, and then let's get out of here."

"Not so fast, ladies," one of the security guards said. "We're going to take a nice little walk to the manager's office and sort all this out. The police and paramedics should be here soon. You'll have to fill out accident forms."

His nonchalant manner led me to believe that he didn't realize I'd almost been abducted at gunpoint. I had no time for what looked like a pimply, fifteen-year-old store security baby to tell me what to do. I started giving orders.

"Call Chief Nick Vincetti of the Oak Forest police. Call Detective Dave Kelly of the Chicago police department. Call Private Eye Erwin Tuppence of God knows where." I dumped out the contents of my purse as I searched for phone numbers. "Is anyone pursuing the guy with the gun?" I looked at the crowd surrounding us. "Did anybody stop that other woman? She didn't get away, did she, Reenee? C'mon, we gotta find her. She can't be far away."

I twisted around too fast, trying to look for Ms. Stalker. The store began to spin.

And then I fainted for real.

I was hoping I'd be revived by a six-foot three-inch paramedic hunk, but I must've got the only fireman in town who was bald, out of shape and grizzled-looking. I was glad I didn't need mouth-to-mouth. All I really wanted was a bag of frozen peas to hold on the bump on my head, but all I got after I woke up were endless forms to fill out and questions to answer.

We formed a procession to the manager's office. By the time we got settled in the compact room, the Orland Park police arrived, as the mall was located in that community. Shortly after they arrived, the Oak Forest boys in blue showed up. Tinley Park detectives joined the party, probably because I informed the store manager that the alleged kidnapper was a resident of that village. All I needed was for the Chicago guy with the blue eyes to make his entrance, and we could have a cop convention. With all the police in the tiny room, I wondered who was chasing Morrow and my stalker.

The ton of paperwork going into folders was amazing, living proof of my tax dollars at work. Why every jurisdiction involved couldn't listen in at one time remained a mystery to me. No doubt some obscure ordinance or restriction didn't allow overlapping authorities accepting explanations at the same time or something.

Macy's store manager acted as if the whole situation was my fault. He extended no sympathy, acting curt and grouchy through the whole interrogation. Mr. Manager was no doubt angry about the extra work I'd initiated by having the audacity to be involved in an attempted kidnapping in his store.

I was allowed a breather while the officials looked over their stacks of forms. Reenee was finally ushered into the room. I supposed she had been going through similar experiences somewhere else. We grabbed onto each other.

"Oh, Sammy, I'll never forgive myself. Some friend I turned out to be. I was so involved in that jewelry video, I didn't see what was happening to you." My pal was extremely upset and looked close to tears. "I caught a glimpse of the guy next to you, but I thought he was a fan of your show and was kibitzing with you." She went on to berate herself. "How dumb of me! Why wasn't I alarmed that a stranger was near you, even though he was a man? And I didn't even notice the woman."

I squeezed Reenee's hand as she continued. "You must've been so scared! I hope you're not real, real mad at me. I wouldn't blame you if you don't want to talk to me."

"Don't be goofy, Reenee. Ms. Stalker and John Morrow are my targets of. . . ."

"That was Frances' husband? How did you know what he looked like?"

"Last time, when I spoke with old blue eyes at the Oak Forest police station, he showed me a picture of John. Morrow thought Ms. Stalker was you."

"What?"

"I couldn't get him to understand the mix-up. He thought she was you. He kept saying how you and I destroyed his life because of our visit to his wife and our insinuations to her about him being involved in a crime. Strange as it may sound, I'm just sorry that we weren't abducted together. Ms. Stalker was useless in overcoming Morrow. You'd have been right by my side, helping me kick the bejesus out of him."

"I wish it had been me, too. We'd have had that sucker by now, hanging by his jock strap . . . do you think the cops are finished with us? I don't know what more I can tell them. How about you?"

"I'm ready to head for home. I've said the same thing over and over so many times that I need a martini and a . . . Harry! Oh, my God, Harry! He is going to kill me for leaving the house, and he's not gonna take a number and wait in line!"

Just then the office door opened. Two patrolmen from the Oak Forest police department had orders to follow us home in their squad car. Although Chief Vincetti didn't make an appearance at the scene, I was told he'd issued orders for the security measures.

As we left the manager's office, shoppers, still abuzz over the incident some of them had witnessed, followed us with eyes and mouths agape. I couldn't believe eyewitnesses to the fiasco had nothing better to do than wait for my reappearance. The questioning must've taken more than a couple of hours. Had they no lives? I was also surprised that the paparazzi weren't lurking behind clothing racks.

Suburban police from three different towns escorted us through the store and then the mall to the parking lot. The cops must've looked like Pied Pipers leading the rats out of the town, or St. Patrick and his army of snakes wiggling after them.

Reenee and I pulled into my driveway, safe and sound. The policemen who had accompanied us got out of their squad cars and approached my car. One of them asked for my house key and instructed us to stay put until he and his partner checked out the place. The officers returned about twenty minutes later and told us the house was secure. All seemed to be quiet on the home front. No love-struck woman hiding under my bed; no madman lurking with a gun. They escorted Reenee and me into the house

"Lock your door behind us, Ms. Lisowski," Badge #153 said. "The chief will contact you later. We're going to look around outside. We'll also be driving by your house regularly to keep an eye on things. Are you two okay alone, or do you want us to wait while you contact your husbands? We can stay parked in front of the house until they arrive."

"No, no. We'll be okay." The last thing we wanted was to contact Harry or Wally. We had to talk a few things over between ourselves first. "Thank you so much, officers."

The policemen left to inspect the outdoor area around the house.

I wondered what the neighbors felt about having a squad car in my driveway and cops nosing around the grounds. Maybe they thought I was running an illicit drug business — or a house of pleasure. Aha, I could hear them saying among themselves, we knew she had something going, wearing those short skirts and long earrings — and in full makeup and high heels just to take out the garbage bins. Humpf!

"Lord, what an experience." Reenee let out an exhausted sigh. "You must be ready to collapse. But I'm proud of you." She began to mix up a couple of martinis. "You kept your head and got yourself out of a dangerous situation that could've gotten worse if that madman had carried out his plan."

"I was running on sheer nerve. Good thing I didn't allow myself to be kidnapped like the dumb women I read about in those books." Rat-tat-tat-tat. I began shooting out sentences in machine-gun mode. "Where do you suppose John is hiding out? And what about the stalker? Do you think she's gonna bother me again? With all the police departments and a private dick involved, someone better start giving me some answers."

I went to get my cell phone to start my inquisition by first calling Detective Kelly. The land phone interrupted my dialing. It was the hunk.

"Are you all right, Samantha? I was told that you've had a terrifying experience." He sounded angry and upset. I was surprised, because I thought cops were cool and detached. "Is someone there with you?" he went on to ask.

"My friend, Reenee, is here, and the Oak Forest police assured me that they'd be driving by the house frequently. I suppose Chief Vincetti phoned you with the news?"

"Yes, and he faxed over the incident report. I've been calling your home every quarter hour or so since then to see how you're managing. I couldn't reach you on your cell."

"I never keep that friggin' phone on. I don't know why I have it anyway. I'll turn it on as soon as we're through talking, and I'll keep it on till the cows come home."

"Excellent idea. Don't forget to charge the phone when the battery gets low. Now, tell me what happened. Unless you're too tired?"

I told him, and damned if I didn't start to bawl. This man drove me crazy with his charisma. In his presence I always felt like the poor helpless princess in the dungeon — Rapunzel imprisoned in the tower without her hair — Sleeping Beauty developing wrinkles. When he was near me, I certainly was not the tough, rough, independent Samantha of *I can handle anything* fame.

"You were very clear-headed and brave. I admire your guts, but I'm also worried about your safety. I'm more than halfway to the Morrows' house. The Orland Park and Tinley Park police are there already and have been there since you filed your reports with them. I'll call you when I know something. If it's not too late, I can probably stop by, if it suits you. I hope you're not going anywhere for the next few days?"

"I'm not going anywhere for the next twenty years, or until you arrest that maniac and hang him up by his *kruszkies*. John couldn't have gone home after his kidnapping attempt, could he? He must be on the loose. I hope I'm still not number one on his hit parade. After this close call, he should be more worried about his own safety."

"As far as I know, Morrow didn't return home and. . . ."

"What about my stalker?" I interrupted. "Is Chief Vincetti concentrating on her? Maybe she crossed me off her list after the scare she got today. She was zombied out during the abduction. Probably won't have to worry about her pursuing me for a long time, if ever."

"Don't be too sure about that. She may now feel protective toward you. You never know how unbalanced minds work. Don't let anything else happen to you, Samantha. You know you're my blond bombshell."

There he went again with his innuendos. I stared at the phone but before I could react to his words, he disconnected after saying, "Take care of yourself. I'll be in touch."

Reenee looked at me as I gawked into space. "Were you crying when you were talking to Kelly? Why? What did he say? You never cry. "

But she knew why.

Reenee figured out that the handsome Chicago detective was getting under my skin, that her pal was susceptible and vulnerable with a man who displayed compassion and empathy . . . and a so-called innocent kiss. But she then said exactly the right thing to toughen me up. "You'd better save some of those tears for Harry, to play on his sympathy."

We heard the garage door go up.

"Oh, oh. I'm out of here." Reenee gathered her belongings and said, "Good luck. Call me." She called out a quick "Hi'" to Harry as he came through the garage and she went out the front door.

Harry gave me a puzzled look. "Wow. Your girlfriend must be in a hurry. I thought she wasn't supposed to come over until the stalker was arrested."

"Great haircut, Harry. Your barber did a nice job this time. Are you hungry? How did your check-up at the doctor go? What'd you have for lunch? I can see you've been working on that suntan — looks great — would you like a drink. . .?"

"All right, Samantha. Stop. Let's have it. What happened?"

The expression beginning to form on Darling's face and the tightening of his jaw made my poor battered head pound like thoroughbreds' hooves on a fast track.

Let the games begin.

"Well. . . ."

Chapter 37

I started telling Harry about going with Reenee to the mall.

"What?" he said, giving me a stare that would wither a weak willy, but I don't wither and I'm not weak.

I told Harry about the stalker.

"What?"

I told him about the aborted gunpoint abduction.

"*What?*"

I told him about my feigned faint and then my real one.

"What? *What?*"

I finished off with all the police officers I had to talk to, the reports I'd had to sign, the cops' search of our home and surrounding area, and the great news that Morrow *and* the stalker were still at large.

Altogether I counted twenty-seven tonal varieties of *what?* although I may be wrong because I was nervous about Harry's increasing agitation. This was the second time within a couple of weeks that I left him speechless but for single word comments.

I stood in front of him as meekly as possible. He just glared at me, tight-lipped and silent. I felt increasingly uncomfortable. Moments, hours, days went by, although the hands of the den's clock ticked away only a minute or two.

I couldn't stand it any longer. "Say something, for God's sake, Harry. Off with her head. Burn her in the fireplace. Get out the rack. Shred her license…."

"Stop the dramatics, Samantha. Calm down. Sit still for a minute and keep quiet so I can digest what you told me."

Digest? *Digest?* Harry should be embracing me, whispering sweet somethings in my ear. I'd bet if ol' blue eyes were here, I'd be comforted all right!

I was ready to explode, but I guess Darling's *digesting* was over because he said in his typical, indifferent Harry-voice, "I give up. No matter what I tell you, how I try to protect you, you do your own thing. You could've gotten yourself killed today. I don't know what to say anymore."

How about, I'm glad nothing happened to you, Samantha, I thought, or Thank God you're okay, or, You really used your head. He could show me a little sympathy, but I wasn't giving him any hints for the way to go. He was even beginning to convince me that I actually *was* to blame for the state of affairs.

So what else was new?

My resentment against him grew, but I remained silent.

The phone and doorbell rang simultaneously, interrupting the stalemate. I opted for Alexander Graham Bell's invention and went into the kitchen to answer it. I could hear Harry arguing with someone at the front door. I gave a big sigh. Now what? I thought.

Into my ear came the welcoming voice of Detective Kelly. "How're you holding up, Samantha? Is your lady friend still there with you? I'm about ready to leave the Morrows' house."

"Reenee's not here, but Harry is. Did you discover the whereabouts of Morrow or the stalker? Are you going to stop by?"

The front door slammed and I could hear Harry swearing in the background. "Can you hold on, Detective? There seems to be a lot of commotion going on."

I put down the phone and rushed to the foyer. Harry stood there with his back against the door and a way-beyond-aggravated look on his face. "Is that a reporter on the phone, or are they all outside on our front lawn?" he asked.

I ran to the front room and looked through the window. Not only did I see reporters with cameras and microphones, but a couple of TV vans also adorned our driveway. I ran back to the phone to inform Detective Kelly of this circumstance.

"I'll be there in twenty minutes," he said. "Don't answer the door, and stay away from the windows. I'll call Chief Vincetti to request crowd control for you. It's his jurisdiction. Just cool it for a few more minutes."

"Harry," I called as I hung up the phone. "Stay away from the windows and chill. The Marines will land within minutes."

"What the hell're you talking about? You're so flippant! Who was that on the phone? Dammit! See what you've caused now."

"Harry, please. Let's just figure out what we're going to do. I suppose I'll have to give some statement to the press. Which channel is the least liberal . . . did you recognize any newscasters out there? Oh, I've gotta check my hair and makeup. . . ."

"Are you listening to yourself? This is not the time to concern yourself with frivolous. . . ."

Sirens interrupted our romantic scene. Looking through the curtains, I was happy to see Oak Forest police bubble lights blinking. It pays to live two blocks from the station. The squad cars pulled onto the shoulder of the road and halfway onto the grass, as our driveway was crowded with press vans.

"Hot damn," I said. "I think the entire police force is out there!"

Harry moaned something about our grass being ruined forever, gave the end table a good whack and sat down on the couch so hard I thought the stuffing would swoosh out of the cushion.

Lord, I told myself, the top of Harry's head is gonna blow. I could almost see steam coming out of his ears. I knew from past experience that the best thing to do at this point was to leave him alone. I went outside to tackle the media mongrels.

I gave a brief, private statement to CLTV, thankful that the anchor who'd interviewed me days ago was not the talking head on the scene this time. I only spoke to a reporter from the *Southtown/Star*, a newspaper that covered Oak Forest and a multitude of surrounding communities. I ignored the rest of the media. Eventually, the police encouraged everyone to leave.

All was quiet on the Central Avenue front. The media and on-lookers had been dispersed; the squad cars were down to two in the driveway. Chief Vincetti had arrived, almost at the same time as Detective Kelly. Harry was not thrilled to see Chicago's finest, barely acknowledging his presence. He turned instead to the chief.

"Have you got a monitoring device that I can strap onto Samantha's ankle, Chief? The minute I turn my back, I know she'll be flying out the door to shop or to get her hair done or her nails manicured." The sarcasm in Harry's voice made my teeth vibrate, and the look he gave me would've broken the spirit of a lesser woman.

Chief Vincetti looked at Harry and gave him a weak smile. "I'm afraid it's not that simple. We have an escalating situation on our hands. Detective Kelly here has told me that Morrow's whereabouts are still a mystery, and I'm sorry to say, so are the stalker's. They'll confront Samantha again; that's a given. As John is the one with the gun, I feel we should concentrate mainly on him."

"I spoke with Mrs. Morrow, who is in a near-collapse state," Detective Kelly added. "She cannot help us establish her husband's whereabouts. The family owns another place in Indiana, and the police down there are pursuing that lead. Our problem is what to do with you, Samantha."

Maybe I could be put in solitary confinement with the fine detective, I mused, but Harry saw the mischievous look on my face and gave me a warning sign to keep any cute comments to myself.

The phone rang. Harry went to the kitchen to answer it, swore, walked back to us and, without a word, went out the front door. He came back with Erwin Tuppence, the useless private-eye who was draining us of our money and doing nothing. Evidently the police in the driveway wouldn't allow him to approach the front door without our consent, so Tuppence phoned and asked Harry to come out and vouch for him. We both had forgotten he was expected to give us an update that evening.

Cold greetings were extended, and it was evident the chief and the detective were not tickled with the private dick's intrusion into the case. I could sense that Tuppence wasn't ecstatic about the lawmen's presence either. But it wasn't every day a girl could be surrounded by a group of handsome men where she was the focus of attention. Well, spoiled by one pipsqueak private eye's presence. I felt I should bring out the chips and dip. Maybe put on some music and have us all relax on the couch and kibitz with each other. Harry wouldn't find those thoughts proper either, so I saved my observations to share with Reenee later.

Said pipsqueak seemed very uncomfortable. He squirmed in his tiny suit. His little feet shifted from one stance to another. I bet myself that his teeny palms were sweating. Chief Vincetti told the private eye that he expected him to share any information he had discovered with the police. The chief set up an appointment for the next morning at headquarters with Mr. Scrawny. Detective Kelly basically mimicked Vincetti's directive. Tuppence fidgeted some more, but agreed.

He turned to Harry and added in his squeaky voice, "I can see Mrs. Lisowski has had a hectic day, so I'll leave now and be in touch with you both tomorrow afternoon."

Humph! Probably to hit us up for more money for doing nothing. He was beginning to get on my last nerve.

I almost screamed, "It's *Ms.* Lisowski to you, little man!" What red-blooded, independent, American female is called *Mrs.* anymore? I was glad when he left, the diminutive twit. What a useless visit, for which we'd no doubt be billed.

"I am going to keep a squad car in your driveway overnight," Chief Vincetti informed us once the pipsqueak was gone. "How long I can offer you this protection is debatable because of the department's budget concerns, but a couple of days and nights should be no problem."

"Must the officers stay in a stuffy car in this heat, Chief?" I asked. "Our air-conditioned house is certainly big enough to accommodate them without their interfering with Harry and me, or vice versa. I could set up a little place for them on this level. We have a bathroom and TV down here."

"Thank you, Samantha, but let's see how it works out come morning."

"What about going on with our lives, Chief?" Harry asked. "Can we go grocery shopping or to the gas station or to the pool at the country club? Should I think about getting back to work?"

Yes, yes, I shouted inwardly, but kept my trap shut. I hoped the expectant look on my face didn't betray me.

"My officers will accompany you wherever you need to go, but it'd be best if you could limit trips only to necessary places for a while. Think about delaying your return to work, if you can, for a couple of days yet."

Damn, I thought. I better get a lot of movies from Netflix. I'd be a prisoner in my own home for the duration. Maybe the Chief should worry about keeping guns and knives away from me.

Detective Kelly had been silent during most of the prior proceedings. I supposed it was because he didn't want to infringe upon the police chief's jurisdiction. As Harry accompanied the chief to the front door, the hunk asked if he could speak to me alone.

Upon Harry's return, I told him the detective had to tie up some loose ends with me. Darling just sighed, shook his head and left us alone in the front room. In a couple of minutes I heard the background noises from the TV in the den.

"Alone at last," I said flippantly, adding a wink.

Detective Kelly gave me a strange, silent look that just about melted me, then said, "Before I leave, I just wanted to know how you're *really* coping with all you've gone through today, as well as the last few weeks. You seem to be holding strong, but you've got to be exhausted and scared, regardless of your bravado. We'll get this guy, Samantha. I promise you. And the woman, too."

I looked at the concern on his face and his beautiful baby blues and, yeah, that's right, my eyes began to tear up. He reached for me but stopped himself in time. I smiled, produced a Kleenex and quickly ended the waterfall. What a full time job it was to keep my mascara from running down my face in front of him.

"I'm okay. Really. Maybe later my situation will hit me like a big ol' semi, but for now I'm dealing with it. Will you call me tomorrow?'

"You got it, Samantha." He took my hands in his. "Keep up that lively spirit of yours. Stay safe."

I escorted him to the door. "Thank you, Detective, for your reassurance." I squeezed his arm. "I'm lucky to have you in my corner." I gave him a big smile and he returned it. I could almost feel his kiss. God, was he handsome!

I sighed and went to join Harry in the den.

"What did Kelly need from you?" he asked.

"He basically wanted to know how I was holding up."

"Hey, yeah, that's right. This has been quite a day for you. How *are* you holding up, Sammy?"

I rolled my eyes and let out a big sigh.
Too late, Harry. Too late.
I went upstairs to call Reenee.

Chapter 38

For the next couple of nights, I experienced nightmares so intense as to awaken me. I'd invariably rouse Harry to explain them in horrific detail, but as Darling never remembered his dreams, he wasn't interested and barely listened.

"Oh, lord, Harry. I went into this room and a woman was hanging from a ceiling beam. She had on one of my nightgowns. You know, the blue one with the flowers? She was swinging slightly and although I couldn't see her face, I knew it was I."

"Must you be grammatically correct at two o'clock in the morning?" he grumbled, punching his pillow to indicate that he was ready for me to stop talking so he could go back to sleep.

On another night, I sat up straight in a cold sweat and jabbed him. "Harry, you won't believe what a nightmare I had! These guys with scary masks on their faces were chasing me, They had machetes, and machine guns. And then some black Doberman pinchers joined the melee, leaping at me and nipping at my heels and biting my legs and *dupa* as I ran through mud and muck and fell down a couple times. I couldn't seem to get anywhere and I couldn't find my car, or my purse."

"I don't know where these dreams of yours come from, Samantha. Probably because you read all those gory books about serial killers and psychos before you go to sleep," my hero said. "You watch too many movies where murderers are chopping up people."

"Gee, Harry, could the reason also be that I'm under a lot of stress and anxiety lately? That I need a little TLC."

"What are you mumbling about now, Samantha? Just relax and go back to sleep. You probably won't dream anymore." Having spent enough time comforting me, he turned over and went back to his visionless paradise.

In my mind I hit Harry over the head with a *Concerned Husband of the Year* trophy and went downstairs to watch TV so that I wouldn't bother His Highness any further.

Detective Kelly had told me to call him any time, day or night, if there was an emergency. I pondered. Would nightmares constitute a crisis?

Nah. Even Reenee wouldn't go along with me on that idea.

Instead, I turned on a jabbering salesman who wanted to sell me pills for my insomnia. I wondered if he had pills for indifferent, blasé husbands.

The days went by with progress — I mean un-progress — reports from the police. The undersized PI, Tuppence, wasn't any closer to identifying my stalker or figuring out where John Morrow was hiding either. I kept dogging Harry to fire Tuppence. In fact, I was shocked Darling hadn't yet let him go. He didn't like to waste money, and it was evident that the little guy wasn't producing.

Chief Vincetti told us that surveillance of the Morrows' second home in Indiana proved fruitless. The Indiana police found no sign that John was using it as a hideout. The place was dilapidated. The house looked as if it hadn't been inhabited in years. The chief also stated that the family's friends and relatives hadn't heard from Morrow either. The investigation was at a standstill.

I believed John was living in his car. Maybe he'd muddied the plates so numbers couldn't be clearly seen. Maybe he had the car repainted. Maybe I was giving Morrow too much credit. Maybe it was just dumb luck that he hadn't been spotted.

My sons were very concerned for me, and for their father, too. They encouraged us to close up shop and come stay with them at their apartment for the duration. Harry wouldn't even consider the suggestion, and I, for once, agreed with him. The problem would just be waiting for us upon our return if we ran out now. Relocating would simply delay the problem hanging over my head, or put our sons in danger.

* * * * *

On the third day since the mall fiasco, we no longer had a squad car in our driveway, but we were assured that frequent drive-bys would continue.

I had already returned to the Oak Forest police department to update the drawing of what Ms. Stalker looked like. I remembered every detail of her appearance from when we wrestle-hugged at Macy's. She was actually quite good-looking. Her dark hair had nary a gray strand. She was around five-foot six and about one-hundred-thirty pounds. It freaked me out that her height, weight and, probably her age as well, were so similar to mine. And, if she had my perfume scent down pat, I certainly also had hers. I'd never wear Chantilly Lace again, even though I've always liked that fragrance.

How could one woman and one madman just fade into the woodwork as they seemed to have done? What kind of a devoted admirer was Ms. Stalker anyway? Why wasn't she driving around in that sharp white car of hers, passing my house, trying to get a glimpse of me? The police who had been parked in my driveway would've grabbed her in a second.

And what about Almost-Kidnapper, Probable-Murderer John Morrow? Didn't he use his credit card to shop for groceries or to buy gas? The cops and detectives I read about in mysteries and watch on TV programs often catch their criminals by tracking their purchases. Besides, wasn't Morrow worried about his family? Didn't he make phone calls to find out how they were? Couldn't he be traced that way?

These thoughts filled my mind most days as Harry and I lived on our respective levels of the house, trying not to get on each other's nerves. I knew he was itching to get back to work as badly as I was eagerly awaiting a return to my own life. Summer would soon be over, and I'd be back to subbing a day or two a week at our local Catholic school, and besides, I missed Reenee. Talking to her over the phone just didn't cut it. I moped over the good times I was missing without her.

In desperation, as the days rolled near the weekend, I said, "Harry, let's go out for a decent meal tonight. I'm tired of eating leftovers and lunchmeat sandwiches. Regardless of what the police tell us, I think Morrow and Ms. Stalker have given up on me."

Darling sighed, put down his paper and started looking through the Golden Opportunity book for restaurant coupons. "Burger King, New China Buffet, Popeye's Chicken . . . what does the Queen want to eat?"

Harry had a tendency to bestow that title on me when he knows any decision, after some bickering, will eventually be mine. So I decreed, "Not damned fast food places, Harry. I want to go to a nice, sit-down restaurant for a change."

"You're impossible to please. Never satisfied with a hot dog." He gave me his best exasperated look. "I don't feel like having soup and salad and dessert. You know I don't eat a lot. A meal of a couple of White Castle hamburgers is good enough for me."

The Queen was going to win eventually, but it seemed we always had to go through the hassle of bitter words and power struggles. After almost twenty-five years of this dance ritual, with no time off for good behavior, I was due for a change of venue. Detective Kelly was filling my thoughts more and more, and I wondered how he would treat me in similar situations.

"Why can't we go to Durbin's, that new restaurant that opened up in Midlothian? Remember me telling you that my staff and I were pleased with the good food and the nice bar area when we taped my television show from there last month? There are TVs all over the place. You could watch the news while we're eating."

The TV and news comment got him. We went to Durbin's.

In less than fifteen short minutes we pulled up to the restaurant. In the parking lot I noticed a sharp white car. Boing! A white car? As I'm terrible about remembering numbers, I couldn't recall the ones Harry'd spouted out to the police after our merry chase a couple of days ago. I'd have to ask Darling what they were, so I immediately dismissed that idea. I wasn't going to spoil a nice meal because I was a Nervous Nellie every time I saw a white automobile.

No, the car couldn't belong to Ms. Stalker. But, then again, yeah, I thought; she probably lives in the area. But, no, that would be too much of a coincidence. If I had written a fictional story about my escapades and put the stalker's car in the parking lot of a local restaurant, my writers' group would call foul. They'd tell me that it was too contrived a happening, that it was too much of a coincidence, too obvious, not believable. . . .

Yes, I agreed. Impossible. Therefore, I said nothing to Harry about my suspicions. But when we were seated in the restaurant, I put on my glasses and looked around. No Ms. Stalker, at least not in the section where we were. The place also had a front patio area and a beer garden in the back. I thought about taking a little tour around the restaurant, but I knew Harry would call the idea stupid and tell me to relax.

After we placed our drink order, I said, "See, Harry? Isn't this better than a fast food joint? Or eating a dry ol' lunchmeat sandwich in front of the TV? They even have young, pretty waitresses for you to check out."

"You know I only have eyes for you, Samantha. Don't start with the nonsense. I'm not too happy about this place anyway. It's too noisy and the menu is limited. I think the Durbin's in Tinley Park is better."

Being used to a person in my life cursed with a negative attitude, I didn't bother to answer. I certainly had found something good on the menu, and I was happy to be out of the house at last.

"I'm going to the john," Harry said. "I don't see it. Must be in the back of this joint."

No sooner did Harry leave for the washroom than Ms. Stalker, or her look-alike, passed him on the way to her table, a little distance from ours.

I gasped and grabbed my chair so I wouldn't fall off. No, it couldn't be. I hurriedly rummaged through my purse for my glasses. My God, it was her! I was so flabbergasted I used the grammatically incorrect pronoun!

I swore as I dug further into the caverns of my purse trying to find the damned cell phone. Tissues, camera, old movie tickets, cookies in a Baggie — how long since these Oreos had seen daylight? — make-up bag, folded up flyers from my TV show, small hairspray, a pair of long earrings — that's where they were; I had searched for them for days! The table began to look like a flea market stand. While tossing out all the paraphernalia I kept mumbling, "Harry, where are you? What's taking you so long?" I let out an irritated sigh and figured he must've bumped into an acquaintance and was shooting the breeze. I was hoping there'd be no shooting of anything at all where I was.

I finally found my phone. I threw the various items back into my purse with one hand and tried in vain to get a strong enough signal with the other. So much for the commercials about the reliable phone service bars. In this bar there were no bars!

I was worried that if I tried to walk around the restaurant to get out of the dead zone, Ms. Stalker would spot me, and I might walk into a dead zone of my own. Desperately I turned around this way and that way in my seat and was finally able to get a signal. With trembling fingers, I punched 9-1-1. Miraculously, I was put through to Chief Vincetti without doing a lot of explaining to the dispatcher.

His advice came across sternly. "Avoid any contact with the woman, Samantha," he said. "Stay put. We'll be there in a few minutes. I'll also contact the Midlothian police, as the restaurant is in their jurisdiction."

Great, I thought. Now I have another police department involved.

Sneaking a look Ms. Stalker's way, I panicked as she gathered up her belongings, placed a tip on the table, and appeared to be ready to leave. Then she looked straight at me!

Something was wrong; there was no recognition on her part. Could I be mistaken? No. I still had on my glasses. It was impossible for someone to look that much like someone else. Maybe she wore glasses and without them couldn't make out faces from a distance any better than I could?

And where the hell was Harry! I couldn't wait for him, or the police. I grabbed my purse, and, amazingly with only one plunge into its depths, got out the spare car keys. I followed Ms. Stalker to the parking lot, keeping a comfortable distance. She wasn't going to get away this time, although I had no intention of stopping her. I was just going to follow her and report back to the police.

Ladies, start your engines!

Chapter 39

I didn't want to back out of my spot until Ms. Stalker made her turn into the street. Because I'm so bad at remembering digits, I needed to write down her license number. All I could find was an eyebrow pencil in my cosmetic bag and a paper napkin in the armrest. Oh, my camera!

I'm not so good at using new-fangled cameras with zooms and flashes and every possible knob and feature. My sons thought they were doing me a favor buying me a jazzy, high-priced one, but I didn't even understand the booklet instructions for taking a simple photo. Did the flash go off in daylight, which would bring Ms. Stalker's attention to me? I should've kept my Brownie box camera that I got from my grandmother for my tenth birthday. At least all you did with that one was snap the button and voila. . . .

I chanced it and took a couple of pictures *sans* flash, thank goodness, and just in time. Ms. Stalker got a break in the traffic and made her turn. Cicero Avenue was a devil to get across from Durbin's parking lot, but I got lucky as I backed out of my parking slot; I was able to make the turn as well. Now all I had to do was let a couple of cars get between us so she wouldn't notice that I was following her.

Although the lights cooperated, and sparse traffic made the pursuit a little less hassled, it's not as easy as you may think to tail someone while keeping your distance so that the tailee doesn't catch on to the tailer. My heart was thumping like the beat of a bongo drum gone wild.

I concentrated on the car, but another one of my silly, irrelevant thoughts entered my over-flowing brain: would Harry consider

buying a hot car like that for me before I got too old to drive one . . .
oh, my God . . . Harry! He was probably going crazy trying to figure
out what had happened to me.

I pulled my cell phone from my bag, then paused. How stupid! I
wasn't thinking. Harry didn't own a cell phone, and I didn't know the
restaurant's number.

Well, call the police, dummy!

Just then, my objective caught the yellow light and turned. I was
stuck behind a few cars as the traffic signal changed to red. Damn.
But at least I could use the phone as I waited. I punched out 9-1-1.

To my dismay, I discovered that I hadn't turned off the phone at
the restaurant and now it signaled *low battery*. I hardly ever used the
dumb thing, so I hadn't recharged it in ages. I tried to press 9-1-1
again, but that made the phone completely shut down. Dead! The
damned thing went dead on me as the traffic light arrow became
green and allowed me to make the turn.

Now where the hell did Ms. Stalker go? I thought, as I cruised
down the side streets. No moving cars were in my field of vision.
Okay, don't panic. She must live on one of these blocks.

I decided to go up and down the side streets, hoping to get lucky
and spot the white car in a driveway. At the same time I was
wondering how to find a pay phone to call the police. Life was easier
with phone booths on corners. What did Superman do nowadays
when he had to change his clothes? And why was I thinking about
such dumb things . . . oh, wait! I had a phone charger in the glove
compartment. I pulled over to look for it. I swore again as it dawned
on me. The device was in my car, and I was driving Harry's.

I took off again. Ninety per cent of me concentrated on finding
Ms. Stalker's auto; the other ten pictured Harry as he fumed over
where I could be. No doubt he was using every swear word available
to mankind and firing up his normal irritability into full-scale volcanic
volume. I could almost feel the heat and smell of the lava from the
eruption. This situation, again, was going to end up being my fault.

All kinds of thoughts went through my head as I kept making
turns up and down streets. I wondered what the police were doing.
They had no way to track me.

Hey, stupid!

It hit me like a slap in the face. Why didn't I just return to Durbin's and give Ms. Stalker's license plate number to Oak Forest's finest? Duh! I was acting like one of those dumb heroines in movies and books who really aggravated me, because she delved head first into the stupid, dangerous route instead of taking the obvious, safer course.

The hell with this, I decided. I'm going back to Durbin's and dump this search into the laps of the police. As I turned down a couple side streets to get back to the main drag, I noticed that a car behind me seemed to be doing the same thing.

Had Ms. Stalker caught on to my tail, changed cars and now pursued me? I made a few more turns; so did the car behind me.

I began to get unnerved and started glowing, because men sweat but women glow according to my friend, Phil. Why would that stupid remark pop into my mind at a time like this? The frigid air blowing from the air conditioner gave me the sweats, yes, the sweats, *and* made me shiver. My eyeballs were playing tennis, alternating between where I was going and the rearview mirror. Beads of sweat, not glow, ran into my baby greens, causing my eyeliner to smear and my eyes to burn and blur, making it impossible for me to figure out if the driver of the other car was male or female.

What should I do; what should I do? Driving back to Durbin's was no longer an option. The restaurant was too far away. My tail could accost me anywhere along the route. Maybe I should turn into somebody's driveway and knock on his or her door for help. But what if the person wasn't home and my pursuer grabbed me before I could get back to my car? Maybe I should pull into a driveway and keep beeping my horn. But, of course, everyone on the block could be at work and not able to help me anyway. I even considered stopping, running to the trunk and getting out the tire iron. Instead I stepped on the gas.

And suddenly I found myself on the block with a white automobile in the driveway. Incredible! I recognized the license plate numbers. After all, I had been staring at them for blocks when I was following her car. Oh, my God!

This must be Ms. Stalker's house.

My foot jammed on the brake which surprised my pursuer. Bam!

The car bumped into my rear fender. Good thing I had on my seat belt. I unfastened it and jumped out. My peripheral vision caught sight of an old man getting out of the other vehicle.

It was John Morrow!

He emerged from his car and ran towards me as quickly as his age would allow. I made a split-second decision. Better the stalker's house than this gun-totin' maniac. I sprinted to her front door as fast as my three-inch heels would take me, Morrow on my tail.

The dash ended in a dead heat.

John grabbed my arm in a vise-like lock. How did this old geezer get so strong? I wondered. He shoved what felt like a gun into my side. With a frightening crazed chuckle, he whispered, "Ring your girlfriend's doorbell and don't get frisky. I'm not glad to see you, so don't think this is my cucumber you feel."

I swallowed. I couldn't believe what I'd heard. Being accosted by a madman spouting ghoulish humor seemed to make my predicament more terrifying.

"Ring the bell," he repeated. His grip tightened, although I hadn't thought that was possible. "It's about time you led me to your girlfriend's house. I almost got the both of you at that store last week." His quiet laughter scared me more than whatever he was poking into my ribs.

I was glowing so much by then that I could probably drown him if he shook me. And if he suddenly let me go, my trembling knees would hit the pavement.

"Th-this is . . . isn't Reenee's hou-house," I began to say.

"Shut up. Don't argue with me and don't think I'm dumb enough to fall for any tricks. Ring that bell! Or do you need to see what a .38 can do?"

I rang the bell.

Chapter 40

The door opened.

Chaos erupted.

Before Ms. Stalker could open her mouth, Morrow pushed me through the doorway against her. She let out a scream and stumbled, and I tripped over her. John steadied himself and waved the gun around like the crazed person he was. He slammed and locked the door behind us.

Déjà vu washed over me, made my heart beat faster. I'd lived this scene before at the mall, but my situation wasn't any less frightening the second time around.

A microscopic ball of fur appeared out of nowhere, yipping like crazy, and began alternately nipping at me and licking Ms. Stalker. Something buzzed overhead, which I hoped wasn't a bat. A caged parrot in the foyer started squawking and shrieking, "Oh, boy. Oh, boy. Awrk! Awrk! Where's Tricky-Dicky? Where's Tricky Dicky?"

"Shut up," Morrow yelled at the bird, brandishing the gun, which made the dog turn his way. Up and down he jumped, trying to reach John's arm and take a chunk out of it.

"Where's Tricky-Dicky! Awrk! Where's Tricky-Dicky!" shrieked the parrot.

"Get this dog off me or I'll shoot him," Morrow yelled.

"Don't shoot my Sweet-ums," cried Ms. Stalker.

All we needed were seventy-six trombones and a big parade.

I figured while everyone was occupied, I'd try to crawl out through the hallway and scoot out the back door.

"Gettin' away, awrk, gettin' away," screeched the parrot.

Shoot the damned bird, I thought, as I nimbly bounded into the den, up the steps, into the kitchen and tripped over a couple of cats. Was this a house or a zoo? The only thing missing was an elephant to block my way to the patio door.

I had just unlocked the kitchen exit when Morrow yelled, "Step outside, missy, and I put a bullet hole through your girlfriend."

Although the offer was appealing for a couple of seconds, I resisted the temptation and called out, "Okay, okay. Leave her alone. I'm coming back."

I took a deep breath, told myself everything would be okay and walked back, grabbing a saucer from the kitchen table and hiding it under my blouse. A dish is no match for a gun, but I figured I might have a chance to fling it at Morrow. Too bad a knife wasn't available.

A more sedate scene greeted me when I re-entered the den. Ms. Stalker was on the sofa, holding tightly to her ball of fluff. John was panting, but kept a steady gun-hand aimed at her. Only the parrot hadn't quieted down and was now going through a litany of swear words, some of which I'd never heard before.

"Why don't you join your girlfriend. . . ," Morrow began above the chatter.

"I'm trying to tell you she is not my girlfriend; she's my. . . ."

"And I'm telling you to shut up and sit next to her on the couch. I want to enlighten you both about the hell you put my family through. Since you visited my wife and told her about the murders and about me making threatening phone calls to you. . . ."

"I never told Frances you were my creepy caller. . . ."

"I'm not going to tell you again to shut up. I'll gag you if necessary. You will listen to me, one way or another."

Just then Ms. Stalker spoke up with a quiver in her timid voice. "Sir," she began, "there seems to be some misunderstanding. I don't know you or this woman. . . ."

I looked at her in amazement. Was she more psycho than I thought: schizophrenic, fanatical, insane? Why didn't she recognize me? Or was she just trying to confuse John?

Morrow waved the gun. "You've got another think coming if you believe I'm falling for some mind trick of yours."

"Tricks. Tricks," the parrot squawked. "Awrk. Where's Tricky-Dicky? Tricks, Tricky-Dicky." Then he began his swear-word recital again.

When John turned toward the parrot in the hallway, I tried a sneaky move with no success.

He whirled my way, and with menace in his every step, he convinced me to stay put.

Queasiness in the pit of my stomach was bubbling up to my throat. I swallowed hard. The sour taste almost made me gag.

"Do you shut that parrot up, missy, or do I?" he asked Ms. Stalker.

Morrow wasn't very creative, I thought. I was *missy* and now my nemesis was *missy*. I mentally socked my head to make those extraneous thoughts go away. I was in serious trouble, and there went my brain again coming up with insipid questions.

Missy slowly got up with a few whimpers and walked to the cage. I thought this would deflect John's attention so that I could throw the saucer at him, but I saw he was in full control of the situation. Why didn't this excitement give the old man palpitations of the heart, or worse? Lord knows that organ of mine was doing a polka in my chest.

As Ms. Stalker approached the cage, the parrot stopped swearing and chattered, "Tiffany wants a martini; Awrk! Tiffany wants a martini."

Tiffany? Martini? What happened to the good ol' Polly parrot and her obsession with crackers? I'm in a snake pit, I thought, as I recalled the old black-and-white movie with Olivia DeHaviland or somebody. There I go again, thinking of all this junk with a gun pointing my way, and my teeth practically vibrating with fear.

Martini-loving Tiffany was not happy. The parrot screeched and shrieked and squawked until the trembling Ms. Stalker finally got the cover over its cage.

"Get back to the couch, next to your friend," Morrow ordered. "You're both wacky women; I can see why you upset my wife so badly."

Scared or not, I was outraged. *We* were nuts? Talk about the outhouse calling the septic tank smelly!

We settled down again. Someone looking through the window would think we were having a pleasant discussion about the gun in

John's hand.

"You couldn't leave well enough alone, could you? You had to come to my house and make allegations against me. Now it's my turn to get even." Morrow continued his rendition of how Reenee and I fouled up his life. He looked more anxious with each mouthful of words. His voice sputtered and quivered. "You caused my wife and daughter to deteriorate to a point from which neither may recover."

Ms. Stalker began to sob and snivel. If she reached to embrace me, I was going to deck her, gun or no gun pointing my way.

"That witch, Carole Langley, was a righteous kill," Morrow continued. "I'd stab her again if I could!" An alarming redness crawled over his face and the veins in his neck seemed ready to jump out. "She caused my precious daughter's irreversible condition. She deserved to die!"

What in the world was he talking about? He'd stabbed Carole Langley, the woman at the writing workshop? How could that be? He didn't even attend the seminar. Only his wife was there. Although Reenee and I had our suspicions that John was covering for Frances, we'd never tagged him as the murderer.

"You don't know anything about me," he went on to say, ignoring Ms. Stalker's hysterics. She was holding on to Sweet-ums so tightly, I thought the poor little thing would pop into pieces.

"I'm a good man. A family man. I love my wife and daughter and would do anything for them. . . ." His voice became weaker. He seemed distracted as he astounded me with his next confession. "Long Tall Sally was a necessity. She saw me kill Langley. Crazy woman singing to herself about the murder, and me stealing the knife. I couldn't let her further mess up my miserable life."

Morrow had also murdered the female impersonator? If he'd already killed two people, what was the likelihood that Ms. Stalker and I would get out of this house alive? I began to shiver. I wrapped my arms around myself. John had killed Carole Langley and Long Tall Sally. Would we women be two more notches on his belt? I couldn't get my mind around the idea.

As my brain tried to adjust to his confession, the two cats came into the room and began to slide up against John's legs. He tried to kick them away, but all he could manage was a series of big sneezes.

Allergic to felines? Now was my chance!

I threw the saucer at him. Because my body was shaking, my aim was off and the dish only grazed the side of John's head. I forced myself to move swiftly and push him down while he was off balance, but Sweet-ums escaped from Ms. Stalker and joined in the fracas. I stumbled over her. Down I went, head first. One of the cats jumped on my back and dug its claws into my skin. The agitated parrot began screeching from under its blanket, "Where's Tricky-Dicky? Awrk, Where's Tricky-Dicky!"

John hit me with the gun, and my shoulder erupted in such searing pain that I never knew existed. The blow must've hurt the cat as well, because it let out a ferocious meow and raced away, taking some of my skin with it.

"Don't shoot her! Oh, God, don't shoot her," Ms. Stalker cried out. I wasn't sure whether she meant me or the damned cat.

Morrow hovered with the gun and bellowed, "Don't try anything like that again. I won't hesitate to shoot next time. Go back to the couch!" The exertion caused Morrow to wheeze and gasp for breath. Our struggle had taken its toll on him as well, but his determination kept him going.

In great pain, I half walked, half crawled to the sofa. Ms. Stalker tried to help me, but I shook her off. My hands were sweaty, and I thought my beating heart would burst out of my chest. My shoulder felt like it was on fire.

Morrow sat down on one of the chairs before continuing. "Long Tall Sally told me I was a bad person," he whispered. He sounded distracted. "She told me she'd go tell the cops that I'd killed somebody, but only after her hair appointment the next day. I couldn't believe my luck when I realized that Long Tall Sally's brain was fuzzy. She wasn't all there!" He let out a maniacal chuckle. "I returned to the area that night to take care of her before she could contact the police. She wasn't hard to find, slipping in and out of buildings, singing to herself."

I was mesmerized by what John was saying. I could tell Ms. Stalker felt the same way, since she quieted down and stared at John with unblinking eyes. Even Sweet-ums sat at attention.

Morrow looked at us as though he expected us to understand, to sympathize with him. "My wife knew nothing ... nothing of this. I drove her home after the workshop with a sense of closure. I had done away with the rotten woman who ruined our cherished daughter's life. I was proud of myself that I finally avenged my Lori."

Morrow looked down and his gun hand dropped as well. But he caught himself, perked up and said in a stronger, louder voice, "Frances would still not know of my involvement in the Langley woman's death if you two didn't invade my home with your accusations and implications. I can still see the horror in her eyes when she confronted me." He gulped and cried out, "Since your busy-body visit, Frances won't allow me to touch her . . . or to comfort Lori."

"Mr. Morrow, please, please." I had to interrupt John even though he might gag or shoot me as promised. My voice was so shaky that I didn't even recognize it. "I knew nothing of what you're telling me. I didn't accuse you during my visit to your home, not of you being responsible for the murders or making the phone calls. I know I messed things up. . . ."

"Messed things up? Is that what you call it? Messed things up? You destroyed my life. Obliterated it." Morrow wiped the sweat from his brow. He looked ready to explode. "You made my wife's fragile health worsen. I can't even visit Lori or hold her in my arms as she deteriorates in the hospital. You and this blabbermouth friend of yours. . . ."

Morrow became more and more distressed, listing a litany of grievances against Reenee and me. I prayed he had the safety catch on the weapon, because as his agitation grew, he could accidentally squeeze the trigger. I was afraid to breathe for fear he would shoot one of us.

But I had to speak out, to try and reason with him. "Mr. Morrow. You don't want to harm us. Think of your wife. Your daughter. What would happen to them? How would they survive, knowing that you killed two more innocent women?" I used as forceful a tone as possible. A trembling, teary-sounding voice might have further angered him. "A jury would probably be able to understand why you committed those other two murders. You could claim temporary insanity. We can work this out. I will help you."

Morrow went on as if I hadn't spoken. Sounding more and more deranged, he continued his tirade. "Frances accused me of calling your home at all hours of the night and threatening you. She thought I would kill *you* next to keep my secret safe." John's gun hand became unsteady as it moved from us to the floor to the wall and back to us. Always back to us. "Since the day of your visit, my wife of fifty years now looks at me with fear and distrust in her eyes. She loathes me because of you both and your big mouths!"

The rage in John's voice sent chills down my body. He was going to shoot us. He was on the verge of shooting us!

And he probably would've if Tricky-Dicky hadn't taken that moment to enter the room. At least it flashed through my mind that it must've been Tricky-Dicky, but who knew in this circus establishment?

The three of us froze.

Even the menagerie took pause.

Tricky-Dicky appeared composed. His big brown eyes danced around in his sockets, sizing up the situation. Only his long tail thumped wildly.

He must not have liked what he saw.

Tricky-Dicky let out a monkey screech and jumped up and down around the room. Tiffany's cage shook as the parrot threw herself against it. Sweet-ums pulled itself away from Ms. Stalker and yipped and hopped up and down like a yo-yo on a string. The cats let out jungle meows and dashed back and forth across the room.

The other animals' sounds were fierce competition for the monkey's and seemed to spur him on. He landed first on Ms. Stalker's shoulder and then leapt onto my lap, which he used as a trampoline. Monkey spit covered us all as he soared off me and bounded up and down the walls. The three of us began screaming and flailing our arms. I feared the gun in John's hand would go off.

The boisterous racket suddenly came to a halt. Shenanigans completed, the monkey made a complete stop in front of a stunned Morrow and looked at him as if awaiting applause and a treat. Receiving neither, he twirled and looked our way for his reward. None coming, he jumped up and down and started leaping and bounding around the room as an encore. His screeches set the parrot, the cats and Sweet-ums off again.

I thought my ears would split from the noise. I worried that the damned monkey would bite me or pull out my hair, as his performance now involved his audience. He was relentless as he leaped in a frenzied state from Ms. Stalker's head to my shoulders. Fur and monkey juices spread over us like a blanket. If there was any justice in the world, Tricky-Dicky would jump on Morrow, too, but he gave the man a wide berth, as though some animal instinct warned him against John's karma.

As I began to pray that Morrow wouldn't shoot at the monkey and get me instead, thunderous banging on the front door and doorbell chimes joined the mayhem. The theme song from *Mission Impossible* burst out in full force.

The theme from *Doctor Doolittle* would've been more apropos.

The sudden silence of the milieu was deafening.

Chapter 41

The silence became mayhem again in two seconds flat.

Tricky-Dicky sprinted to the door and began jumping straight up and down as if he were pounding nails into a board with his feet.

Parrot Tiffany began screeching, "Awrk, trouble, Awrk, trouble, Awrk." The covered cage hadn't stopped her output.

Sweet-ums yipped. Ugh. My flesh prickled. The dog's shrill bark brought back memories of fingernails scratching across a blackboard.

Only the cats didn't join in. They licked each other ferociously, as if to show the rest of us they were truly above it all.

The doorbell rang again, and the knocking became louder and more insistent. Voices, barely heard over the pandemonium, demanded to be let in.

Morrow darted toward Ms. Stalker and put the gun against her head. "Who would that be knocking at the door?" The threat in his voice paralyzed us both.

"P- probably my sisters," she sputtered. "They . . . they . . . they're p-p-probably back from the psych-psychia . . . d . . . d . . . doctor."

"Sisters? How many sisters? Who else would be with them?"

"N-nobody else, just the t-two of them, I th-think." Ms. Stalker was shaking; a waterfall of tears flowed from her eyes. "Pl-pl-please don't shoot m-m-me," she whimpered.

Morrow ran to the door, unlocked the deadbolt and pulled it open so violently that the two newcomers stumbled in. He shoved them, and they fell against each other as he closed and relocked the door. He pointed the gun at their faces before they even had time to right themselves.

The two women were in a daze as they tried to get up. Their faces registered shock from the madness they had stepped into. The noise from the menagerie, Morrow waving the gun at them, and Ms. Stalker screeching loud enough to wake up Rip Van Winkle didn't help their traumatized state.

I thought about tackling John when he was distracted, but I was afraid the gun would accidentally go off and shoot one of us. Besides, I was still in shock myself. Not only was our situation horrifying, but I was also staring at two identical faces, glazed with fear, each mirroring the features of the third sister on the couch! As if in slow motion, I watched as recognition dawned on one of the identical triplets.

"Samantha! Samantha!" she screeched. "My darling, my sweetheart! You're here, you're here!"

"Shut up, all of you," Morrow yelled as he fired a bullet into the ceiling.

Only we humans got the message. Rather than quiet down, the animals became even more agitated. In desperation, John fired at Tricky-Dicky. Unfortunately the monkey was passing right in front of me at the time. The bullet would've hit me if my cumbersome purse hadn't deflected it into the sofa. Thank God it was always filled with a lot of junk.

The real Ms. Stalker threw herself at me. "I will take the next bullet for you!" she screamed, as she covered me with her body.

"Drop the gun, Morrow!" a voice in the rear doorway yelled. "It's over. Drop the gun!"

It was the pipsqueak!

Sweet-ums jumped off her mistress's lap and attacked Tuppence. We all began yelling and moving. I pushed Ms. Stalker off me and dived for John. He and I went down as my admirer plopped on top of us both, with Tricky-Dicky completing the picture. That damned monkey liked to jump. His feet kept pounding our backs, cementing us together. We must've looked like a layered human/animal sandwich.

Tuppence dragged Sweet-ums, still clinging to his pant leg, into the mayhem. Taking advantage of the confusion, the PI kicked the gun out of John's hand. I couldn't believe Morrow held on to it through all that bedlam.

Sniveling Triplet #1 rushed to detach Sweet-ums from the private eye's leg. As she pulled at the dog, the trouser material ripped off, causing her to fall backwards. That little monster sure had a tight hold on Tuppence.

Triplet #2 calmed down the rest of the zoo. She sped to Tricky-Dicky and talked some monkey gibberish. The ape jumped into her arms, embraced her, causing spit and fur to cover her face. Animal and human then proceeded to the screeching parrot's cage. The woman took off the cloth, and, with a treat from her pocket, soothed that savage beast as well. The cats rubbed against her leg, yawned with loud mews and plunked down to nap.

I loosened myself from Ms. Stalker and pushed away from Morrow. Tuppence grabbed him from the floor and shoved him onto a chair on the other side of the room. He sure was strong for such a little guy.

Tuppence put John's gun into his pocket. The PI was puffing and wide-eyed, but to me he never looked more handsome. I was already sorry for thinking he was a pipsqueak. He was my hero.

"The police should be here any minute. Everyone relax and take a seat," he said, keeping his gun aimed on John Morrow.

Before I could ask any questions of Tuppence, my stalker became agitated. It seemed she could hardly contain herself with me in the room. I made sure I kept my distance. She looked toward me with mad, adoring eyes and began to chatter. "Sisters . . . this is my Samantha . . . when this is over . . . we'll live happily ever . . . I saved her . . . from that nasty man's bullet."

Her monotone and unblinking stare unnerved me almost more than the gun in Morrow's hand did earlier. Her voice sounded eerie as she whispered. "I love her. She is my soul mate."

"Sorry, sister," I said under my breath. "I've already got a soul mate."

Her lips continued to move, but no sound came out as she sank into a conversation with herself.

Her sisters looked at Ms. Stalker in sorrow and shook their heads. Triplet #2 put her arm around her sibling and led her to the couch. She apologized to me on her sister's behalf. "We're so sorry about this, miss. We thought she was progressing in her treatments. Even the psychiatrist was hopeful today during her appointment. She must've had a relapse."

Relapse? In my opinion, Ms. Stalker needed a thousand more visits to the psychiatrist. She could use a straight jacket, as well. I wasn't too sure about her siblings, either. They all seemed wacky. I tried to feel compassion for them, but right now I only had enough sympathy for myself. I was furious and uptight.

Morrow began whimpering. "I'm sorry, I'm so sorry. . . ."

A calm Tricky-Dicky in funny monkey-stride walked over to John and put a long arm over his shoulder. His show of affection only made John shake and blubber more.

The identical triplets sagged into their couch with Ms. Stalker in the middle. They had their arms around her and were making soothing sounds as her chatter turned into maniacal babbling. Their attention, however, was aimed at the private eye and me.

The PI took out his cell phone. "I'm calling Chief Vincetti to let him know everything is under control. We don't want the police coming in with guns blazing, now, do we?"

If he thought his little joke was cute, the triplets didn't. Two of them let out a little moan and almost shuddered out of their skins. Their eyes were as big as TV dish satellites.

"Tuppence." I took a deep breath, as I suddenly began gasping for air. I felt cold and started trembling. I hugged myself to keep my teeth from chattering. "How did you know where to find me? How did you get in?"

"This situation would've been messier if you hadn't unlocked that kitchen patio door, Ms. L, when you were trying to make a run for it. I called the police immediately and entered shortly afterwards. I was waiting for an opportunity to join the mayhem so that no one would get hurt, and also to give the police a chance to get here. But when I heard the gun go off, I knew I had to act and rushed in. It's amazing no one got shot or killed."

Amazing, indeed! A rescue like this only happens in the movies. Wait till Reenee hears about this dandy day!

"But how did you know where to find me?"

"Your husband called me a couple of days ago and told me to

follow you. He said he was going back to work and was worried that you wouldn't behave yourself and stay at home. Although you both went to the restaurant together today, I thought I'd tag along anyway. I'm glad I did."

"Not as glad as I am!" I gave the PI a big, toothy grin, although, considering my condition, it probably looked like a demented grimace to him.

No sooner had Tuppence finished his explanation than we heard sirens blaring. As in any TV show, the cops arrived en masse after all the danger and mayhem was over and peace on earth had been restored.

Orland Park, Tinley Park, Oak Forest, Midlothian police departments, they all pulled up in their respective squad cars.

Here we go again, I thought. I supposed because of overlapping jurisdictions and today's screwy lawsuits, no force wanted to do anything illegal or questionable to botch up a future court case. It must've been a slow crime day in the 'burbs, judging by the emergency vehicles and personnel who showed up. Two ambulances were also on the scene. A fire engine arrived as well. A fire engine? All we needed now was the FBI.

Curious neighbors flowed from surrounding houses like bees to a jar of honey. I could actually hear the buzzing. Adding to the melee was the press, who'd showed up as if directed by radar.

I began to worry about my makeup when I saw the lights and cameras. No doubt I looked awful with mascara smeared all over my eyelids, making streaks down my cheeks. I pinched myself. Rhyming even at a time like this!

My head spun as I watched the squad cars parking at all angles in front of the house. Seeing Harry emerge from one of them made my head spin even faster. My brain began whirring like a fan in a wind tunnel as I tried to think of what my first words to Darling should be. At the moment, he was restrained from entering the house by a couple of cops. I supposed the police wanted to be sure the situation was secure and under control before they let Harry enter.

"Would you open the door for the police, Ms. L?" Tuppence asked. "I'm not taking my eyes off Morrow."

I could feel testosterone enter with the burly policemen. Under different circumstances, Reenee and I would've been in heaven, seeing all these men in attack mode. We always felt that squeaky leather on big hunks sporting holstered guns was sexually stimulating. Extraneous thoughts like that helped lower my intense fright level from the harrowing experience of the last couple hours.

The boys and girls in blue who entered the house had stern looks on their faces, and no one had a smile for me or anyone else. I was so happy when I finally spotted Chief Vincetti that I almost hugged him. He gently squeezed my arm as he passed by to speak with the private eye.

"Looks like you have things under control, Mr. Tuppence," he said. "I'll talk to you later. You can wait by the fireplace with Patrolman Rizzs here. We'll take over now."

Tuppence turned Morrow's gun over to the police tech, then followed Rizzs to the other side of the room. Chief Vincetti conferred with a Tinley Park big shot cop and they both started giving orders. A couple of female officers walked behind the couch where the sisters were sitting. Morrow was cuffed and a cop led him out to a squad car.

I was tempted to trip John as he walked past me, but I behaved myself. He looked his years, and then some, when he left the house. His wife and daughter would now have an even harder time ahead of them. I wondered why he'd killed that Langley woman at the writing workshop. I speculated as to what she'd done to cause his daughter's horrific condition.

The sisters were still seated. They looked like convicts awaiting sentencing. The female officers behind their couch seemed ready for orders about handling the real Ms. Stalker.

I figured everything would be explained in good time, but right now I had to face Harry. I squeezed my elbows into my sides and waited. I didn't know what to expect; I hoped he wouldn't embarrass me by berating me and lecturing me in front of four police departments.

Harry rushed into the house. He looked distraught and disheveled. I was just ready to open my mouth and start talking fast when he shocked the hell out of me. He took me in his arms and gave me a first-year marital hug and even kissed my hair!

I almost fainted. I tried to pull away and take another look to be sure it was Harry, but he held me in a tight embrace. If he started whispering sweet nothings in my ear, I'd have *The Big One*, like Red Foxx in the TV series, *Sanford & Son*. Clutching his heart, Foxx would say to his wife in heaven, "This is 'The Big One,' Elizabeth. I'm comin' to join you!"

The police were occupied, probably sorting out jurisdictions, and I was so involved with Harry's loving behavior, that none of us realized Ms. Stalker was on the move. She had pulled herself away from her sisters and started to attack Harry with her shoe. She pummeled his head and back, screaming her litany: "Samantha is mine; Samantha is mine; she's mine, *mine*!"

I pulled away from Harry as she dug her nails into his face. I tried to drag the crazed woman away from him.

"Samantha, Samantha, I love you. I love you!" Her shrieks made my gray roots jump out of my scalp as I struggled with her.

Two female officers descended upon her. They subdued her and kept a firm grip on her squirming body.

"Get the paramedics in here," Chief Vincetti shouted.

Ms. Stalker's sisters were wringing their hands. They wanted to approach their sister, but the police told them to stand back. We all watched helplessly as the paramedics conferred with the sisters, then gave Ms. Stalker an injection to calm her down. They placed her on a gurney.

"We'll be taking your sister to the psychiatric wing of St. James Hospital," one of the paramedics told the women. "I'd advise you to call her doctor and meet us there; you might want to bring some clothing and personal items for her as well."

The paramedics proceeded to wheel Ms. Stalker out of the house. Although in a groggy state, she smiled a sad, almost stupid, smile and mumbled something as she passed by me. Her limp hand sought mine, but no way was I going to go near that psycho. I had absolutely no sympathy for her. Harry's torn skin and bloodied face were more than enough reason to feel incensed toward that woman.

Chief Vincetti came up to us accompanied by a Tinley Park police official. He introduced us and said, "Have the paramedics take a look at your face, Harry, and see to those cat scratches on your back,

Samantha. Then, if you would, please reiterate what happened here for Detective Hurlee. After that, you and Harry go home. Have a drink; get a good night's rest. You can come to my office in the morning to give your statement."

"Bless you, Chief," I said.

A female paramedic led me into the kitchen for privacy. I carefully removed my blouse. The material caught on the scratches from the cat and the dried-up blood. I winced each time the paramedic disinfected, then treated, each gouge. She gave me a couple of aspirins and instructed me on post-care of the lesions.

Feeling better already, I found Tinley Park Police Detective Hurlee and summed up my ordeal as best as I could. He then had me repeat my story, this time stopping me with a question here and there.

When I thought my jaws were too tired to work anymore, he said, "Thank you, Ms. Lisowski. I'll want you to sign a sworn statement tomorrow at the Tinley Park police station. Would two p.m. be okay with you?"

I told him that would be fine and went to see how Harry's face looked after being cleansed and medicated.

"You're as handsome, as ever, Harry," I told him. "I'm ready if you are to get the hell out of here."

Harry smiled, and as we prepared to leave, he actually put an arm around me. I don't know who was comforting whom, because I could feel his trembling body.

One of the triplets approached us.

I stiffened for a second, thinking she might attack us as well.

"Would you both like to stay for a while and have some coffee?" she asked.

I looked at her as if she was nuts. I wasn't staying in this loony house a second longer than necessary, and Harry's gruff "No" led me to believe he felt the same way. The woman began to cry as she apologized for her sister's behavior. I relented and offered a smile and a few comforting words. After all, it wasn't her fault that her deranged sister was my stalker from hell.

With Harry's arm still around me, we gratefully left the house of horror. Damn, it's awkward walking with someone's arm around your waist. How do those people do it, hanging on to each other or walking with a hand on the other's butt? Maybe I'm just not a romantic soul. Or the wrong person had his arm around me? I wanted to move away but didn't want to hurt Harry's feelings. He'd become his old self soon enough, so I figured I might as well enjoy his affection, uncomfortable as it was, while it lasted.

The police handled crowd control and the media in order for us to get our car out of the vehicle mess in the driveway. Harry assured the police that he could drive home, but a squad car was assigned to accompany us. A few reporters poked microphones into our faces and asked stupid questions about how we felt, but as I knew all my makeup must be messed up or completely gone, I kept my head down and said nothing. I was not going to be on the evening news looking like a ghoul from a haunted house. Now, if they wanted to speak to me tomorrow, well. . . .

I was anxious to get home and call my sons, Reenee, my dad, and maybe Detective Kelly, too, but those calls would have to wait. Harry'd be all over me with questions. I felt I owed him first consideration. I hoped he wouldn't spoil this sudden warmth by insinuating that the mess I'd found myself in was my fault.

I still had a long night ahead of me.

Chapter 42

"I'm so glad to see you up and around," a teary-eyed Reenee said as she gave me a bear hug even before she stepped over the threshold of my front door. "I've been so worried that you might be sick in bed from the after-effects of your ordeal."

Three days had passed since my encounter with pandemonium. The first two were spent reliving the hell again with the police. I had to go over the entire horrible story from the moment I discovered the body of Carol Langley at the writing seminar, through the stalker phone calls and notes, to the incidents with Morrow, and ending with the nightmare at the triplets' house.

First I had to tell my story to Chief Vincetti because I'd originally lodged a complaint with Oak Forest police regarding threatening phone calls. Then the Tinley Park police wanted my version of the encounter, since Ms. Stalker and the killer lived in that community. And because the murder of Carole Langley took place in Chicago, Detective Kelly also had follow-up questions for me. Each session was grueling. I now understand why some suspects admit to being guilty even though they're innocent — anything to stop the constant questioning and backing up and retelling.

I'd practically slept the day before away. Now I was looking forward to reliving my encounters with Reenee, because I knew she'd help me heal and expunge any *kruskies* left in my body.

"I don't know where to start," I told my friend, as I returned the hug and led her into the house. "While talking to the police, I felt more and more like it had all happened to someone else — like I was watching a movie unfold." I gave her another hug as we headed for the family room. "I couldn't wait till you got here. I've got Krispy

Kremes and a full pot of coffee set up. We're gonna need these cathartic donuts to get through my story."

As the jelly-filled heaven hit my lips, I didn't miss a beat in going over the nightmare involving the triplets. Reenee shuddered as I described my fear and squeezed my hand amid her "oh, my Gods" and "wows." As I explained the danger I'd been in, I stuffed my mouth, and she matched my eating frenzy. I could feel her empathy each time she gave me a warm touch as I hurried through my story like a mad woman.

After I finished, and feeling entirely spent, I let out a big sigh and slumped further into the couch. The initial high-energy rush from the sugar in the donuts had now made me lethargic. Reenee looked as tired and worn out as I felt.

"You could've been shot. Murdered," she whispered with a catch in her voice. "I would've killed you if you died on me! You promised me that we'd live as best friends into our hundreds."

We looked at each other, green eyes to brown. Tears began to flow. Seconds later bubbles of laughter percolated from deep within us. We giggled and cried at the same time. Chortles and snuffles swept away my harrowing experience and her fright and concern for me.

Half a box of tissues later, we were emotionally exhausted. "I love ya, girlfriend," I said, as I hugged Reenee.

"Pshew! Listening to your story was rough enough. I can't even imagine living it," she said, taking a deep breath. "Now tell me about the last couple days with the police — and Harry. How in the world is he taking all this?"

Ah, yes, Harry. He, who hated to have his staid life disturbed, was behaving astoundingly. Darling actually took me out for a lovely dinner the night before at an expensive restaurant, and he didn't even have a coupon for the place. He was so attentive and sympathetic until I wanted to scream, "Enough already!" I don't think I liked Harry being the soul of empathy. Or maybe his caring manner came too late after his years of irritable, loveless indifference.

"I changed my mind," Reenee went on to say. "Save Harry for later. First I want to know the reason behind the two murders, and what happened to Ms. Stalker. Did you ever find out her name? But," she added with a wink, "I especially want to know about your encounter with Detective Kelly. Did he use his billy club on you? Were there handcuffs involved — leather straps. . . ."

We began to giggle again. We were both on a roller coaster of emotions.

"Stop! Stop, Reenee. I can hardly breathe. The hell with these donuts; let me get out the booze."

I didn't even bother to shake up a martini for me or a Manhattan for her. We just sipped the good ol' Jack Daniels from the bottle, like the aged geezers in movies do on their bench in front of the general store.

I took a sip and plunged right in with my story. "Let me start with that Morrow guy. He's in police custody. Detective Kelly called this morning to say that John's daughter, Lori, suffered a fatal seizure last night, related to the bacterial meningitis." The news was so horrible, it hurt me to repeat it. "As a result, his wife had a heart attack and is on the critical list at Palos Hospital. I don't think John will live to face a court trial, considering this escalating heartbreak in his life."

"Good lord!" Reenee exclaimed. "You gotta feel for them, and him, too, right?"

"Yep. I do. Who knows how any of us would act under the circumstances that he faced? But to go on, John drove Frances to the seminar and intended to stay in the neighborhood to drive her home after the sessions. It turned out that he unexpectedly spotted Carole Langley at the writing seminar." I shook my head and paused before going on. "The hatred he had stored in his heart for decades toward that woman must've been too much for him. The knife was available and, I suppose, his emotions exploded into action. Killing Langley must've been the final blow in driving him over the line of sanity."

"Yeah, the poor guy. But the poor woman, too, losing her life. Both caught in a tangled web. How did John know the Langley woman was responsible for his daughter's condition?"

"I learned what I'm going to tell you from the hunk. He felt I'd earned a right to an explanation after what I went through."

"Uh-huh. And did he also say he needed to cross-*examine* you over dinner and?"

"Reenee! Wipe that smirk off your face. He was in his highly professional and matter-of-fact mode. Anyway, not to digress, remember when we found out that in their hey-day the Morrows held very successful positions and that they entertained famous people in their home? Well, during John's interrogation, Detective Kelly found out that the victim Langley and Morrow's wife, Frances, had been very close. Carole Langley came to every one of their parties and seemed star-struck. In fact, she got out of her sick bed one night to attend a dinner there because she wanted to meet Sean Connery, one of their guests."

"Yikes! Double 07? I would've crawled on my hands and knees to sit next to him at dinner."

"Yeah, well, the problem was that, besides being ill that night, Langley was a carrier, a Typhoid Mary. A person who didn't get sick herself from some deadly disease but passed the bacteria or virus on to others used to be called Typhoid Mary. The reference had something to do with Mary Mallon, a cook who lived in New York in the early 1900s. She supposedly infected tons of people with typhoid fever. Many died, hence the name."

"Okay, Sam, okay. Nix the history lesson. Wet your tonsils with JD and get on with it."

I took a slug of whiskey and continued. "Well, before the party, Langley went up to Lori Morrow's room. She was the girl's godmother. She hugged and kissed the little girl and held her close as she read her a bedtime story, and I guess she sneezed and coughed on her as well."

"Yuck." Reenee let out a squeal. "Weren't there handkerchiefs or tissues available in those days?"

"It gets worse. Unfortunately the girl was cursed with fragile health and was already afflicted with childhood diabetes. Evidently, bacterial meningitis carried by Langley attacked Lori's delicate condition. To complicate matters, a few days after contact, the young girl was stricken with paralysis and seizures." In the retelling, I began to feel down in the dumps. I couldn't even imagine how the Morrows survived those depressing circumstances. "Although it wasn't that long ago, very little was known at the time about meningitis or, more importantly, its need for immediate treatment." I sighed, then added, "Before the doctors correctly diagnosed Lori's condition, her brain was further attacked by the bacteria, which resulted in mental retardation for the girl."

"Oh, my God, Samantha. It's mind-boggling, what happens to people." She shook her head, then took a sip from the bottle. "One unfortunate incident, and the lives of that pitiful girl and her parents were ruined forever."

"You got it. The Morrows stopped all contact with Carole Langley, whom obviously they resented and probably hated. They moved, divorced themselves from their lifestyle and friends, and spent the rest of their lives quietly devoting themselves to the care of Lori."

Reenee interrupted. "I know how this ends. Suddenly, John sees Carole Langley at the writing seminar and goes bonkers. The decades-long resentment toward her for the dreadful disease she passed on to Lori, and its consequences in their lives, probably hit him like an Amtrak express."

"I guess. Anyway, you're right. Frances was able to merely give her ex-friend, Carole, those killer looks throughout the seminar, but John snapped. When he saw the knife in the empty cooking room of Unique World, he made his choice. I think he would've killed Langley even if she weren't alone in the room."

I shook my head as I thought of the sheer coincidence of everything that had happened. Reenee's eyes met mine, and I knew she was having similar thoughts.

I took a deep breath and continued. "Long Tall Sally witnessing the murder was just a stroke of fate. John would probably never have returned to kill Sally, had the transvestite not confronted and threatened him with the police. That threat must've given Morrow a few sane moments of reflection. He realized what he had done and how it would affect his wife and daughter if he got caught, so Long Tall Sally had to go."

"Wow. Have a sip of Jack. It sounds like you need it. You look pale, too."

She passed the bottle to me. "Did you figure out how *you* got involved in the chaos, Sam?"

"Our trip to visit Frances did it. She must've been suspicious of her husband considering the victim was Carole Langley. Then, when

I told her I was being harassed by phone calls, she wrongly assumed that John was making them, and that I was his next threat to shut up."

"Right. You know, Sammy, we never did tell Frances why we wanted to speak with her."

"Uh-huh, and then, as you know, my phone buddy, Khara, told me that Frances confronted her husband the ill-fated day of our visit and attacked him physically."

"Didn't Frances suffer heart palpitations after that fight and end up in the hospital?"

"Yep. Lori also had a serious seizure and a setback at this time. John blamed you and me for his family's descent into even worse health problems." I closed my eyes and shuddered. "He also became obsessed by the erroneous idea that I knew he was the murderer and that I had exposed him to his wife, as well as accusing him of hounding me with threatening phone calls. I can see why he believed our visit to his home was responsible for their mounting problems."

"Lordy, lordy, Sam, hand over that bottle. But what I don't understand is why Frances needed to attend a writing seminar in the first place. She was top dog at a publishing company before disaster struck the family."

"Yes. I was curious about that also. I found out, again from phone-buddy Karla, that the speaker at the seminar was Frances' niece and needed one more *body* to keep the event from being canceled. What a senseless reason, huh, for the tragedy that followed?"

"Yeah," Reenee said, "little did anyone know what kind of *body* it would turn out to be."

We both sipped and tossed that image around in our brains for a while.

Reenee perked up first. "Now. What about Ms. Stalker?" she asked.

"Sad. Seems she became obsessed with me because of my TV program. I'm told she'd kiss my image on the damned TV screen and became hard for her sisters to handle whenever I was on. Creepy!"

"Just your luck that the stalker was a female and not a six-foot, three-inch, fortyish, handsome, male admirer."

"No, thank you. Don't want *any* admirers. I think I'll grow a mustache for the show."

Reenee wiggled her index finger across her upper lip in Charlie Chaplin mode.

I laughed and then laughed some more.

Her imitation was priceless. "Proceed, my little sugar plum," she said, then went on to further mimic W. C. Fields.

I felt like I was stuck in a 1920s silent movie.

"You're bad, girlfriend. This really isn't funny stuff. I understand Ms. Stalker's being re-evaluated and will probably end up in a private sanitarium. Her sisters are financially well-off, and there's also family money, so expense for her upkeep shouldn't be a problem. Her name, by the way, is Alexandra Cummings. Such a lovely name for so sick a lady."

"Hmm. Do you realize the odds of those women being identical triplets?" Reenee asked, now through with her pantomime shenanigans. "I looked up the stats on the Internet. Birth rates of identical female triplets range from one in one-hundred-fifty thousand to one in two-hundred million, depending upon age, nationality and birth order of the mother."

"Holy shit! And I had to end up with a screwy one. Look that stat up in your *Funk and Wagnalls.*"

Reenee was already on a different thinking track. "I wonder if all the Cummings' triplets are lesbians. I bet they're going to be in touch with you. Those women must feel terrible about what happened and what their sister put you through. Besides, Alexandra's doctor probably would like to know about the stalking to help him with her treatment."

"Could be. But nobody better ask me to visit Ms. Stalker Cummings. My sympathy has its limits."

We both sighed and fell silent for a while, nipping at the Jack Daniels, absorbed with our own thoughts.

Reenee recovered first. "Enough bad stuff. Now tell me what I've been dying to hear since I got here. Give me the dirt on Detective Kelly."

"Oh, Reenee, there is no dirt. But the hunk did tell me that he applied for a position with the Tinley Park police force. There's an opening for a deputy chief. He said he's tired of fighting Windy City politics, which plays a large part in who gets promoted and...."

"And he's applying for the position to be closer to you," Reenee interrupted with a shriek. "Why, that big, bad wolf!"

"Oh, please. He'd been thinking of a move into a suburban police force for some time now, and this opportunity just popped up."

"Uh-huh, and if you buy that story, I've got a five-carat diamond ring you can have for a buck ninety-nine."

The twinkle in Reenee's eye actually made me blush. "You're screwy, girlfriend. He knows I'm married."

"Kelly also senses your relationship with Harry isn't all it might be. After all, he's a detective, isn't he? Part of his job is to delve into people's lives. Besides, you're married, not dead."

"Reenee, stop. And speaking of Harry, not that you were, he's been overly caring recently. I always wanted him to be more attentive to me. Now I'm finding out that I might have preferred him the other way."

"Just stick around, Tootsie. The old Harry will be back before you know it. In time, a chameleon goes back to its original color; I learned that on the Discovery channel."

"What in the world are you talking about now, Reenee? I think you've sipped of the JD fountain too freely and. . . ." The jingle of the phone interrupted our chitchat.

"Let's go get some big hamburgers and greasy French fries after I answer this call, okay? Yesterday I received a letter from that magazine I've been writing for," I said as I ran to the kitchen to answer the phone. "They're keeping me on as a regular contributor, and I want to tell you about it."

Reenee's big, happy screech followed me to the kitchen. "Way to go, girlfriend!"

As I rushed to get the phone before the answering machine kicked in, I figured the call was from Harry. Part of his new persona was a daily call from work. He never bothered to phone me daily for twenty-five years, and now he called to see how my day was going. I felt like he was checking up on me to make sure I wasn't involved in another adventure to upset his world. I found myself not appreciating the calls.

But it wasn't Harry. It was the hunk. I began to wonder if he was going to phone me constantly, too. This was his second call today.

"Detective Kelly! I haven't heard from you for such a long time," I said with a little hint of sarcasm.

As he apologized for bothering me again, I was surprised by his voice. I didn't remember it being so sexy. Or was it the booze I'd consumed making it sound that way?

"I'm going to be in your area tomorrow, Samantha," he went on to say. "I have an interview with the Tinley Park police chief. How about joining me for lunch? If I get the job, you can be the first to toast to my success."

You know the old saying that your life flashes before your eyes when you think you're going to die? Well, that's how the thoughts exploded through my brain as I considered my answer.

No, of course I wouldn't accept the invitation . . . on the other hand didn't I owe it to myself to enjoy lunch with an appealing man after what I'd been through?

Forget it! What was I really doing here? Did I want to jeopardize a sound, comfortable, although boring, life, with Harry, who had been trying to make strides in our relationship. . . .

But, hell, I could handle a lunch, couldn't I?

Or was I fooling myself, tempting fate? I remembered how exciting that kiss had been.

Excuses and rationalizations, reasons and counter-reasons spun around in my brain at a velocity that would put Superman's faster-than-a-speeding-bullet power to shame.

My alter ego kicked in its opinion. For God's sake, it's not a rendezvous at the Steaming Flesh Motel. Be sensible. What could happen in a restaurant with bright lights and loads of people around?

It's only lunch!

But. . . .

"Samantha, are you still there? Did you hear me? I asked if you'd have lunch with me tomorrow."

I stared hard at my reflection in the kitchen window.

I took a deep breath and said, "Well. . . ."

ABOUT THE AUTHOR

Lydia Ponczak is a retired Chicago schoolteacher who is presently program director and host of a community cable television program. She is married and states that her two sons and daughter-in-law are to die for.

Lydia considers Oak Forest as her "grandbaby" and is very involved in volunteer work in the community, for which she has received numerous awards of recognition. She claims being chosen first runner-up in a Ms. Illinois Seniors Pageant was one of the highlights of her life.

Lydia loves to read mysteries and to polka dance with Lee, her husband of too many years to count. She is busy writing a sequel to this, her first novel.

CPSIA information can be obtained at www.ICGtesting.com
Printed in the USA
LVOW090300280412

279504LV00001B/1/P